"So, umm, do you want to try being friends, Hank?"

He pulled the brim of his hat down to shade his eyes while he considered his answer. When Emily let down her guard, he felt a powerful attraction toward her that had a whole lot more to do with sex than with friendship. But it wouldn't hurt to give friendship a try, would it?

"Yeah," he said slowly. "Why not?"

Emily turned toward the house. Hank walked along beside her, draping his arm around her shoulders. He laughed at the dubious glance she shot him and gave her a quick hug.

"Relax, Em," he said. "Friends do this kind of stuff."

To his surprise and immense satisfaction, Emily placed her arm about his waist and shyly hugged him back.

Dear Reader,

Welcome to Silhouette **Special Edition** . . . welcome to romance. Each month, Silhouette **Special Edition** publishes six novels with you in mind—stories of love and life, tales that you can identify with—romance with that little "something special" added in.

July is a wonderful month—full of sizzling stories packed with emotion. Don't miss Debbie Macomber's warm and witty *Bride on the Loose*—the concluding tale of her series, THOSE MANNING MEN. And *Heartbreak Hank* is also in store for you—Myrna Temte's third COWBOY COUNTRY tale. Starting this month, as well, is Linda Lael Miller's new duo BEYOND THE THRESHOLD. The initial book is entitled *There and Now*.

Rounding out this month are more stories by some of your favorite authors: Bevlyn Marshall, Victoria Pade and Laurie Paige.

In each Silhouette **Special Edition** novel, we're dedicated to bringing you the romances that you dream about— stories that will delight as well as bring a tear to the eye. For me, good romance novels have always contained an element of hope, of optimism that life can be, and often is, very beautiful. I find a great deal of inspiration in that thought.

Why do you read romances? I'd really like to hear your opinions on the books that we publish and on the romance genre in general. Please write to me c/o Silhouette Books, 300 East 42nd Street, 6th floor, New York, NY 10017.

I hope that you enjoy this book and all of the stories to come. Looking forward to hearing from you!

Sincerely,

Tara Gavin
Senior Editor
Silhouette Books

MYRNA TEMTE
Heartbreak Hank

Silhouette Special Edition

Published by Silhouette Books New York

America's Publisher of Contemporary Romance

To Pam and Maggie, who remind me every day what it was
like to be a little girl. I couldn't have written this without you.
Thanks for being so special.

ACKNOWLEDGMENTS

My thanks to the following people for help with research:
Mrs. Gerry Sperling, Principal, Brentwood Elementary
School, Spokane, Washington; Sharon Ziegler, Pinedale,
Wyoming; Robin and Irv Lozier and Chera Temte of the
Box "R" Ranch, Cora, Wyoming; and Melody Harding of
the Bar Cross Ranch, Cora, Wyoming.

SILHOUETTE BOOKS
300 East 42nd St., New York, N.Y. 10017

HEARTBREAK HANK

Copyright © 1992 by Myrna Temte

ISBN: 0-373-09751-4

First Silhouette Books printing July 1992

Printed in the U.S.A.

Books by Myrna Temte

Silhouette Special Edition

Wendy Wyoming #483
Powder River Reunion #572
The Last Good Man Alive #643
For Pete's Sake #739
Silent Sam's Salvation #745
Heartbreak Hank #751

*Cowboy Country Series

MYRNA TEMTE

grew up in Montana and attended college in Wyoming, where she met and married her husband. Marriage didn't necessarily mean settling down for the Temtes—they have lived in six different states, including Washington, where they currently reside. Moving so much is difficult, the author says, but it is also wonderful stimulation for a writer.

Though always a "readaholic," Myrna Temte never dreamed of becoming an author. But while spending time at home to care for her first child, she began to seek an outlet from the never-ending duties of housekeeping and child rearing. She started reading romance novels and soon became hooked, both as a reader and a writer.

Now Myrna Temte appreciates the best of all possible worlds—a loving family and a challenging career that lets her set her own hours and turn her imagination loose.

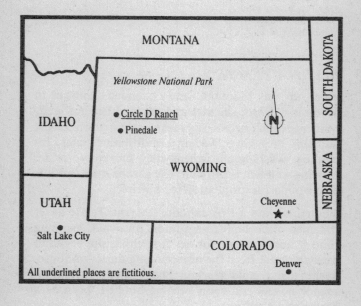

All underlined places are fictitious.

Chapter One

"Emily, you've *got* to help me."

Principal Emily Franklin looked up from the latest copy of the Pinedale Elementary School budget and found Mary Jovanovich, one of the best teachers on her staff, invading her office.

"Sit down, Mary," she said with a smile. "What's the problem?"

Mary plopped her five-months-pregnant body into the chair in front of Emily's desk and tossed both hands into the air in a typically melodramatic gesture. "I'll give you three guesses."

"Tina Dawson?"

"Who else?" Mary heaved a gusty sigh, then patted her rounded belly before turning a look of mock horror on Emily. "That kid is such a corker, I'm beginning to wonder if I haven't made the biggest mistake of my life. If Junior turns out to be as inventive as Tina, I'll lose my mind before he gets to preschool."

Emily chuckled in sympathy. "All right, I'm ready, now. What's her latest inappropriate behavior?"

"You're not going to believe this one."

"That's what you said the last time."

Mary rolled her eyes toward heaven. "Well, she's topped herself again. Arnie Bevins caught her chewing tobacco out by the Dumpsters with three of the sixth-grade boys. And get this, the boys said Tina supplied the snoose. Only in Wyoming, right?"

Emily bit down on her lower lip in a vain attempt to stifle a startled laugh. "That little devil," she finally said, shaking her head in reluctant admiration.

"It's not funny," Mary grumbled. "She was one of my best students until Thanksgiving, but now I'm not sure she should be promoted to third grade next fall."

"I'm sorry, Mary. You haven't had any luck with the notes you've sent home?"

"Knowing Tina, she probably pitched them out the bus window."

"I wouldn't be surprised," Emily agreed. "Have you tried phoning her father?"

"Of course, I have," Mary answered indignantly. "Hank keeps telling me he'll handle it, but I haven't seen any change in Tina's behavior. Frankly, she was a lot better when she was living with her Aunt Becky and Uncle Peter. I tried calling them, but they're out of town for the next month."

"What about her Uncle Sam or Grandma D? Have you contacted them?"

Mary stared at Emily in amazement. "Don't you ever listen to the gossip around this town?"

"Not if I can help it," Emily replied. "What did I miss?"

"Sam's on his honeymoon. He married Dani Smith last week. You know, Kim's mother?"

"Kim Smith in Abby's class?"

"That's the one. Grandma D is helping Hank take care of Tina and Dani's kids. I talked to her, but she insisted that Hank's working on the problem."

Emily winced inwardly at the second mention of Hank Dawson's name. Though she hadn't seen him for years—not since they were both in high school—she dreaded the thought of having to deal with him again.

Mary leaned forward, a pleading expression in her eyes. "I really need your support, Emily. Tina's a good kid headed for disaster. I'm at my wit's end with her."

"All right. Have her report to me after school. I'll convince Hank to come in for a conference."

"How?" Mary demanded. "By putting a gun to his head? Holding Tina hostage?"

Emily gave her a grim smile. "Whatever it takes."

Exhausted, filthy and discouraged, Hank Dawson unsaddled his blue roan gelding, Sioux, and gave him a good rubdown. He turned the horse into the pasture, then limped toward the house as fast as his throbbing left leg would allow. After the lousy day he'd put in, he wanted a beer, a shower and a hot meal, in that order.

The minute he opened the door to the back porch, however, his eighty-six-year-old grandmother appeared in the kitchen doorway on the other side of the room, a worried frown creasing her forehead. Hank stiffened his posture and tried to walk normally, but Grandma D's eyes narrowed behind her big, red glasses.

"I *told* you, you should have listened to the doctor," she scolded, rushing forward to help him. "You're not supposed to be ridin' for another three months."

"Tell that to those damn heifers," Hank muttered. Then he sighed and patted the old lady's shoulder. "Don't fuss at me, Grandma D. I just lost a calf."

"Oh, dear, what happened?"

"It was a breach. I couldn't get him out in time. Saved the heifer, though."

Grandma D pushed her glasses up farther on her nose and said worriedly, "We shouldn't have let Sam go off until all the calves were born. You're just not up to runnin' the ranch yet."

Fearing he might say something that would start another in a long line of arguments since Grandma D had come to help him take care of the kids, Hank clamped his jaws together until he could speak calmly. He loved his grandmother dearly, but her continual praise for his older brother was really starting to gravel Hank's drawers.

Yes, Sam had successfully run the Circle D since their father's death fourteen years ago. Yes, Hank hadn't always been as responsible as he should have. But dammit all, he was doing the best he could.

"I doubt even Sam could have saved this one, Grandma," he said. "What's for supper?"

The old lady clapped both hands over her cheeks, her mouth forming a perfect O. "Land sakes, I forgot to tell ya."

"What?"

"We can't have supper yet. You've got to go into town and pick Tina up at the school. The principal called about two o'clock and said she wouldn't be comin' home on the bus unless you came in for a conference."

"That sounds pretty weird, Grandma. Sure you understood him right?"

"Course, I am. And the principal's not a him. She's a Ms. Franklin. I reckon Tina's been actin' up again. You'd better find out what the little stinkpot's done this time."

Glancing down at his muddy boots and blood-stained jeans, Hank cursed under his breath, then sighed. "Well, I can't go lookin' and smellin' like this. Call her while I grab a shower, and tell her I'll be there as soon as I can, will ya?"

"Sure thing," Grandma D replied, scurrying into the kitchen.

Hank pried off his boots and stormed upstairs to his bedroom in his stocking feet. The hot water eased the ache in his bum leg somewhat, but his mind was so busy with the problem of Tina, he barely noticed. The kid had declared war on him five months ago, and he had a sinking feeling deep in his gut that he was losing.

Damn and double damn. He loved his daughter with a tenderness that probably would have surprised a lot of folks who knew him. Shoot, the way that little girl could grab his heart and turn it inside out even surprised him sometimes.

She'd had a rough time during the past year, and he'd tried to be patient with her, but the little wretch still treated him like a first-class skunk. Well, she was about to find out who was in charge...and it wasn't a seven-and-a-half-year-old hellion. He might not be the best parent in the world, but he was the only one Tina had, and she'd damn well better start accepting that.

And when he was finished with his daughter, Hank thought darkly, as he rushed out to his pickup, he had a thing or two to say to a principal who had the damned gall to keep a little kid at school until suppertime.

The street lamps had already come on by the time Hank arrived in Pinedale. A fierce March wind whipped against his denim jacket and tried to rip his hat off as he limped toward the front door of the school.

Except for a light shining through the windows of an office set behind a long counter, the building was dark and eerily quiet. Brightly colored bulletin boards and the scent of chalk dust triggered old feelings of frustration and inadequacy in Hank, and he hesitated. God, he'd almost forgotten how much he'd hated school.

Then a slender woman of medium height, five-seven, or so, Hank guessed, stepped out of the office. She wore a navy suit with a prim white blouse and sensible, low-heeled pumps, about what he'd expect a female principal to wear. She was younger than he'd imagined, though, maybe a few years younger than he was. Her blond hair fell straight to her shoulders and curved under, without so much as a single strand daring to stray out of place.

There was something familiar about her oh-so-correct posture as she approached him, but he couldn't place her until she spoke.

"Hello, Mr. Dawson. I'm glad you could finally make it."

Hank's mouth dropped wide open, and he stared at her intently. The glasses and braces were gone. The skinny, angular body had developed some mighty nice feminine curves. The jaw and cheekbones had a leaner cut than he remembered. But he'd know that soft, low voice, those big green eyes and those sweet, vulnerable lips anywhere.

Grinning in delight, he yanked off his hat and whacked it against his thigh. "Well, I'll be damned. If it ain't the Worm!"

Her mouth twitched at the corners, and a glint of amusement appeared in her eyes. "I was hoping you'd forgotten that awful nickname."

Though he'd rather give her a bear hug, Hank shook the hand she offered. Emily Jackson had never been one to tolerate much touching, at least not from him.

"Never, Em," he said with a chuckle, looking her up and down all over again. "By golly, I can't get over how much you've changed."

"I'll take that as a compliment," she replied.

"Yes, ma'am, you sure should," he drawled, letting a husky note creep into his voice.

Her smile fading, she immediately released his hand and gestured toward the lighted windows. "Let's go into my office, Hank. We need to talk about Tina."

He walked along beside her, trying to hide his limp. "Where is she?"

"Back in the nurse's office with a stack of library books. I wanted to talk with you in private before bringing her into the discussion."

Hank settled into the chair Emily indicated and plunked his hat back on his head while she moved behind her desk. Gazing around the room, he decided maybe she hadn't changed that much, after all. Everything looked incredibly neat and organized; the stack of files on her desk was in such perfect alignment, it wouldn't surprise him to find out she'd used a ruler to straighten it. She flipped open the top folder, but he wasn't ready to discuss his daughter yet.

"How long have you been back in Pinedale?" he asked.

"Since last July. It's amazing we haven't run into each other before this."

"Not really." Hank shrugged and rubbed his left leg. "I was laid up for over a year. Couldn't get around without crutches until just before Christmas. I didn't get out much."

"I guess that explains why I haven't seen you around the school. Was it a rodeo accident?"

"Nope. Happened out at the ranch, but that's a long story." He inclined his head toward the nameplate on her desk top. "Why is your last name Franklin now? I don't see a wedding ring."

Emily's gaze skittered away from his, and she tucked her hands in her lap. "I'm divorced."

"Me, too," he admitted. "Bummer, huh?"

"You might say that. Now, about Tina. Do you have any idea what's going on with her?"

Hank slid down in his chair, laced his fingers together over his stomach and gave her a wry grin. "I know she's been ornery as the devil lately. I've talked to her every time her teacher's called me, but I haven't had much luck gettin' through to her. What's she done this time?"

He stared at Emily in disbelief for a second when she told him, then threw back his head and roared with laughter.

"Did she puke her guts out?" he asked when he finally regained control. "Good Lord, what'll she think of next?"

"It's not funny. Her behavior is totally inappropriate," Emily said in a stern principal's voice Hank had heard more times during the course of his own academic career than he'd care to admit. God, did these people take classes in lecturing, or what?

"Aw, c'mon, it's not *that* bad—"

"As an isolated incident, it's not," she agreed, fixing him with a piercing glare that set Hank's back teeth on edge. "Unfortunately, this is hardly an isolated incident."

Picking up the file with Tina's name typed on the tab, she ran her index finger down the margin of the paper inside. "During the last four months, Tina has repeatedly sassed her teacher, refused to do her assignments, called other children names, cursed at the music teacher—"

"Yeah, she's a real delinquent," Hank muttered, shoving his hands into his pockets.

Ignoring the interruption, Emily continued. "She gave Bobby Hartwell a black eye and bit Shelley Thompson. Last week, she wrote, 'School *s-u-c-k-s* and so does Mrs. Jovanovich,' across the bulletin board next to the lunchroom."

"Hell, Em—"

Emily drew herself up ramrod straight and gave him another one of those beady-eyed glares. "I'll thank you not to use that kind of language, *Mr.* Dawson. I am *not* your classmate or your algebra tutor now. I am your daughter's principal."

"Well, pardon me all to he—heck," Hank retorted. He'd been right about one thing—other than turning into one fine-lookin' woman, Emily Jackson hadn't changed a bit. She'd been so damn prissy back in high school, he used to think her mother starched her underwear. Now, he figured, she probably starched her own.

"I'm sure you can understand that I can't allow this kind of behavior to continue."

"Well, whaddaya want me to do about it? Beat her? Wouldn't that be a little *inappropriate?*"

"Of course it would," she said patiently, making him feel about ten years old. "You may want to revoke some of her privileges, such as watching television, or—"

"So, she's pulled a few childish pranks. I pulled my share of 'em when I was her age." The dubious look Emily shot him forced him to amend his statement. "All right, maybe I pulled more than my share. It's probably genetic and the kid can't help herself."

"She's gone far beyond childish pranks," Emily said, picking up a pen as if preparing to take notes. "And I doubt genetics has anything to do with her problem. Judging from her past records, Tina was a model student until just prior to the Christmas vacation. Has there been a major disruption of some kind at home?"

"Such as?"

"Such as a recent divorce or a death in the family?"

Now that she'd mentioned it, there'd been all kinds of disruptions in Tina's life in the past eighteen months. But Hank wasn't about to discuss them with this prune-faced, judgmental witch. "That's none of your dang business, *Ms.* Franklin."

Emily studied him for a long moment, then sighed and shook her head. "Look, Hank, I'm sorry if I offended you," she said quietly. "But any child as unhappy as Tina most certainly *is* my business. Especially when she's disrupting an entire classroom and tormenting one of my best teachers. We need to find a solution before she does something that will force me to suspend her. Mrs. Jovanovich is already threatening to retain her, next year."

"It's really that bad?"

"I'm afraid so. Tina has got to learn to accept responsibility for her actions."

Hank bit into his bottom lip and studied the scars and calluses on his hands while he racked his brain for answers. Finally he said, "All right. I'll take care of it."

"Good." Emily stood and crossed to the door. "You can start right now. I'll be back with Tina shortly."

Sighing, Hank straightened in his seat and crossed his left leg over his right. True to her word, Emily returned a moment later with his daughter in tow. Tina shot him a defiant glare as she took the chair beside his. Then she turned to face the principal's desk, her little mouth settling into a sullen line.

When Emily had seated herself again, she looked expectantly at Hank. He cleared his throat to buy time. "Ms. Franklin tells me you've been actin' pretty ugly lately, Tina," he said.

"I didn't do nothin'."

"C'mon, don't lie to me. What have you got to say for yourself?"

"Nothin'," the little girl mumbled, refusing to look at him.

"That's not good enough," Hank replied. "I wanna know why you've been givin' everybody such a hard time, and I wanna know *now.*"

"I didn't do nothin'." Tina lifted one shoulder in an I-don't-care shrug. "An' even if I did, maybe I just felt like it."

"Why? Is it because you're still mad at me for not takin' you to Oklahoma? If it is, you're not bein' fair to your teacher and everybody else here at school."

She shrugged again and shook her head, but didn't utter another word. The silence stretched out, prickly as ten miles of barbed wire fence. Because she was exposing just how ineffective a parent he was in front of Emily, Hank wanted to grab the kid and shake her until her teeth rattled. He'd never lay a hand on his daughter in anger, of course, but the urge was definitely there.

Finally Emily spoke, her voice soft and low, and somehow reassuring. "Tina, I know you're really a very nice little girl." She held up the folder. "It's all right here in your records, honey. It sounds to me as if you're really angry and hurting inside. Is there some way we can help you? Your father loves you and he's worried about you. So am I."

Tina's throat worked down an audible gulp, and her chin started to quiver. Then her little face crumpled in anguish, a flood of tears gushed down her cheeks and she ran around the desk and threw herself into Emily's arms. Emily automatically scooped the child onto her lap and cuddled her close, while Hank looked on in astonishment.

"He don't love me!" Tina wailed. "Nobody loves me or wants me around any-m-more."

Ignoring the pain in his leg, Hank bolted out of his chair and hobbled over to his sobbing daughter as fast as he could. He braced his backside against the desk and leaned down, gently stroking her cinnamon-colored hair.

"That's not true, baby," he whispered hoarsely. "I love you more than anything else in the whole world."

Tina shook her head violently and buried her face in Emily's neck. "No you don't. You never did."

Hank shot Emily a desperate glance. She nodded and smiled, as if in encouragement.

"Well, let's go home and we'll talk it over," he said.

"No!" Tina wrapped her arms around Emily's neck in a strangling hold. "I don't *wanna* go home with you. I wanna stay with Ms. F-Franklin."

"Now, honey, I know you don't like me much right now, but do you want me to call Aunt Becky and Uncle Sam? I know they'll come home if you need them."

She raised tear-filled eyes to meet his. "They g-got their own kids now. They don't got t-time for me anymore. I'm j-j-just in the w-way."

"Aw, sugar, don't cry so hard," Hank begged, his heart shattering at her distress. "Want me to go get Grandma D?"

"She only likes Aunt B-Becky's dumb ol' baby now. An' besides, she'll prob'ly die pretty soon."

"Where on earth did you get an idea like that? Grandma D's fine."

"Well, Billy's grandma died, an' Grandma D's really my great-grandma, so she's bound to die before long, Dad."

"Believe me, Tina," Hank said with a wry smile, "Grandma D's such a tough old bird, she'll probably outlive the rest of us. But no matter what happens, you'll always have me, baby. Honest."

"You never pay attention to me," she said, wiping her nose with the back of her hand. "An' you're always crabby an' goin' off an' l-leavin' m-me."

"That's not gonna happen anymore, Tina. I promise."

"Oh, *sure,* Dad."

He raked one hand through his hair and sucked in a deep breath for patience. "Listen, honey, I know things have been crazy at home lately, and you've kinda gotten lost in the shuffle. But my leg's a lot better now, and from here on out, wherever I go, you're comin' with me."

"You m-mean it?"

"Cross my heart and hope to die," he answered, making the appropriate sign on his chest. "So whaddaya say? Ready to go home?"

She eyed him warily for an endless moment, then stubbornly shook her head. "I wanna stay with Ms. Franklin."

Completely at a loss as to what to try next, Hank looked to Emily for help. She mouthed the word "dinner" over the top of Tina's head.

Hank nodded. "I don't know about you, Tina, but I'm so hungry, my belly thinks my throat's been cut. How'dja like to go out and get some supper? You can even choose the restaurant.''

"Not unless Ms. Franklin comes, too."

"Ms. Franklin might have other plans, honey," Hank said gently. "We've taken up enough of her time."

A fresh batch of tears puddled in the little girl's eyes, and she turned a pleading expression on the principal. "Do you?" she asked, her voice quavering. "I really want you to come, Ms. Franklin."

Emily hesitated, then shot Hank a questioning glance. "Tina, I—"

"Please?" the child begged. "I promise I'll be good."

Hank added his own pleading look to the effort. Lord, he was willing to do just about anything to keep the kid from cryin' again. The principal gave in with a soft chuckle.

"I'd love to join you and your father for dinner."

Chapter Two

Her heart filling with emotion, Emily returned Tina's exuberant hug, then blinked back tears when the little girl went willingly into her father's arms a moment later. Hank gathered his daughter into a desperate embrace, repeatedly kissing the top of her head and murmuring silly, affectionate nicknames that made Tina giggle. This was the part of her job that made all the headaches worthwhile, Emily thought with a smile.

Hoping to give Hank and Tina a bit of privacy, she turned away and packed her briefcase with paperwork to complete over the weekend. When she'd finished, she took the child into the teachers' rest room. Tina washed her face and hands while Emily repaired her own makeup, and then Tina stood as still as a little doll while Emily brushed out the girl's tangled, waist-length, auburn hair. Without the sullen scowl she'd worn for the past few months, Tina Dawson was a beautiful little girl.

The feminine ritual brought a lump to Emily's throat. The one real regret Emily still carried from her failed marriage was that she'd never had a child of her own.

At age thirty-seven, her biological clock ticked more insistently with each birthday, but there didn't seem to be anything she could do about it. She hadn't been seriously attracted to a man since her divorce five years ago. That situation wasn't likely to change, especially since she'd come back to live in a community as small as Pinedale.

What about Hank? a quiet voice inside her head demanded.

Emily nearly snorted with laughter at that suggestion. Though she would readily admit that Hank Dawson still possessed a kind of earthy, sexual magnetism to which she had very little immunity, he was absolutely the last man on the planet with whom she would ever allow herself to become involved.

Oh, his looks had improved with age—she'd come close to blushing like an adolescent when he'd turned those sinfully gorgeous dark eyes of his on her with blatant admiration. Her fingers had itched to touch his thick, wavy hair, which was two shades darker than his daughter's.

If she were to be completely honest with herself, Emily would also have to concede that her stomach had done a series of funny little flip-flops every time she'd noticed his impressive physique and handsome features. When a man who stood well over six feet tall and had a face and body that had haunted your most private sexual fantasies for over twenty years, sat barely ten feet away from you, it was more than a bit difficult to ignore his attributes.

Fortunately, Emily was no longer the impressionable fifteen- and sixteen-year-old girl who had suffered a heartbreaking crush on seventeen- and eighteen-year-old Hank when she'd tutored him through his high school math classes. Even with her help, he'd barely managed to maintain his eligibility to play football, which had been his sole reason for putting up with the tutoring sessions in the first place.

Lord, how he used to frustrate her with his devil-may-care attitude toward academics. Always at the top of her class, despite having skipped a grade in elementary school, she'd never been able to understand Hank. He'd certainly been intelligent enough to handle the work himself, but unless he saw an immediate, personal benefit from learning the material, he simply couldn't dredge up the motivation necessary to do his assignments.

It had been as if his brain was too full of sports and rodeo, fast cars and cheerleaders, and cramming as much hell-raising as was humanly possible into each and every day, to leave any room for schoolwork.

Hank hadn't understood her any better. He'd delighted in teasing poor, studious Emily. He'd called her Worm, short for Bookworm, until his rowdy friends and eventually everyone else in school had picked up on the wretched nickname. She shuddered at the thought of the torment he would have put her through if he'd known how she really felt about him.

Considering the condition of his relationship with his daughter and the things Tina had said in her office, Emily doubted that Hank's basic personality had changed much since those days. No matter how sexy or charming the man might be on occasion, the idea of developing any kind of involvement with him was positively ludicrous.

"What's the matter, Ms. Franklin?" Tina asked.

Emily started at the sound of the little girl's voice and looked up to meet her worried gaze in the mirror. "Oh, nothing, honey. I was just thinking."

"You looked kinda sad."

"I did? Well, I didn't mean to," Emily replied with a smile. "There, you look gorgeous. Let's go get some dinner."

Tina nodded vigorously in agreement. Taking Emily's hand, she skipped along beside her, chattering like a normal second grader. Hank was waiting for them outside her office, his shoulder braced against the door casing, one booted foot crossed casually over the other.

When he straightened to his full height at their approach, Emily experienced that disquieting sensation of a sudden drop one sometimes feels in an elevator. Heaven help her, the man really *was* an impossibly good-looking hunk.

With his black Stetson tipped back on his head, those broad, muscular shoulders and long legs encased in tight jeans, he was enough to give any woman heart palpitations. Add in that cheerfully wicked grin, those dark, sexy eyes and his deep, pleasantly husky voice, and he could almost make a sensible woman forget what a rogue he truly was.

"Well, ladies?" he said. "Are we ready to hit the road?"

"I'll get my things," Emily replied, utterly grateful that she'd learned to mask her emotions years ago.

During the few moments she spent alone in her office while Hank bundled Tina into her coat, Emily inhaled deep, calming breaths and silently chanted the word *ludicrous* over and over again. Then, squaring her shoulders, she marched out to join her dinner companions.

After locking the building, she followed Hank and Tina to the parking area, pausing to stare in amazement at the lone vehicle waiting there. It wasn't just a pickup, like one of the hundreds that daily lined the streets of Pinedale. It was the biggest, blackest, shiniest pickup she'd ever seen, with acres of chrome, oversize tires and, she didn't doubt for a second, a souped-up engine.

Hank glanced over his shoulder at her. "What's the matter, Ms. Franklin? Don't you like trucks?"

Emily smiled and shook her head in amusement. It wouldn't be appropriate for a principal to call a parent a show-off, certainly not in front of his child. But that vehicle was so brash, so arrogant, so...Hank, she couldn't help chuckling over it. He hadn't changed one whit.

He opened the passenger door for her and watched her struggle to lift her leg high enough within the confines of her slim-fitting skirt, to reach the step. Of course, the blasted thing sat so high off the ground because of the oversize tires, she couldn't do it without hiking her skirt halfway to her waist. And, of course, Hank just stood there, his dark eyes dancing with impertinent glee at her dilemma, challenging her to give him a show.

If it weren't for Tina, who had already scrambled into the cab and was looking out with tear-reddened eyes, Emily would have walked the three blocks to her house without so much as a backward glance. But she would never renege on a promise to a child, especially one as vulnerable as Tina. The wretched man knew that, too.

Determined not to let him rattle her composure, Emily turned away, gritted her teeth, then let out a startled yelp when his hands closed around her waist and boosted her onto the seat in one smooth motion. Before she could say a word, he shut the door in her face and walked around the front of the pickup. The man swaggered, even when he limped, she thought, silently fuming.

Hank settled in behind the steering wheel, started the engine and turned to his daughter. "All right, Miss Tina, where should we eat?"

"I wanna go to The Diner, Dad."

His jovial grin slipped. "Aw, c'mon, honey, we'll starve before we get there. How 'bout McGregors Pub instead? That's a nice restaurant."

Tina's eyes narrowed. "You *said* I could choose the restaurant."

"Well, yeah, I did. But that's way out north of the ranch."

"I wanna go to The Diner," the little girl insisted, her chin raising in a gesture that positively reeked of stubbornness.

Emily had to look out the window to prevent herself from laughing out loud at the battle of wills taking place beside her. While she would have felt more sympathy for any other parent in a similar situation, at the moment she couldn't think of a soul who deserved to have a child like Tina more than Hank Dawson. The kid wasn't going to give him a millimeter, much less an inch.

To his credit, he gave in with a shrug and affectionately tweaked his daughter's nose before driving away from the school. Emily leaned back, determined to enjoy the evening, despite Hank's disturbing presence. After all, this wasn't a date; she was only going along for Tina's sake, and they both knew that.

Still, there was something...intimate about riding off into the gathering darkness, enclosed in the pickup's cab with Hank and his daughter. Tina snuggled close, strands of her long hair clinging to the wool fabric of Emily's coat. Putting her arm around the little girl's shoulders, Emily felt another pang of wistfulness when Tina tilted her face up, giving her a sweet, gap-toothed smile.

Emily exhaled a silent sigh and turned her attention to the windshield. Hank had already made the turn to the north toward Cora on Highway 352, and the broad valley between the Wind River and Wyoming mountain ranges lay open ahead of them. A familiar lump rose in her throat at the sight. Her mother had always loved this view. Though she had lost her battle with cancer a little over a year ago, Emily still missed her.

Tina leaned forward and switched on the radio. Emily started at the sudden blast of noise and chuckled when she saw Hank had done the same thing. They exchanged sheepish grins over the top of the little girl's head. Then Hank turned the music down to a more tolerable level.

"Last I heard, you were doin' real well down in Cheyenne, Em," he said. "What made you come back to Pinedale?"

"I wanted to be closer to my father," she replied.

"He's all right, isn't he?" Hank asked, his tone laced with a sincere concern that surprised Emily. To her knowledge, he'd never had anything to do with her father or the congregation he'd served until his retirement. Perhaps Hank was simply being polite.

"Oh, he's fine. But after Mother passed away, I realized he wasn't getting any younger, and I wanted to be able to spend more time with him. I was lucky the principal's job opened up."

Hank nodded in understanding. "Have you missed livin' in a bigger town?"

"To tell you the truth, my job's kept me so busy, I haven't had time to think about it," Emily said with a smile.

"Oh yeah? I thought all principals ever did was sit in the office and yell at kids."

"She hardly ever yells, Dad," Tina piped up. "But she does lotsa other stuff."

"Like what?"

"She's the announcer at assemblies, an' she's always runnin' around the building talkin' to the teachers, an' she plays with us at recess sometimes. She's real good at jump rope."

"No kiddin'?" Hank asked, raising a doubtful eyebrow at Emily's prim suit.

Tina followed the direction of his gaze, and informed him with a giggle, "Sometimes she wears pants, Dad."

Hank shook his head, as if in amazement. "Principals must have changed since I went to school."

"Did you get yelled at a lot?" Tina asked.

"Yeah," he admitted.

"What didja do, Dad?"

Hank looked at Emily. She shrugged, then bit her lower lip, desperately trying not to laugh at the predicament he'd gotten himself into now. After scowling at her, he turned his attention back to his daughter.

"A lot of things I'm not very proud of, Tina. There've been plenty of times I've wished I'd paid more attention in school. I hope you'll do better than I did."

Tina suddenly found the scuffed toes of her sneakers extremely interesting. "I'll try. But I don't think my report card's gonna be too good. I'm real far behind everybody else now."

Emily patted the little girl's shoulder in reassurance. "I'll talk to Mrs. Jovanovich on Monday and we'll help you get caught up. But you're going to have to work hard and stay out of trouble."

"I will, Ms Franklin," Tina replied earnestly. "Honest."

They finished the rest of the drive in a comfortable silence. The parking lot at The Diner was crowded with cars and pickups. Hank found a space at the north end of the long, one-story log building, then hurried around to the passenger side to help Emily down.

She put her hands on his shoulders, digging her fingers into the soft, well-worn denim of his jacket when his hands closed around her waist and lifted her off the seat. Suspended in midair, she caught a whiff of a spicy after-shave, and saw in his dark eyes the same intense awareness she was feeling as he slowly lowered her to the ground.

Gravel shifted beneath her pumps. His big hands tightened, steadying her, lingering a second longer than necessary. Their gazes locked for a heartbeat, then another and another, until Tina jumped out of the pickup, sending up a clatter of rocks that effectively broke the spell.

Emily shivered and turned toward the building, silently assuring herself that one breathless moment of attraction meant nothing. Still, she had to admit it was a relief to enter the small restaurant section and join the company of other people. All of the chrome stools with brown leather seats at the L-shaped counter were occupied by men wearing jeans, boots, Western shirts and cowboy hats, but one of the two chrome-and-Formica tables was available.

While they removed their coats and settled in, Tina beside Emily and Hank directly across from her, a chorus of greetings went up from the group at the counter. Hank acknowledged them with a smile and a wave. If he failed to notice the surprised glances he received when his friends took a good look at his companion, Emily didn't. Remembering the girls Hank had pursued in high school, she wasn't particularly surprised by their reactions.

Back then, he'd liked his women stacked, wild and hot to trot—he'd told her that once in exactly those terms. Evidently, his tastes hadn't changed much over the years. Telling herself that Hank's love life, past or present, was none of her concern and never would be, she picked up the menu and studied it.

The jukebox in the bar next door blared out a country-and-western song. Whoops of excitement and groans of disgust followed the cracks of the billiard balls at the pool tables. A low rumble of masculine conversation competed with the sizzle of hamburgers frying on the grill and the clank and rattle of silverware and dishes.

Then a short, stout waitress with frizzy red hair planted her feet beside Hank's chair and propped her elbow on his shoulder. "Hi there, stranger. Good to see you back on your feet again. What'll it be?"

Chuckling, he gave her a one-armed hug, then rested his hand on her ample hip. "Good to see you, too, Bonnie. I'll have the usual." Directing his gaze across the table, he said, "What do you want, Emily?"

"I'd like a cheeseburger with a salad instead of french fries, ranch dressing on the side. Hot tea to drink."

"Me, too," Tina said. "Only I want a chocolate milk shake."

Bonnie scribbled furiously on her order pad, tipped her head to one side when she'd finished and inspected Emily for a moment. "Ya know, you look kinda familiar. Have we met before?"

"You went to high school with her, Bonnie," Hank said with a teasing grin for Emily. "Think skinny, glasses, braces, a year behind us, smart."

Tapping her pen against her watch, Bonnie scrunched up her nose and squinted at Emily, softly muttering her name. Then a broad smile spread across her face. "Emily Jackson? The preacher's kid? The Wo—"

Desperate to prevent the woman from blurting out that despised nickname in front of Tina and everyone else, Emily interrupted. "That's right. My last name is Franklin now. I'm sorry, but I can't quite place you, Bonnie."

Bonnie laughed at that. "Can't say as I blame you there. Think fifty pounds less, long, straight hair and pompoms." She nudged Hank with her elbow. "I used to go with ol' Heartbreak Hank here, until he went off and joined the rodeo circuit."

"Bonnie Atkins?" Emily guessed, shaking her head in amazement.

The woman nodded eagerly, but before she could reply, the burly man at the grill swiveled around and shouted across the room. "Dawson, get your hand off my wife's fanny, will ya? You gonna stand there and flap your gums all night or take that order, Bonnie?"

The men at the counter roared with laughter, then glanced over their shoulders to catch the next line, as if they'd witnessed this kind of byplay a thousand times before. Bonnie didn't disappoint them. Clamping her hands on her hips, she threw back her shoulders and turned to face the cook, her massive breasts jutting out like a pair of torpedoes.

"Aw, keep your shorts on, Jerry, and mind your own business," she shouted back. "Hank's my friend and he can pat my fanny any time he wants."

Jerry leaned across the counter toward his wife, puckered up and kissed the air with a loud smacking noise. Then he smacked his rear end and returned to the grill.

Bonnie screeched with laughter and retorted, "Yeah, you can kiss mine, too, honey," before turning back to the table as if nothing out of the ordinary had happened. "Let's see now, where were we? Oh yeah. Emily, are you just here for a visit, or what?"

Still a bit shocked by such a crude display, Emily cleared her throat, then took a sip of water. "I, uh, live here now," she finally managed to reply.

"She's the principal at my school," Tina said with a proud smile.

"You're kiddin' me." Bonnie looked from Emily to Hank and back to Emily again, then let out another screech of mirth that drowned out the jukebox and once again drew every eye in the room. "Hey, did you guys hear what the kid said? Hank's datin' the grade school principal! Do you remember the stunts he used to pull when we were in school?"

The laughter that followed reverberated against Emily's eardrums in time with the hot blush climbing higher up her cheeks at every beat of her heart. She slid a little lower in her chair, wishing she could simply disappear under the table and slither out the door unnoticed, taking Tina with her. This was not an appropriate place for a child.

And then, as if she wasn't already embarrassed enough, the chairs at the other table scraped against the worn linoleum. The two couples who had been sitting there filed past Bonnie, the women's mouths tight with disapproval as they made their way to the door. The first man walked by, fishing a wallet out of his hip pocket, but the second man stopped beside Emily's chair, silently demanding her attention.

She slowly raised her eyes and met the stern gaze of Keith Daniels, a member of the school board. Forcing a smile, though it was definitely a sick one, to her lips, she nodded. "Hello, Mr. Daniels."

"Ms. Franklin."

He didn't say anything else, but then, he didn't have to. During her job interview, he'd made it plain that he hadn't wanted to hire her, or, she suspected, any other woman. In the months since, he'd also made it plain that he hadn't changed his mind.

Though the other members of the board had voted against him, he still had the power to make her life miserable. The long, reproachful look he'd just given her told her he planned to do exactly that. Emily gulped when the door closed behind him, then glanced at the man sitting across the table from her, chatting with Bonnie as if he hadn't a care in the world.

Wasn't that the way it had always been for her with Hank Dawson? She helped him out and ended up feeling completely mortified by something he or one of his rowdy friends said or did? Well, it had happened for the last time.

She would help him get Tina fed. Then she would make him take her home and she would never have anything to do with him again. No matter how handsome or sexy or charming he was, she wasn't willing to pay the price an association with him could cost her.

Hank watched the color flood into Emily's face and felt like a first-class idiot for bringing her here. For that matter, he wasn't really happy to have Tina here, either. The kid's eyes were as big as Grandma D's biscuits, and he could just imagine the kinds of questions Bonnie and Jerry's little scene would inspire.

But how was he supposed to know they'd get into one of their public snits tonight? He hadn't been in The Diner since he'd come home from the hospital, and he'd forgotten how raunchy they could be. To tell the truth, when Tina had said this was where she wanted to eat, he hadn't thought about much of anything but makin' the kid happy.

Dammit all, though, he *should* have thought about that decision before he made it, which was the story of his life. Oh, The Diner wasn't a dive by anybody's definition. As cafés went, it wasn't bad at all. The food was good, the atmosphere relaxed, the prices reasonable.

But on a Friday night folks tended to come in here and let down their hair after a hard week's work. It had never bothered him, but he should have realized Emily would feel about as comfortable as a maiden aunt in a strip joint.

She wasn't a snob, exactly—at least he didn't think she was. She'd just been raised with different standards and expectations than a rancher's kid. Back in high school, he used to get quite a kick out of offending her delicate sensibilities and watching her blush redder than a tomato.

He didn't feel that way anymore, though. In fact, while it seemed weird after he'd rebelled against conventional behavior all his life, he wanted Emily Franklin's respect more than he'd wanted anything in a long time. Considering the way he'd treated her all those years ago, it was a daunting prospect. Still, he figured it'd be worth the aggravation it would cause him.

Tina obviously adored the woman. He'd give just about anything to have the kid look at him with that much trust and admiration. By earning Emily's respect, maybe he could earn his daughter's, too.

The first logical step in meeting his new goal was to get this supper over with and get Emily out of The Diner before Bonnie and Jerry said or did anything else outrageous. With that in mind, Hank gave Bonnie's rump a final pat and winked at her.

"Put a rush on that, will ya, Bon? We're all about to starve to death."

"You bet, Hank," she answered, returning his wink. She turned toward the counter and shouted, "Order up, Jerry! One heartburn special, two cheeseburgers, hold the fries, put a ranch garden on 'em and get the lead out."

Bonnie hurried off to get their drinks, and Hank looked over at Emily. She gave him a glare hot enough to melt the chrome on his chair, then pointedly turned her attention to Tina. He bit back a disgruntled sigh and kneaded his throbbing left leg.

Jeez, it wouldn't be easy getting Emily to like him. Contrary to popular belief, however, he wasn't a quitter. There just hadn't been many things in his life that had seemed important enough to make a real effort. What most folks didn't understand about him was that when something *was* important to him, he'd bust his butt trying to get it.

Rodeo was a prime example. He hadn't made it all the way to the top, but not for any lack of effort on his part. He'd been bucked off, kicked and stomped by more broncs than he cared to remember. That had never stopped him from climbing onto the next one and trying again, enough times to make the national finals twice.

Tina was even more important to him. As far as he was concerned, Emily could be as mad at him as she pleased, but it wouldn't do her any good. She knew some things he needed to learn. Whether she wanted to or not, she was gonna teach him about kids, just like she'd hammered the basics of algebra into his thick skull.

By the time Tina finally swallowed the last bite of her cheeseburger, Emily was ready to run screaming into the night. Though she'd seen all sorts of behavior in school cafeterias over the course of her career, she had never seen a child dawdle over a meal for so long. It flattered her immensely that the little girl wanted to spend as much time as possible with her. Unfortunately, being this close to the little girl's father was driving Emily crazy.

Hank hadn't said or done anything to tease or offend her, which had certainly been a surprise. In fact, he'd gone out of his way to be pleasant and polite, and he'd definitely worked hard at getting himself back into Tina's good graces.

Nevertheless, Emily had to wonder how long he could hold out against the urge to provoke her. Furthermore, she didn't trust the sparkle of amusement she'd glimpsed in his eyes at least twice during the meal when he'd looked at her. It reminded her too much of the kind of man he'd always been—the kind who would start an uproar for the sheer fun of it. Then he would sit back, looking as innocent as a kindergartner in a Christmas program, and watch it unfold with fiendish delight.

They made it out to his pickup without a mishap, however, and Emily buckled her seat belt with a silent sigh of relief. Tina snuggled up next to her. A moment later, or so it seemed, the little girl's head fell back against the seat and a quiet snore emitted from her mouth. Smiling, Emily pulled her closer and gently brushed the child's shaggy bangs out of her eyes.

Hank's deep, gravelly voice reached out from the other side of the darkened cab. "Thanks for helping her, Emily."

"That's my job, Hank," she said quietly.

"You went above and beyond the call of duty tonight. I appreciate it." They rode on in silence for several miles before he spoke again. "Mind if I drop her off at the ranch? I know you must be anxious to get home, but—"

"That's fine. She should be in bed."

He made a left turn onto a gravel road. Tina slept through the thunder of rocks kicked up by the tires and the bouncing from potholes and ruts. But when Hank parked in back of the big white ranch house and killed the engine, the little girl bolted upright, shaking her head in confusion.

"Where are we?" she asked.

"We're home," Hank said, reaching for her. "C'mon, sweet potato, time for you to hit the sack. Grandma D'll help you get tucked in while I take Ms. Franklin home."

Leaning away from her father, Tina latched on to Emily's arm with both hands. "No. I wanna stay with Ms. Franklin."

"Don't start that again," Hank warned her. Emily couldn't see his face clearly, but she heard exhaustion and impatience creeping into his voice. "I did what you wanted. Now it's your turn to do what I want. Get out of the pickup and let's go."

He reached for her again. Tina kicked and hit at him with her fists, shrieking, "No! I wanna stay with Ms. Franklin. Soon as she's gone, you won't be nice to me anymore."

"Tina, stop it!" Hank roared, protecting his face with one hand while he grabbed at her flailing feet with the other.

"No! I hate you! I really really really hate you! An' I hate Grandma D, too!"

Unable to bear the child's hysteria, Emily wrapped her arms around Tina, trapping her fists at her sides. "Hush, Tina. It's all right. It's all right."

Hank finally gained control of Tina's feet, and the little girl's shrieks gradually quieted into choking sobs. Emily crooned reassurances and rocked her until she exhaled a ragged little sigh and laid her head on Emily's breasts. Hank retreated to the driver's seat without saying a word, but Emily felt tension radiating off him in waves.

At the moment, however, Hank was not her first concern. Lifting Tina onto her lap, she turned the child to face her and opened her door. Doing so turned on the pickup's dome light. She had to see Tina's face.

"I need to ask you some questions," she said softly, wiping the little girl's tears away with her thumbs. "They're really important, and I need completely honest answers. Do you understand?"

Tina nodded.

"Has anybody here at home ever hit you or done anything else to hurt you?" Emily ignored Hank's muttered curse, focusing all of her attention on the child.

Tina shrugged. "Well, Uncle Sam swatted my bottom once when I sassed him. But it didn't leave a bruise or nothin'."

"How about your dad? What does he do when he gets angry with you?"

"Aw, he just yells. Mostly he's not around, an' he doesn't care what I do anyhow."

"Nobody beats her," Hank snarled.

Emily glared at him. "That's for Tina to tell me, Hank. Not you." Softening her voice, she turned back to the little girl. "Is that true, honey?"

Tina nodded.

"Good. I'm glad to hear that. I just have one more question, and remember, you can tell me anything. Has anyone been touching you in a way that makes you feel uncomfortable?"

"You mean like when we talked about strangers and stuff at school?" Tina asked. "Like, on my private parts?"

"That's right. But it doesn't have to be a stranger, sweetie. Has *anybody* ever touched you like that?"

Much to Emily's relief, Tina shook her head. "No, Ms. Franklin. I just don't want you to leave."

Emily hugged her. Then she leaned back and met Tina's gaze again. "I'm glad you feel that way about me, Tina, but you're going to have to find some other ways to let people know what you want. And, you have to understand that people can't always do what you want. I have pets at home waiting to be fed. You wouldn't want them to be hungry, would you?''

Tina slowly shook her head. ''Would you maybe come in and tuck me in bed?'' she whispered, her eyes welling with tears again.

''I'd enjoy that,'' Emily assured her. ''Are you ready to go inside now?''

The child nodded and climbed out of the truck after Emily. Hank slammed his door hard enough to make the vehicle shudder and stormed ahead of them to the house. He yanked open the back door and held it for them. Emily winced inwardly at his rigid posture and the fury in his eyes when she passed him under the porch light, but she held her head high and followed Tina into a warm, homey kitchen.

Chapter Three

Too angry and shaken to speak coherently, Hank let Tina introduce Emily to Grandma D and Sam's new stepson, Colin. Evidently, she already knew Colin's sister, Kim. He stalked across the kitchen and drew himself a tall drink of water. He guzzled it straight down, then had to fight an almost overpowering urge to smash the glass into a million pieces against the porcelain sink.

After taking five deep breaths, he set the tumbler on the counter, shoved his hands into his pockets and stared through the window at the darkness outside. Dammit all to hell and back in a hay wagon; he'd thought he was doing the right things for Tina. He'd been planning to settle down and make a real home for the two of them as soon as he could talk old man Gunderson into a reasonable price for his place and Sam and Dani came back from their honeymoon.

But after that scene in the pickup, he wasn't sure about anything as far as Tina was concerned. Not one *damn* blessed thing. Maybe he just wasn't cut out to be a parent. Maybe he was doing her more harm than good.

His throat closed up at that thought, and he nearly jumped clean out of his boots when Grandma D laid her gnarled little hand on his shoulder.

"What's goin' on, Hank?"

He turned to face her, steadied somewhat by her calm, quiet tone. God bless her, Grandma D could be a real termagant when she felt like it, but she was a valuable ally in a crisis. She wouldn't pull any punches if he asked for advice, and he figured that's what he needed. Since everyone else had taken off for other parts of the house, now seemed as good a time as any to get it.

When they were seated at the kitchen table, he told her exactly what had happened at the school and an edited version of what had taken place in the pickup. He couldn't bring himself to repeat what Emily had halfway accused him of doing to Tina. Lord, just the memory of the questions she'd asked made his stomach clench and his skin crawl.

Grandma D listened intently. After he'd finished, she set her big red glasses on the table and rubbed her eyes. "Land sakes," she murmured, shaking her head in dismay. "The poor little tyke. None of us meant to hurt her feelin's like that."

"I know that and you know that, but now we've got to convince Tina," Hank replied. "I don't have the faintest idea how to go about doin' it, either."

"We'll just have to keep lovin' her, that's all," the old lady said.

"Grandma, you didn't hear her. That kid hates my guts. Do you think she'd be happier if I left? Got out of her life and stayed out?"

"Is that what you want to do, Hank?" Grandma D demanded, shoving her glasses back onto her nose. "Give up and abandon her like her mama did?"

"No, dammit!" He sighed, then ran both hands through his hair in frustration. "You wanta know what really got me back on my feet when the doctors kept sayin' they didn't know if I'd ever walk again? It was the thought of not bein' able to walk Tina down the aisle at her wedding. I'd lay there in that hospital bed and imagine Sam gettin' to do that, and I was damned if I was gonna let it happen."

"Well, then," Grandma D said, "you'd better start actin' like a father, hadn't you?"

"You mean like my dad acted with me?" Hank demanded with a bitter laugh. "Yeah, that oughtta *really* make her love me."

"No, Hank, of course not," she said quietly.

Hank stared at her in amazement. Jack Dawson had been her only child, and Hank had never once heard his grandmother criticize him. Or allow anyone else to, either. She noted Hank's reaction with a small shrug.

"I know he wasn't fair to you, and I warned him about bein' so damned hard on you plenty of times. So did your mama."

"You did? Why haven't I ever heard about it before?"

"Because we didn't want to get caught in the middle. A kid hears somethin' like that, and then next thing you know, he's playin' you off against each other. But that doesn't mean we agreed with the way he handled you. He never could get it through his head that all you wanted was some of his attention."

"Yeah, well, I got it, didn't I?"

"You sure did. And I think that's exactly what Tina's tryin' to do with you now. Get your attention."

"Hey, she's got it, Grandma. She can have anything she wants from me."

"That's part of the problem, Hank. What she needs from you right now is some limits. You've always relied on Becky and Sam and me to give 'em to her, 'cause you were tryin' so hard not to be like your dad. But kids need 'em to feel secure. And since Becky and Sam and I've been distracted one way or another, Tina thinks nobody cares about her.''

"So now I've gotta be tough with her?" Hank asked, hating that thought with every last bit of his soul. Tina was his baby, his little sweetheart. He wanted her to laugh and be free and enjoy her childhood. Life would get tough for her soon enough, just like it did for everyone.

"Not necessarily tough," Grandma D said. "God knows, you don't hafta be mean about it. But you've gotta be firm with her. Let her know what you expect and then hold her to it.''

"I don't know if I can do that," Hank protested. "I mean, she does so well with Becky and Pete, maybe she'd be better off with them.''

"From what you said, that's not what she wants. She wants an adult who's all hers, and you're the only one who fits the bill, Hank.''

"But what if I screw up with her?"

Grandma D snorted with laughter. "You think there's a parent alive who doesn't screw up with their kids now and then? Get real, boy. You just do the best you can and pray a lot. That's about all any of us can do.''

"You're sure it's not too late?"

"When it comes to kids, there aren't any guarantees," she said, patting his hand. "But you're a smart enough guy and you love her. You can get through to her if you want to bad enough.''

"All right," Hank said slowly. "I'll give it my best shot, Grandma.''

"You'll do well, Hank. I know you will." She pushed back her chair then, and stood. "I'm gonna sneak upstairs and see how Ms. Franklin's gettin' along.''

Hank propped his left leg up onto the empty chair and drummed his fingertips on the table, struggling to digest everything his grandmother had said. Deep down inside, he knew she was right about a lot of things, but he still couldn't quite picture himself in the role of a father for Tina or anyone else.

To Hank, the word *father* always brought up a mental picture of his old man berating him. No matter how hard Hank had tried, he'd never been able to measure up to Sam or do anything well enough to suit Jack Dawson. Eventually, he'd stopped trying and set out to aggravate the hell out of his dad any way he could.

During his early rodeo years, he used to dream about bringing home a national championship belt buckle. Even then, he'd wondered if his dad would have respected the accomplishment, because he'd been the one to do it instead of Sam. But his dad had died before he could get close to his dream, and there was no way he'd ever know now.

All he'd been left with were memories of a stern disciplinarian he couldn't please, and he'd sworn never to be that way with his own kids. Hank laughed and shook his head. Well, he'd done that with a vengeance, and his daughter had ended up thinkin' he didn't care about her. Go figure.

Logically, there had to be a middle ground somewhere, and that's where Grandma D was tryin' to point him. It wasn't as if he'd never been around kids at all. He'd bossed teenagers some, kids who'd worked on the Circle D as hired hands during the summer. Of course, Sam had handed out most of the orders and it just wasn't the same as coping with a little girl.

Teenage boys didn't cry when you yelled at 'em. God, he'd never been able to stand Tina's tears, and the little varmint knew it, too. It sure as hell looked like he was gonna have to learn, though. If he didn't, he'd lose his daughter for sure.

The back of his neck prickled with the sensation that someone was watching him. Hank glanced over his shoulder and saw Emily standing in the doorway to the living room. The memory of what she'd implied in the pickup washed over him. Blood boiling, he swung his bad leg to the floor and climbed to his feet.

"Is Tina all right?" he asked gruffly.

Nodding, Emily walked hesitantly into the kitchen. "She's sound asleep."

"Let's go, then."

She followed him outside without a word and scrambled into the truck on her own. That was just dandy with Hank. He intended to drive her to town, dump her at her house, and if there was any justice in this world at all, never have to lay eyes on her again. She tolerated his brooding silence until they hit the highway.

"I'm sorry I offended you, Hank, but—"

"Hey, I always knew you didn't think much of me," he retorted, shooting her a scathing glance before looking back at the road ahead, "but I sure as hell never dreamed you'd believe I could beat or molest my own daughter."

"I won't apologize for asking Tina those questions," Emily replied. "For your information, I couldn't imagine anyone in your family doing something like that. But Tina was so adamant about staying with me, and with the sudden change in her behavior last winter, it was a possibility I couldn't afford to ignore. It wasn't meant as a personal attack."

"It felt pretty damn personal from where I was sittin'."

She blew out an exasperated sigh. "I'm bound by law as well as basic human decency to protect children. I've seen too much abuse in all kinds of families to pretend it couldn't happen here or anywhere else. If the governor's daughter acted the way Tina did, I'd have asked her exactly the same questions."

"You mean that?"

"Yes. And so would any other professional who works with children. Ask Dr. Sinclair, if you don't believe me. I had to know she was safe. Surely you can understand that."

"Yeah, I guess I can," Hank grumbled.

He unclenched his fingers from around the steering wheel and rubbed the back of his neck in an effort to ease the knot that had formed there. Neither of them spoke again until Emily had to give him directions to her house. The second the truck stopped rolling, she reached for her door handle.

Hank's conscience jabbed at him, and he forced himself to listen to it. He owed the woman an apology and a thankyou. Before she'd royally ticked him off, he'd decided she knew some things he needed to learn. That was still true. Even if Emily wouldn't help him, it wasn't in Tina's best interests for him to be at odds with her principal.

"Emily, wait," he said. She turned and looked at him expectantly, and though it stung his pride like the iodine his mother used to put on his cuts, he forced himself to go on.

"I'm sorry. You were right to do what you did, and I'm glad there are people like you lookin' out for kids. It just seemed to me like those... accusations came outta nowhere. Tina was so mad at me, I was afraid she might say I did those things out of spite."

Emily shook her head. "Children rarely lie in that situation, Hank. If anything, they usually try to protect their abusers. Especially if the abuser is someone in their family."

"Well, see, you know all this stuff about kids, but I don't. And I'm finally wakin' up and realizin' I need to know about 'em. I love my little girl, Emily, no matter what she says."

"I can see that. She loves you, too, no matter what she says."

Hank's bum leg cramped up. He shifted his weight in search of a more comfortable position, but after all he'd put it through in the past sixteen hours, he couldn't find one. "Look, I need to talk to you some more about Tina. Could I come inside with you for a little while?"

Emily glanced up and down the street. "I guess it would be all right, but only for a little while."

"Still the preacher's kid, worried about her reputation?" Hank asked with a grin.

"No. Now I'm the elementary school principal, and believe me, that's even worse," she replied seriously. "I really can't afford any gossip, Hank."

"Well, jeez, you want me to park my pickup a block away?"

"That's a good idea." She slid out of the vehicle and added, "I'll make some coffee," before closing her door and heading up the sidewalk.

Hank stared after her in disbelief, then shrugged and drove to the next block. If Emily was willing to let a few busybodies run her life, it wasn't any skin off *his* behind. He thought it was a weird thing for a thirty-seven-year-old woman to do in this day and age, but that was Emily.

She met him at the door with a fat, yowling cat in her arms and two more twining around her feet. A big mutt, part husky, part German shepherd, part God only knew what, ran out of the kitchen. He planted himself beside Emily, hackles raised, low, vicious growls coming from his throat.

"Ivan, sit," Emily commanded. The dog obediently dropped to his haunches and like a besotted lover, accepted her soft, "Good boy," and affectionate pats on his misshapen head. "It's all right, Hank. You can come in now."

Keeping a wary eye on the dog, Hank stepped into an extremely tidy living room furnished with sleek Danish furniture. Floor-to-ceiling bookshelves covered the longest wall. There wasn't a doubt in Hank's mind that Emily had read every single one of those books, and that they were arranged in alphabetical order by the authors' last names.

At her invitation, he sat on one end of her sofa, then took off his hat and set it on the armrest. Emily shooed the animals away from the door and closed it. Released from his "sit" command, Ivan came over to inspect Hank.

"I suppose Ivan is short for Ivan the Terrible?" Hank asked, holding out his less favorite hand for the animal to sniff, just in case.

Emily chuckled. "How did you guess?"

"I don't mean to hurt your feelings, Emily, but that is the ugliest excuse for a dog I've ever seen. Where in the he— heck did you get him?"

"He adopted me about five years ago."

"Same with those cats?"

She nodded and held up the one in her arms. Hank noted that half of its left ear was missing and its right eye appeared to have been sewn shut. The other eye, a surprisingly brilliant green, studied him with malevolent fascination.

"Attila's been with me for three years." Pointing to the other two at her feet, she continued, "The gray one is Napoleon, and the calico is Cleopatra. Napoleon found me about eighteen months ago. Cleo moved in just before Christmas."

Hank laughed and shook his head. Napoleon had more bald patches than a ten-year-old tire. Though Cleopatra's hide was in better shape than either Attila's or Napoleon's, her left rear leg and a third of her tail were missing.

"If you'll excuse me for a moment, I'll feed them and bring in the coffee," Emily said.

Turning sideways so that he could prop up his left leg without getting his boot on the pale peach fabric of the sofa, Hank shut his eyes and heaved a deep, weary sigh. God, what a day. It was a good thing Emily was making coffee. He hoped it wouldn't be that decaf crud, or he was liable to fall asleep in midsentence.

He heard Ivan's toenails clicking on the tile floor in the kitchen and smiled to himself. So that mangy menagerie had adopted finicky, straitlaced Emily. The thought surprised and tickled him no end.

As far as he was concerned, her choice of pets said some pretty nice things about her. Underneath that starchy manner, she must be one helluva softie at heart. He probably should have figured that from the way Tina had latched on to her.

If only she could loosen up a little, he just might find himself powerfully attracted to her. Not that he would ever do anything about it, or that she would let him do anything about it if he wanted to. But she sure had filled out in all the right places.

She strode briskly into the room a second later, carrying a tray decked out fancy enough for a ladies' aid meeting at her dad's church. Feeling a little ridiculous, he accepted a cloth napkin and a dainty china cup and saucer that practically disappeared in his hands. Then she perched on the edge of an overstuffed chair across from the sofa.

"How can I help you with Tina?"

Hank fidgeted beneath her steady gaze, uncertain how much he wanted to reveal. He decided that if she was going to help him, she'd probably need to know everything, if she didn't already. It was damn near impossible to keep a secret in a town the size of Pinedale, and he hadn't even tried.

"How much do you know about us?" he asked.

"Only that you're divorced." He raised a skeptical eyebrow at her, and she smiled and shrugged. "That's the truth, Hank. I don't like gossip and I refuse to indulge in it. Is there something you think I should know? About Tina's mother for instance?"

"There's not much to know about Christine. She took off about three weeks after Tina was born and we haven't heard from her since. My sister Becky's pretty much raised Tina."

"She's the one with the 'dumb ol' baby' Tina resents?"

"Yeah. Becky and Pete have gone back east to show the baby off to Pete's friends and relatives."

"I did hear that Sam married quite recently. I take it that's upset Tina, too?"

"You've got that right. So that leaves me. Grandma D says I've got to learn how to set limits with the kid, but I'm not sure how to do that. I guess I've acted more like a doting uncle than a father."

"Why haven't you been more involved with her, Hank?"

"She was so tiny when Christine left, I felt pretty... helpless. Becky and Grandma D moved in on the kid, and I was grateful that they knew what to do for her. It just kinda got to be a habit. I mean, Tina didn't really seem to need me much. And, I guess..."

"You guess what?" Emily prompted.

"You'll probably think I'm a real jerk for admittin' this, but a part of me kinda wanted to go back to the rodeo circuit. See, I quit when I found out Tina was on the way, 'cause that's no life for a family. But I'd come so close to a national championship, I always wondered if I couldn't win one. Maybe I didn't want Tina to depend on me too much, or I didn't want to let myself get too close to her in case I ended up taking off someday."

"Do you still want to go back?"

Hank gestured toward his left leg. "I couldn't if I wanted to. I thought about getting into the stock-contracting side of the rodeo business. Even went down to Oklahoma last fall to look into it—that's the trip I mentioned to Tina in your office. Boy, that really ticked her off."

"Why?"

"She wanted to come with me, but I didn't think she should miss that much school. I don't know, maybe she didn't think I'd come back."

"But you did."

"Of course I did. Shoot, I took one look at all those young guys out there competin' and knew my bronc-ridin' days were over, crushed leg or not." He grinned ruefully at the memory. "Lord, they made me feel about a hundred years old."

"I feel that way sometimes when I work with first-year teachers. They have so much enthusiasm and energy."

Hank nodded in understanding, then held out his cup for a refill. "Anyway, gettin' back to Tina, she's had another upset, besides Becky and Sam getting married. We had some trouble at the ranch about eighteen months ago. A bunch of drug runners bought the place north of us and tried to force us off the Circle D."

"I read about that in the Cheyenne newspaper," Emily said. "How did it affect Tina?"

"Well, I'm not real sure, 'cause she won't talk about it at all. But I was engaged to a gal who was workin' with 'em, and she ended up goin' into the Witness Protection Program."

"Was Tina close to her?"

Hank shook his head and gave her a wry smile. "Not exactly. In fact, she didn't like Janice much at all. I figured once we were married, the kid would accept her and it'd be all right. As it turned out, Tina was instrumental in us finally realizing who was tryin' to sell us out."

"In what way, Hank?"

"She was playin' dress-up with Jan's clothes. When Becky scolded her, Beck looked over some of Janice's clothes and made the connection from a button missing off one of her blouses. I was so mad, I took off before the sheriff came to arrest Jan. That's when I hurt my leg."

"How did it happen?"

"They had a sniper out waitin' for one of us to ride by. He shot my horse. Barney fell on my leg, and I laid there until Becky and Sam and Pete found me the next morning."

"It's been a long recovery for you."

"Yeah, and I wasn't real nice to live with. Tina ended up gettin' shuffled back and forth between Becky's place and the Circle D. I was so wrapped up in surgeries and physical therapy, I didn't think much about what she must be feelin'.''

"That's quite a story, Hank."

"Isn't it just. What I want to know is, how do I go about makin' it all up to Tina? I had some big plans for us, but now I'm not sure I should go through with 'em. It'd mean uprooting her again."

"Would she still have contact with your family?"

"Oh, sure. I want to buy the old Gunderson dude ranch and see if I can make a go of it. I thought if Tina and I could live by ourselves for a while, it'd kinda force us to get closer, you know? She'd hafta depend on me, instead of runnin' to Grandma D or Sam or Becky when she needs something. But now..."

"Actually, Hank, I think that's an excellent idea."

"You do?"

Emily nodded. "I think she may be feeling responsible for your injury."

"What? She didn't have anything to do with that!"

"Children don't always see things the way adults do. Try to look at it from her viewpoint. She was playing with Janice's things, and she probably knew she wasn't supposed to do that, right?"

"Yeah."

"The next thing she knows, the sheriff arrests Janice, you're in the hospital, everyone's upset and her life hasn't been the same since."

"You're right about that."

"To her, it may seem as if her misbehavior caused all the problems. Children whose parents divorce often take the responsibility for the breakup of the family."

Hank rubbed his chin and thought about that for a moment. "It does make sense in a weird kinda way."

"She may be saying she hates you, because she's afraid you'll blame her for what happened. She rejects you before you can reject her."

"Good Lord," Hank muttered. "How do I help her with that, Em? Sit her down and tell her it wasn't her fault?"

Emily shook her head. "I'd be inclined to wait until she brings up the subject. If you're living by yourselves, that's more likely to happen. It may not even be a conscious feeling on her part."

"How do you know so much about kids when you don't have any?" he asked, running one hand through his hair in frustration.

"I've got a master's degree in child psychology, Hank, and," she said gently, "I was a classroom teacher for twelve years. They're not really all that mysterious."

"Well, they are to me," Hank grumbled. "Can you teach me what I need to know?"

Chuckling, Emily rose and walked to the bookcase. She selected a paperback volume from the second shelf, then handed it to Hank. "As a matter of fact, I'm going to be teaching a parenting class every Wednesday night for the next eight weeks. That's the text we'll be using. Are you interested?"

"Yeah." Hank studied the cover, flipped the book over and read the back copy. "Yeah, I'm interested." He looked up and smiled at her. "That's quite a library you have there. Got any more I should read?"

She turned back to the bookcase. "Come on. We'll see what we can find."

He crossed the room and stood beside her, accepting one volume after another until he hollered, "Uncle!" in self-defense. Emily looked at him, her green eyes sparkling with laughter, her nose wrinkled up like a mischievous imp's. It was such a change from her normally sober expression, Hank's breath caught in his chest.

She was standing so close to him, he could smell a light, citrus fragrance on her hair. An adorable little dimple formed in her right cheek, and her skin looked so soft, he wanted to touch it. He would have, too, if he hadn't had books piled halfway to his chin.

"You did that on purpose," he said after clearing his throat.

"You always hated homework so much, I couldn't resist," she admitted. She shook her head at the stack in his hands, then chuckled and took back the top six books. "I was beginning to wonder if you were ever going to stop me."

"Oh, I get it. It's payback time."

She arched an eyebrow at him and sniffed in disdain. "If I wanted to pay you back for all the rotten things you did to me, Hank Dawson, you wouldn't get off so easily."

Struggling to keep a straight face, Hank stepped closer to her, leaning down until they were nose to nose. "Most of that was your fault, Emily."

"*My* fault! How did you come to *that* brilliant piece of rationalization?"

She backed up, as if being this close to him bothered her. Hank decided he really liked the idea of bothering her. Grinning, he invaded her space again. Oranges. That's what her hair smelled like. Oranges.

"You were so much fun to tease, I couldn't help myself."

Her chin came up and she propped her hands on her hips. "Next you'll be telling me the devil made you do it."

The sight of Emily in that challenging stance brought back a slew of memories, and with it, a warm rush of affection. Though her prissy ways had often irritated him, he'd always admired her spunk. He cradled the books in his left arm and reached out with his right hand, tenderly brushing her flushed cheek with the backs of his knuckles. Her skin was every bit as soft as it looked.

"Would it help any if I apologized after all these years?" he asked.

She didn't flinch away from his touch as he'd expected. Instead, her gaze searched his face with all the seriousness of her nature, as if she were trying to see down into his heart. Her breath came out in sweet, warm puffs against his face.

"It might. If you meant it."

Teasing her had seemed harmless enough back in high school. It had eased his tension and humiliation over needing her help to learn stuff he'd hated, and Emily had always returned his wiseacre remarks in spades. But the hint of vulnerability in her eyes and the remembered pain in her quiet words gave his heartstrings one helluva yank. Damned if he didn't want to kiss her and make it all better.

"Well, then, I'm sorry, Em," he said, his voice sounding huskier than usual in his own ears. "I'm real sorry I was mean to you."

She gazed at him for another long moment, then nodded and glanced away as if she didn't quite know how to handle his sincerity. He dropped his hand to his side and stepped back, needing a little more space himself.

"I hope you'll find the books helpful," she said.

"They can't hurt," Hank replied, giving her a lopsided grin. When she didn't return it, he went back to the sofa and grabbed his hat. "I'd better go now. Thanks for the coffee and for your help, Emily."

"You're welcome, Hank."

She opened the door for him and stood to one side, obviously anxious for him to leave, though he could see she was trying hard not to show it. He plunked his hat onto his head, wishing he could think of something to say that would make her smile or laugh. Nothing came to mind, however.

He finally muttered, "See you in class," and stepped out into the darkness.

*   *   *

Emily closed the door behind Hank, then leaned back against it, closed her eyes and sighed, her emotions in more turmoil than she cared to admit. If she hadn't seen it with her very own eyes, she never would have believed he could be so concerned about his daughter, so serious, so thoughtful. She'd always found the old, devil-may-care, teasing Hank Dawson attractive, but the man who'd just left her was absolutely devastating.

For an instant there, just before he'd apologized, he'd looked as if he might be thinking about kissing her. Her lips had tingled with anticipation. Her mouth had gone dry. Her heart had started to pound. Lord, but she'd wanted him to do it.

In short, she'd come dangerously close to making a complete idiot of herself.

Ivan nudged her knee with his nose and whined softly. Emily opened her eyes and chuckled at the quizzical look he gave her, his big head tipped to one side. Remembering what Hank had said about Ivan's appearance, Emily scratched behind the animal's ears.

"You're a big, ugly brute, all right, Ivan," she crooned, "but you're *my* big, ugly brute, aren't you, baby?"

The dog closed his eyes, as if in ecstasy, and rubbed his head against her legs. Ignoring the danger to her panty hose, Emily dropped to her knees and wrapped her arms around Ivan's neck. She felt off balance and emotionally fragile at the moment, and she'd always found comfort in her pet's unconditional love.

It was a shame people couldn't be as uncomplicated as animals, she thought, burying her fingers in Ivan's thick fur. He slurped the side of her face with his big, rough tongue and she pulled back, laughing. He slurped her again and wagged his tail hopefully.

"Want to go for a run, boy?" she asked.

Ivan woofed and did a canine dance of joy at the sound of his favorite word. Emily hurried into her bedroom, changed into her sweats and running shoes and found the dog waiting for her at the front door, his leash in his mouth. She slipped the choke chain over his floppy ears and let herself out into the cool night air.

A disciplined and dedicated jogger, she ran her usual five-mile route, then added on another two miles because she still felt edgy and restless. By the time she returned to her house, she was exhausted and dripping with sweat and Ivan's sides were heaving. Leaving him panting in the living room, she went into the bathroom and stripped off her clothes.

Unfortunately, despite the vigorous workout, a pair of troubled green eyes stared back at her from the mirror over the sink. Muttering, "Ludicrous," under her breath, she cranked the shower to cold and stepped inside.

Chapter Four

On Monday morning, as usual, Emily walked to work before the sun came up. She needed at least an hour at her desk before the staff and students arrived and the phone started ringing, to create a cushion of time for dealing with the inevitable emergencies that cropped up during the day. Though the temperature still felt more like February than late March and patches of snow lingered in shady areas, she detected a hint of spring in the air.

After spending a quiet weekend at home, she had finally put her encounter with Hank Dawson into perspective. He was a handsome, virile man, who had played an important part in her life during her adolescent years. It was perfectly understandable that she might still feel a certain amount of attraction toward him.

Granted, he had surprised her by exhibiting more depth to his character than she ever would have dreamed possible. And he had occupied her thoughts far more than she would have liked during the past two days. But he didn't have to become a problem for her unless she allowed him to do so.

In any case, she doubted he wanted anything from her, other than assistance in becoming a more effective parent. He was the father of one of the students attending her school, and she intended to relate to him on that basis in the future. Her personal feelings for the man were solely her business and her responsibility, and need not, indeed *should* not, enter into her contacts with him.

Smiling with satisfaction at having the whole disturbing incident neatly filed away in her mind, Emily entered the school building. By the time Margaret Sheridan, the school's secretary, arrived at seven-thirty, Emily had already completed one of the lengthy evaluation forms she had to fill out for each teacher before the end of the school year.

A striking, dark-haired woman in her mid-fifties, Margaret had occupied the front desk at Pinedale Elementary for the past twenty years. Emily had formed a comfortable working relationship with her, and felt that they were on the way to developing a close friendship, as well.

"So, did you get the Dawson dilemma solved?" Margaret asked, depositing a fresh cup of coffee on Emily's desk.

"We made a good start," Emily replied, setting the evaluation form to one side of the desk. She briefly related what had happened on Friday night.

Margaret listened with interest, then shook her head in admiration. "You sure know how to get to these kids, Emily."

Emily shrugged. "I do my best, Margaret."

"Spare me the modesty. You really love them and they know it. Even the rotten ones."

"Tina wasn't a rotten kid. She was an angry kid."

"That's where you're different from the other principals I've worked for. You don't just browbeat them into obedience, you find out why they're acting like little jerks. By the time you're done with them, they feel good about themselves and about school. It's amazing.''

"That's why we're supposed to be here, Margaret."

"Yeah, well, you convince a couple of teachers, who shall remain nameless, of that, and we won't have any problems around here at all."

Emily gave her a wry smile of understanding. "Don't hold your breath."

Margaret chuckled, then propped one hip against the corner of Emily's desk. "Tell me, what did you think of Tina's father?"

Oh, boy, here it comes, Emily thought with a silent groan. Though her outlook on most things was decidedly modern, Margaret firmly believed that every woman needed a man in her life to be complete. Emily's single status had become a jovial bone of contention between the two women.

"He seemed very concerned about her."

"That's not what I meant, and you know it," the secretary replied. "Hank Dawson fills out a pair of jeans better than just about anyone, except maybe Patrick Swayze."

Emily raised both eyebrows in feigned shock. "Does Bill know you have a fetish for men's tushes?"

"He knows I didn't marry him for his wit," Margaret replied with a lascivious grin.

Unable to maintain a stern expression any longer, Emily threw up both hands in surrender and laughed. "Honestly, Margaret. You're terrible."

"I know. It's part of my charm. Come on, Emily, admit it. Don't you think Hank's a good-lookin' cuss?"

"Well, yes, of course he is. So what?"

"So, he's single, that's what!"

"I don't have anything in common with him."

To Emily's relief, the bell rang at that moment, signaling the start of another day. Margaret snorted at the interruption and headed for the reception desk muttering, "Battle stations. Battle stations."

Emily followed her from the office, then took up her usual post in the hall as the front doors crashed open and an exuberant herd of children pushed their way inside. She loved greeting them, hearing their laughter and animated conversations, watching them bring life and energy and excitement into the building.

She coordinated the flow of traffic, broke up a shoving match and helped a kindergartner untangle knotted strings on the hood of his coat. Then a little girl wearing a hot pink ski jacket raced through the doorway, her steps slowing automatically when she caught sight of Emily. She dug something out of her backpack, then approached the principal with a hesitant smile, one hand tucked behind her back.

"Good morning, Tina," Emily said, crouching down to eye level with the child. "Is that a new coat you're wearing? I thought yours was blue."

Tina nodded eagerly. "My dad took me shopping in Jackson on Saturday."

"Well, it's very pretty. I love that color."

Tina stuck out one foot, displaying a high-topped sneaker with purple trim and laces. "I got new shoes, too."

"Hey, those are cool," Emily said.

"Yeah, and he took me ridin' yesterday. All afternoon."

"That sounds like fun. Do you like horses?"

"Uh-huh." Tina gave her a shy grin. "I made you something, Ms. Franklin."

"You did?" Emily leaned to one side, as if trying to see behind the child's back. "Is that what you're hiding back there?"

Tina slowly drew her hand in front of her and held out a folded piece of paper.

Emily unfolded the sheet and said, "Oh, Tina, what a pretty picture. My goodness, you drew so many different animals, and I love that smiling sun. And you put in the mountains and green grass. Did you draw this all by yourself?"

"Uh-huh."

Emily had to hug the little girl. "Thank you. I'm going to put this up in my office so I can look at it all day long."

"I got one for Mrs. J., too. Think she'll like it?"

"I'm sure she will. Speaking of Mrs. Jovanovich, you'd better scoot off to class now, or you'll be tardy."

Tina hung her head and scraped the toe of one shoe across the freshly waxed floor. Then she raised pleading eyes to meet Emily's gaze and whispered, "Will you come with me, Ms. Franklin? I've been awful bad, lately. I'm afraid Mrs. Jovanovich'll still be mad at me."

"All right." Emily took Tina's hand and set off down the hall toward the second grade room. "You know, one of the things I like best about Mrs. Jovanovich, is that she's a very fair and forgiving person."

"Will she like me again if I say I'm sorry?"

"It wouldn't hurt to try. Besides, I think she's always liked *you*. She just hasn't appreciated your behavior lately."

"Oh."

A smiling Mary Jovanovich greeted them at the door of Tina's classroom. Emily left the little girl in her teacher's capable care and went back to the office. When she stepped behind the counter, Margaret glanced up from a phone conversation and motioned Emily to her desk.

"She just walked in, Mrs. Matheson. If you'll hold for a moment, I'll put you through to her office." Margaret pushed the appropriate button, then gave Emily an apologetic smile. "She's all yours."

Violet Matheson had been incensed by the school board's decision to hire Emily for the principal's job instead of her son, Harold, who taught fifth grade at Pinedale Elementary. She had made it a ritual to phone at least three times a week to voice her opinions, all of them negative, about the way the school was being run.

"What's she upset about this time?" Emily asked with a sigh of resignation, feeling her sense of accomplishment with Tina draining away at the prospect of another round of criticism.

"She wouldn't say, but she sounds pretty steamed."

Emily went into her own office, sat behind her desk, took a deep breath, then picked up the receiver. "Good morning, Mrs. Matheson. This is Emily Franklin. How may I help you?"

"You can start by cleaning up that playground. With the snow melting off, you can see all the litter those kids have thrown around. I swear, it's nothing but a garbage heap out there. Why haven't you taught them anything about trash cans?"

"I hadn't noticed there was a problem, Mrs. Matheson, but I'll look into it," Emily said calmly.

"And another thing," Vi went on, as if Emily hadn't responded to her first attack. "I hear you're still playing with those kids out there at recess. Alma Smith told me just the other day that you were actually playing jump rope! That's not a very dignified way for a principal to act, and I'm not the only one who thinks so."

"You're certainly entitled to your opinion."

"But you obviously don't agree with it."

"Mrs. Matheson, we've discussed this before, and I don't believe either one of us is going to change her mind. Perhaps we should simply agree to disagree."

Vi replied with a disgruntled, "Hmmph!" After a moment of tense silence, she continued with an even sharper edge to her strident voice. "Since you won't listen to my advice about that, I suppose you won't listen to this, either, but I consider it my Christian duty to warn you about goin' out with that reprobate, Hank Dawson."

"I beg your pardon?"

"Don't try to act innocent with me, Ms. Franklin. I heard all about how you were out at The Diner with him on Friday night, carryin' on right in front of his little girl. Now, you may have forgotten what it's like to live in a small town, seein' as how you lived down there in Cheyenne for so long, and you can ignore me all you want—"

"Mrs. Matheson—"

"—but I'm telling you in no uncertain terms, that this community will not tolerate indecent behavior from a school official."

"I think you've said quite enough, Mrs. Matheson," Emily broke in when the woman finally had to pause for breath. "I had dinner with Mr. Dawson and his daughter. I did *not* carry on with him. Furthermore, my personal life has nothing to do with my job performance, and is nobody's business but my own."

"Well, we'll just have to see what the school board thinks about that, now, won't we?"

There was a loud crash in the receiver. Enraged, Emily banged it into its cradle, pushed her chair away from her desk and paced back and forth across her office.

Margaret stuck her head through the doorway. "What's ruffled Vi's feathers this time?"

Emily threw up both hands beside her head in frustration. "The playground's a garbage heap. It's not dignified for a principal to play with the children at recess. And, last, but not least, if I value my job I'll stay away from that reprobate, Hank Dawson."

"Why, that nasty old battle-ax," Margaret said, coming inside and closing the door behind her.

"You can say that again," Emily muttered.

The secretary seated herself in the chair in front of Emily's desk and grinned at her boss. "Why, that nasty old battle-ax."

Emily shook her head, then chuckled and returned to her own chair. "Thank you, Margaret. I've had my tantrum and I'm fine now. You may go back to work."

"You're not going to listen to that woman, are you?"

"About playing with the children at recess? Of course not."

"No, about Hank. There aren't many single guys your age in this town. Of the three or four I can think of, he'd be my first choice."

"In the first place, Margaret," Emily said briskly, "Hank and I have never been friends. In the second place, he hasn't shown any personal interest in me whatsoever. And in the third place, Mrs. Matheson may have a point. A lot of people wouldn't approve if I dated him."

"Oh, horsefeathers, Emily. I know his reputation isn't the best, but the stuff people talk about happened a long time ago. Hank's a nice guy, and he's had a rough time of it the last couple of years. He just needs a good woman like you to settle him down a little."

"No thanks. I already have a full-time job, and I'd like to keep it."

"Nobody with half a brain is going to listen to Vi Matheson, Emily. Everybody knows she's got a grudge against you. The school-board members have been awfully impressed with your performance this year."

"Not all of them," Emily replied. "Keith Daniels was out at The Diner Friday night. Believe me, he'd be delighted to find an excuse to fire me, and this is exactly the kind of issue to help him do it."

"Keith is nothing but a male chauvinist hog. I can't believe you're going to let him and that old biddy Vi dictate your social life."

Emily sighed in exasperation. "This is a ridiculous conversation, Margaret. I suggest we drop it and get back to work. Hank Dawson isn't interested in dating me."

Margaret pushed herself out of the chair and walked to the door. She opened it, then turned back for a final parting shot. "Don't underestimate yourself, Emily. There aren't many single women his age in this town, either. It's time you got out and had some fun. You're too young to live such a boring life."

The door closed with a snap before Emily could utter a suitable reply. *Boring.* How she despised that word. It brought back too many painful memories, too much self-doubt.

Yes, she preferred a quiet life-style. Her job provided so much stimulation during the day, she was perfectly content to spend her evenings at home with her pets. Besides, she enjoyed reading and puttering around the house.

If that made her boring, so be it. She didn't need Hank Dawson or any other man to spice up her life. After all, *she* wasn't bored. And she wasn't lonely, either. Not really.

On Wednesday, Hank showered and shaved after he'd finished working and put on a pair of black slacks and the light blue shirt his sister-in-law, Dani, had made for him. He combed his hair and splashed on some after-shave, trying to ignore the butterflies zipping around in his belly. He figured a little anxiety was normal enough, seein' as how he hadn't been to a class in years.

What he hadn't counted on, though, was the keen sense of anticipation he felt about going to this thing. Of course, that was because he knew Emily would be there. She hadn't been far from his thoughts since he'd left her on Friday.

He'd tried to convince himself that his interest in the woman was simply the result of gratitude for her help with Tina. The kid hadn't magically turned into a little angel overnight. Far from it. But at least she was talking to him, even if he didn't always like what she had to say.

Still, Hank had to admit, he'd thought about Emily's figure and her soft low voice and those big green eyes of hers every bit as often as he'd thought about her in connection with his daughter. The admission didn't please him any. Shoot, the two of them had never gotten along worth spit. Given their backgrounds and personalities, they probably never would.

And yet, she intrigued him. What kind of a man had she married? Why had her marriage failed? What would it be like to make love with her? Would she stay cool and reserved? Or was there a passionate side to her personality nobody ever got to see?

It was dumb to consider those questions. Hell, with all her college degrees, he'd bet she thought *he* was pretty damn dumb. What would a woman like her want with a guy who hadn't even tried going to college? To Emily, he was probably nothing but a broken-down old rodeo bum and a lousy excuse for a father, to boot.

There was no doubt about it. The smart thing for him to do would be to treat her as an old friend and his daughter's principal and leave it at that. He grabbed his textbook, which he'd already read twice so he wouldn't come off as a complete idiot in class, then checked his hair one last time in the mirror over his dresser.

Oh, damn. He didn't like that gleam in his eyes one bit. Unfortunately, over the past few days, he'd come to think of Emily as a challenge, and he'd never been able to resist a challenge yet.

"Yeah, well," he muttered at his reflection, "since when did you ever do the smart thing, Dawson?"

By the time he arrived at the elementary school an hour and a half later, Hank had almost convinced himself that there was nothing all that special about Emily. He'd probably imagined feeling attracted to her because he hadn't been with a woman for one helluva long time. Once she started lecturing, it wouldn't surprise him if he discovered he didn't like her at all.

The school library was more crowded than he'd expected. Hank found a seat at a table near the back of the room and glanced around, smiling and nodding at folks he knew. From the strained smiles some of them gave him in return, he figured maybe he wasn't the only one having a problem with parenting.

Then Emily breezed into the room, wearing a mint-green pair of slacks and blouse with a white blazer. She looked professional and approachable at the same time, her warm, friendly smile going a long way toward relieving the tension in the atmosphere. To Hank's surprise, she bypassed the podium and sat on top of the table at the front of the room, facing the crowd as if this were nothing more than an informal bull session between friends.

Damn, but she was pretty. As she made her opening remarks, she became even prettier. Her eyes sparkled with good humor and enthusiasm. Her body language was inviting. Her voice soothed and reassured.

"Everybody relax," she said with a smile. "We're not here to judge anyone. This is not a contest. There aren't any right or wrong answers. There won't be any tests or grades."

"Then why the heck are we here?" grumbled a man at the left side of the room. His wife blushed and swatted his arm.

"That's a reasonable question," Emily replied with a chuckle. "I'll tell you why I'm here, and then I'd like you to do the same for me. Does that sound fair enough?"

"Yeah, it'll do," the man replied, giving her a sheepish grin.

"My primary goal for this class is to teach you techniques that will make it easier for you to communicate with your children. I'm also hoping to learn some things from you, especially how the staff at Pinedale Elementary can better support you and your kids. While I'm not a parent myself, I appreciate how difficult your job is. It will be to everyone's benefit if we all work together."

Hank noted heads nodding all around the room and smiled in appreciation of Emily's smooth delivery. Even the guy who'd asked why they were there was leaning forward with an interested expression on his face. Before long, she had a lively discussion going. From there, she divided the crowd into small groups and made them all role-play conversations with their kids.

For the first time in his life, Hank was sorry to see a class end. He hung back until almost everyone else had left, then approached Emily as she was packing her briefcase.

"You're quite a teacher, Ms. Franklin," he said.

She turned and smiled at him. "Thank you, Mr. Dawson. Did you learn anything helpful?"

"Darn right. I was real impressed."

"I'm glad to hear that. Tina seems to have settled down here at school. How is she getting along at home?"

"Better. We've got a ways to go, but I think I've got a handle on her now."

"That's wonderful." Emily snapped her briefcase shut and gestured for Hank to precede her from the library.

He accompanied her to the doorway. "Would you like to go out for a drink, Emily?" he asked when she reached for the row of light switches.

"No, thank you," she said, softening her refusal with a smile. "I don't patronize the local bars."

"Not good for a principal's image?"

"Basically." She started off down the hallway. "I enjoy an occasional glass of wine, but I'm not much of a drinker."

"Well, then, how about if I give you a ride home and we could have a cup of coffee," Hank suggested, matching his step to hers.

Emily hesitated a moment before firmly shaking her head. "I'd rather not. It's been a long day and I have to work tomorrow. The walk home will help me unwind."

Hank studied her face intently, wondering whether she was simply giving him a brush-off because she didn't like him, or if she really was tired. Whatever the truth, this didn't seem like a good time to push. He hid his disappointment behind a shrug. "All right. See you next week, Emily."

"Good night, Hank."

Emily watched him limp toward his truck, gnawing her lower lip to prevent herself from calling him back. Despite frequent reminders that Hank was no more important to her than any other parent, she'd spent the whole day fighting a sense of nervous anticipation. One minute, she'd been afraid he wouldn't show up tonight. The next minute, she'd been afraid that he would. Then she'd worried that if he *did* show up, he'd be every bit as obnoxious as he'd been to his high school teachers.

He hadn't done anything of the sort, of course. In fact, he hadn't said much at all outside of his small group. He'd participated in the role playing without complaint and asked several questions that had led her to believe he'd actually read the textbook.

"Big deal," Emily muttered to herself as she locked the building and headed for home. "Even class clowns and troublemakers have to do a certain amount of growing up in twenty years."

Still, she couldn't deny that his favorable comments had meant more to her than the ones she'd received from a number of other parents. She couldn't pretend she hadn't been delighted to see him again, either. And, she had to admit, she would have enjoyed listening to more of his observations and reactions to the class over a cup of coffee.

Sighing, Emily hurried the rest of the way home. She greeted her pets, hung up her coat and decided a glass of wine would be just the thing to help her relax before going to bed. She turned on the kitchen light, then halted after taking two steps into the small room when her shoes crunched on a shard of broken glass.

"What in the world . . ." she murmured.

The curtains covering the window beside her dinette set fluttered, as if from a gust of wind. Emily cautiously approached, pushed them aside and gasped at the jagged hole in the center of the windowpane. More glass covered the table and chairs, and there on the floor, about a foot from the wall, sat a large, flat rock. The back of her neck tingled with uneasiness.

Ivan brushed against her and whined, obviously sensing her distress. Emily grabbed his collar and led him out of the room, assuring herself that if an intruder were in the house, the dog would be barking like crazy. After checking to make certain he hadn't cut his paws, she shut him in the living room and went back to take another look at the rock.

There was something red and shiny drizzled across the surface, but she couldn't see it clearly because the table blocked the light. She grabbed a flashlight out of the cupboard and directed its beam toward the rock's surface, then jerked back when she saw "Bitch" written in red nail polish.

That was enough for Emily. It wasn't uncommon for teachers and principals to receive harassment in one form or another from disgruntled students and even parents, but this person had gone too far. She marched to the phone and called the sheriff's office.

Ten minutes later, Sheriff Andy Johnson arrived at her front door. He was a tall, rangy man with red hair and freckles. He'd graduated from high school with Emily, and though he hadn't been nearly as wild as Hank, it was hard for Emily to imagine him doing his present job. Still, his presence was reassuring.

She explained what she'd found and followed him into the kitchen. He squatted beside the rock and studied it.

"Did you touch it?" he asked.

"No. I didn't know if it would hold fingerprints."

He grinned up at her, his blue eyes warm with approval. "I'm not sure it will, either, but that nail polish might. I'll take a look around outside."

Emily made a pot of coffee, more to give herself something to do than because she wanted any. Andy returned, shaking his head.

"Ground's still too hard to leave footprints. Have you got a board or something we can cover that window with so you don't freeze?"

"I think there's one in the garage."

He patted her shoulder and turned toward the back door. "I'll get it. Pour me a cup of that coffee, and I'll be your friend for life."

By the time he'd taken care of the window, Emily had set out cups and a plate of oatmeal cookies she'd baked the day before. Andy pulled a small notebook and a pen from his pocket and took the chair at a right angle to Emily's. He sipped his coffee and devoured two cookies before getting down to business.

"Now then, Emily, who have you ticked off so bad they'd do a thing like this to you?"

Emily shrugged. "There are always people who resent some of the decisions a principal has to make."

"I hear ya," Andy said, nodding in understanding. "There's a few folks around here who don't like me much, either. But give me a list. Who calls the school and complains the most?"

"Mrs. Matheson," Emily answered automatically. "But I don't think she'd resort to vandalism."

Andy tipped back his head and laughed. "You're on ol' Vi's list, too? I swear, that woman thinks she should be running the whole world. But I agree with you. A rock through a window's not really her style. Who else?"

"Well, Mr. Paxon did get awfully upset when I told him his son Ned needs some special help."

"Lawrence Paxon?" Andy asked, sitting straighter at the mention of the man's name.

"Yes. I still don't understand his reaction. Ned's dyslexic and he needs help or he'll never learn to read. Actually, he's lucky we discovered it so soon. It's certainly nothing to be ashamed of, but Mr. Paxon didn't want to listen to me."

"That doesn't surprise me," Andy said. "Larry's a hothead who never could take any kind of criticism. He thinks that kid has to be better than anybody else. I don't like the sound of this, Emily."

She gulped. "Do you think he's dangerous?"

"I don't know. I *do* know that his wife's had a lot of black eyes over the years. I'll have a little talk with him, but I want you to be careful and let me know right away if you have any other problems."

"I'll certainly do that."

"Anybody else I should check out?"

"Not that I can think of."

Andy tore a page out of his notebook, wrote something on it and handed it to Emily. "That's my home number. Don't be afraid to use it. I'll leave word at the office that I want a patrol car driving past your house on a regular basis." He stood, and Emily walked him to the front door.

"Thank you, Andy," she said, trying to force a smile.

"It's all part of the service." He chucked her under the chin and grinned. "Keep that chin up. It'll be all right. By the way, you datin' anyone?"

Emily laughed and shook her head. "Not at the moment."

"You interested in datin' anyone?"

She looked into his friendly blue eyes, flattered by his question, but unwilling to give him any encouragement. Smiling, she shook her head again. "Not at the moment."

He accepted her refusal with a good-natured shrug. "Well, let me know if you change your mind. And keep that dog handy. He looks like a pretty good deterrent."

"I'll do that, Andy."

After he'd gone, Emily locked her doors and got ready for bed. She snuggled under the covers with Ivan curled up on the floor beside her, wondering if she'd been hasty in turning away Andy's interest. After all, who could complain about her dating the sheriff?

Unfortunately, she hadn't felt attracted to him, not the way she'd felt attracted to Hank. Past experience had taught her that that wasn't a feeling she could force, much as she might want to. No, it was either there or it wasn't, and Andy Johnson didn't deserve any false hopes. Life certainly was perverse sometimes.

Chapter Five

Too restless even to think about going home, Hank drove his bruised ego to the Cowboy Bar. He ordered a beer from Bob Williams and proceeded to catch up on the local news. When he'd finished about half of his drink, the door banged open and Gusty Edwards stomped into the room.

Gusty was a sawed-off runt of a guy, with big ears and a hatchet-blade nose. Even in the dim light, it was easy to see his face was flushed with temper. He climbed onto the stool beside Hank's, slammed a five-dollar bill onto the bar and demanded a shot and a chaser.

"What's the matter, Gusty?" Hank asked, trading a quick grin with Bob. "You look mad enough to spit lead."

The little man knocked back his drink, gasped, then banged the shot glass down and reached for his beer.

"Goldanged woman," he said, after cutting loose with one of the thunderous belches responsible for giving him his nickname years ago. "If I live to be a thousand, I'll never understand her. I musta been out of my mind to marry her.''

''Aw, c'mon, Gusty,'' Bob chided him. ''You were in here just last week, bragging about Peg.''

''I was probably drunk when I said it,'' Gusty grumbled. ''I'm tellin' ya, Bob, women are just plain unreasonable. First, she wants me to stay home with the kids while she goes off to some fool class over at the grade school to learn how to be a better parent, right?''

Hank and Bob nodded.

''So, she takes off before supper's even over, and there I am, all alone with them four hellions, tryin' to watch a little TV, right?''

The two men nodded again.

''Now, get this. She gets a night off, an' then she comes home and has the damn gall to be mad at me, 'cause I didn't do the dishes. And then, she's yellin' at me, 'cause I didn't give 'em all a bath and put 'em to bed.''

''That's rough,'' Hank said, choking on suppressed laughter.

''Yeah, no kiddin'. I mean, hell, I changed the baby's pants and kept the other three from killin' each other. In my book, that's about all anybody oughtta expect from a man who's been workin' his butt off all day.''

''Maybe she worked hard all day, too,'' Bob observed.

Gusty snorted. ''Baloney. That woman would complain if ya hung her with a new rope. I ain't buyin' that women's lib line. The kids are *her* job.''

''You had a little somethin' to do with producin' 'em,'' Hank pointed out.

''Well, yeah. But if she wants to be a better parent, it seems to me like she oughtta stay home and take care of the kids. The little brats won't mind me, no matter what I do.''

''Maybe next week, you should hire a baby-sitter and go to the class with her,'' Hank suggested.

"That's what Peg wanted me to do tonight," Gusty grumbled. "I figured I'd be the only man there."

"Naw, there were lotsa guys there."

"*You* went to that class, Dawson?" Gusty demanded, his eyes bulging as he stared at Hank.

Hank slid off his bar stool and towered over the shorter man. "I've got a kid, don't I? Wanna make something of it?"

"Who, me?" Gusty hastily shook his head and held both hands up beside his face. "Hell, no. I was just a little surprised, that's all, Hank."

"Good." Hank tossed a couple of bills on the bar. "See you guys later."

Then he strolled out the door, grinning to himself when he heard Gusty griping to Bob, "Well, I *still* say there's no understandin' women."

Hank climbed into his pickup and fired the engine. Without consciously thinking about it, he headed toward the school, turned left and cruised down Emily's street. Once he knew she'd made it home okay, he could go back to the ranch and rest easy.

Damn. She was home, all right, but she wasn't alone. His jaw clenched and his gut knotted. That was Andy Johnson's patrol car, and she hadn't made *him* park on the next block. No, his car sat smack-dab in front of her house like an advertisement the size of a billboard.

Hank hit the gas and raced out of town, jealousy clawing at his insides. He slowed down as he turned north toward Cora, telling himself it wasn't as if Emily owed him anything. Shoot, they'd never even been out on a date. Besides, the sheriff was a good-lookin' bachelor, and it wouldn't be the first time a woman had chosen somebody else over Hank Dawson.

Furthermore, he'd had it with women who couldn't be honest. Hell, he'd had it with women, period. He didn't understand 'em any better than Gusty did, and he wasn't sure he gave a rip anymore, either.

The house was quiet when he got back to the Circle D. Hank took off his boots on the back porch and went upstairs, turning out the lights Grandma D had left burning for him. He paused at Tina's door, then crept inside to check on her.

She was sprawled on her stomach, an arm and a skinny leg flopped out of the covers. Hank moved closer, studying her face in the faint glow from the night-light. She looked so sweet and vulnerable with her thick lashes fanned out over her freckled cheeks, a lump formed in his throat.

He gently pushed her arm and leg under the sheet and pulled the blankets up around her neck. Stroking the tangled hair from her eyes, he silently promised to do better by her, even if it meant he had to go back to that dumb ol' class and see dumb ol' Emily again.

The next morning, Hank got up earlier than usual, put on a set of thermal underwear under his jeans and flannel shirt and went out to feed the herd. He planned to head into town after breakfast, and see how the real-estate agent was coming along with old man Gunderson. On his way back to the house, he saw Sam's car parked by the back door and hurried inside.

The kitchen was in an uproar, with everyone talking at once. Grandma D hugged Sam's waist, while a batch of pancakes turned black on the stove. Kim and Colin bounced up and down on their toes, competing for Dani's attention. Somehow Sam's Australian shepherd, Bear Dog, had snuck inside, climbed onto one of the chairs and was making short work of a platter of link sausages.

Tina sat at the table by herself, turning a plate of syrup-soaked pancakes into a gloppy mess with a fork and watching all the excitement with big, sad eyes. Hank's heart went out to the kid. How many times had he sat in that same spot and felt left out when his folks came back from a trip and fussed over Sam and Becky?

He greeted his brother and sister-in-law, and after learning that they'd come home early because they missed Colin and Kim, Hank scooped Tina out of her chair and gave her a piggyback ride upstairs.

"How'd you like a ride to school this morning?" he asked, setting her down outside her room. "We need to have a talk in private."

"What about, Dad?"

"Get dressed quick, and you'll find out."

"Am I in trouble again?"

"Not that I know of. Got a guilty conscience?"

"Nope."

"Good. I'll meet you downstairs in ten minutes."

When he returned to the kitchen, he found everyone gathered around the table. Tina stood beside Grandma D's chair, getting her hair brushed out. He poured himself a cup of coffee, then leaned back against the counter and watched his grandmother gather Tina's hair into a ponytail and tie it with a ribbon.

He figured he'd better start paying attention to things like that, because he'd have to get the kid ready for school by himself before long. It didn't look all that hard, but maybe he'd try it a time or two when Grandma D could coach him. Five minutes later, he hustled Tina out to the pickup.

"What didja wanna talk about, Dad?" she asked once they were under way.

"Remember when I went to Oklahoma to see if I wanted to get into the stock-contracting business?"

"Yeah. I thought you said you weren't going to do that."

"That's right, I'm not. But I don't plan to stay at the Circle D for the rest of my life, either."

Her bottom lip jutted out so far that a chicken could roost on it. "Why not? Don't you like Uncle Sam anymore?"

"Of course, I do, honey. It's just that, well, I like bein' around lots of people more than he does. I get bored with plain ranching sometimes."

"So what are you gonna do, Dad?"

"Not just me, Tina. Us. I promised wherever I went, you were comin' with me, and I meant it."

"Okay, so what are *we* gonna do, then?"

"I'm thinkin' about buyin' a dude ranch. We'd have folks come in from all over the country in the summer and stay with us, and we'd take 'em ridin' and campin' and fishin', maybe a little white-water raftin'. And in the fall, we could have huntin' trips for 'em. Whaddaya think?"

"Would we have to move far away?"

"Heck, no. The place I want to buy's only fifteen miles from the Circle D."

Tina thought about that for a moment, then shrugged. "I guess it might be okay, then."

"It's gonna take a lot of work to get it started," Hank warned her. "And I'll need your help."

"I'm a kid, Dad. What can *I* do?"

"You're gonna have to be the lady of the house, and I'll teach you how to do lotsa stuff outdoors, too. We'll have to learn how to be a family all by ourselves."

The ear-to-ear grin his daughter gave him convinced Hank he was on the right track. "Wanna give it a try?" he asked.

She nodded. "Yeah."

They fell into a comfortable silence for the next five miles. Gazing out her window, Tina crossed one ankle over the other and swung her feet back and forth, kicking the seat with her heels. Then she turned to Hank with an impish grin.

"I think you should ask Ms. Franklin for a date, Dad."

"What makes you say that?"

"Real families have a mom around."

"Not always, honey."

"Yes, they do. And Ms. Franklin likes me. She's lots nicer than ol' Janice was."

Chagrined, Hank stared at Tina for a second, before turning his attention back to the road. Now, how the heck was he supposed to answer that? Finally, he chuckled and shook his head.

"Well, I'm glad you like Ms. Franklin, darlin', but I'm not gonna have time for any gals but you for a long, long time."

Tina gave him a smug, we'll-just-see-about-that kind of look, and didn't say another word until Hank dropped her off at the school. He watched her scamper off, her backpack clutched in one hand, lunch money in the other. An uneasy feeling settled into the pit of his belly, but he shook it off. He was just hungry 'cause he'd missed breakfast.

He stopped in at the grocery store for a cup of coffee and some doughnuts. His mood darkened when he spotted Andy Johnson visiting with the county attorney at one of the small tables in front of the bakery section. Rather than join any of the regulars, Hank took his breakfast back to his truck and drove to the real-estate office.

Eric Jordan arrived at five minutes before nine and motioned Hank inside after he unlocked the building.

"What can I do for you, Hank?" he asked, turning on the lights.

"Had any luck getting Gunderson to come down on his price yet?"

Eric shook his head. "Not much. I think he'll come down ten thousand or so, but that's about it."

Muttering a curse under his breath, Hank lowered himself onto the chair in front of Eric's desk and crossed one foot over the other. "Well," he said thoughtfully, "offer him fifty thousand less than his askin' price and remind him it'll be a cash sale. Anybody else wantin' to buy the place'll probably want a contract for deed."

"You want me to do it now?" Eric asked.

"Yeah. I want to get this deal sewed up."

While Eric made the phone call, Hank shoved his hands in his pockets and gazed around the room. His chest tightened, and he tried to convince himself it wasn't fear causing the sensation. So what if he'd never been a businessman before?

All he was gambling was the money he'd gotten from the civil suit he'd won against the bastards who'd damn near crippled him for life. Sam was banking his share of the Circle D's profits for Tina's education, so he wouldn't lose everything if the dude ranch didn't pay off like he hoped. It was a risk, all right, but it wasn't that much different from the risks Hank had taken every time he'd climbed onto a bronc.

He'd taken that correspondence course in accounting last winter and done all right. And he had a buddy in the business over in Jackson. Charlie'd be glad to give him advice; Hank was sure of it.

Eric waved to get his attention, and covered the phone's receiver with one hand. "He'll come down twenty-five thousand."

"Tell him to make it thirty-five, and I want immediate possession. Remind him how decrepit everything is out there and that taxes are comin' due pretty soon."

The real-estate agent went back to his conversation. Hank listened intently, holding his breath until Eric started to smile and nod at him.

"Congratulations. You've just bought yourself a dude ranch," he said, hanging up the phone.

Hank shook the man's hand, feeling a surprising sense of relief wash over him. So, he was finally committed. Until this moment, he hadn't fully realized just how much he'd wanted to try this. Now all he had to do was go home and convince the rest of the family he hadn't lost his mind.

He shored up his arguments while he drove back to the ranch. He'd discussed the idea with Sam once, and his older brother had grudgingly agreed that it might work. But it had only been an idea at the time, and knowing Sam's worrywart tendencies, Hank knew he'd have to go through the whole thing again. Shoot, Sam had probably figured he'd never really go through with it.

And then, there was Grandma D. Imagining what she'd have to say about the whole thing, Hank rolled his eyes and prayed for patience. Damn. He wished Becky was home. If anyone understood him, it was his little sister.

Well, it was time to stand up for himself and stop expecting other folks to run interference for him. Not with Grandma D and Sam. And not with his daughter.

The discussion went just about the way he'd expected. Grandma D predicted he wouldn't last a year. Sam trotted out the same arguments he'd used before and added a few more for good measure.

It sure would be nice if a guy's own kin would have a little faith in him, Hank thought darkly. Granted, outside of rodeo, he'd never demonstrated much ambition, but he'd appreciate it if they'd give him the benefit of the doubt. The third time Sam shook his head and used the word *impulsive,* however, Hank received some support from an unexpected quarter.

His sister-in-law, Dani, laid down the knife she was using to spread frosting on a cake, her eyes glinting with determination. She marched over to Sam, pushed his coffee cup out of the way and plunked herself down on his lap. Grasping his face between her hands, she kissed him with such fervor that Grandma D had a coughing fit and even Hank found himself glancing away in discomfort.

"What was *that* for?" Sam asked when she finally let him up for air, his neck and ears flushed a dull red.

"Do you think our marriage is going to work?" she demanded.

Sam's dark eyes filled with tenderness and his voice took on a husky note. "Of course I do, honey."

"Well, I'm awfully glad to hear it. If I remember correctly, you thought I was pretty impulsive when I came to Wyoming to meet you."

"And you were," he said with a chuckle. "But just because it worked out for us, doesn't mean it'll work out for Hank, too."

"It doesn't mean it won't, either," she retorted. "My parents gave me the same song and dance you've been giving Hank. If I'd listened to them, we never would have met, Sam. Give him a chance to show you what he can do before you try to discourage him."

"Yeah," Hank agreed. "Besides, I'm not askin' anybody's permission here. I gave Gunderson my word. As far as I'm concerned, it's a done deal."

Sam and Grandma D exchanged guilty looks, but before they could say anything, the phone rang. Dani jumped up to answer it, then held the receiver out to Hank. "It's the school."

Hank gave Dani's shoulder a thank-you squeeze before taking the call. She winked at him and went back to work on her cake. After listening to the school secretary for a moment, he hung up, grabbed his keys from the kitchen table and headed for the back door.

"What's the matter, Hank?" Grandma D called after him.

"Tina got sick at school," he explained. "I need to go pick her up."

"I'll come with you," she offered.

The offer was tempting, but Hank forced himself to refuse it. "No thanks, Grandma. She'd my kid, and from now on, I'm gonna be the one who takes care of her."

The drive back into town seemed endless. Mrs. Sheridan had said she didn't think Tina's illness was serious, but Hank couldn't help worrying. What if it *was* serious? What if he didn't know how to take care of her? Man, sometimes this responsibility thing was about as much fun as gettin' bucked off in a cactus patch.

Mrs. Sheridan greeted him at the front desk and escorted him to the principal's office. He found Tina curled up on Emily's lap, her head resting against Emily's breasts. Hank's stomach took a nosedive when Emily looked up from stroking the little girl's forehead and smiled at him.

"That was a quick trip," she said.

Hank walked around to stand beside the chair and leaned down toward his daughter. "What's goin' on, sugar?"

Tina gave him a pitiful smile. "My stomach hurts."

"You didn't eat much breakfast. Maybe you're just hungry," Hank suggested, watching her closely. Something didn't smell right here, although he wasn't sure what it was. The kid just looked a mite too pitiful.

"Oh, no," she said, shaking her head. "I feel like I'm gonna barf, too."

"We'd better get you out of here, then. You wouldn't want to do that all over Ms. Franklin."

When Hank reached for her, Tina shrank back against Emily. "I don't think I should move yet, Dad."

"Give her a minute, Hank," Emily said softly, stroking the little girl's ponytail.

The beatific smile Tina shot at Emily raised Hank's suspicions even more. The kid's color was good, and she didn't seem the least bit upset. In fact, she looked downright content. He sat on the edge of Emily's desk and crossed his arms over his chest.

"Boy, Tina, it's a real shame you're feelin' lousy," he said, putting a sad note into his voice. "I had somethin' real special planned for when you got home from school."

"What was it, Dad?"

"I bought that dude ranch I was tellin' you about."

She sat up a little straighter. "You did?"

"Yup. I thought maybe you'd like to take a ride out there with me and we'd look the place over."

"Oh yeah?"

"Yeah. But, hey, if you're sick, you're sick. You prob- ably won't mind waiting to see our new home. We can al- ways go next week."

Hank glanced at Emily. She smiled at him and nodded her head once in approval. Knowing she agreed with his assessment of the situation, he relaxed a little.

"Ya know, Dad, I don't feel so barfy now. Maybe I do just need some lunch."

"I think that sounds like a good idea," Emily said. "You can always come back here if you start feeling sick again."

Tina hopped off her lap, then looked up at Hank for a moment. "I think I'll be okay now, but thanks for comin' to get me."

"You're welcome, honey. Anytime."

Hank followed Tina to the door, and would have kept right on walking if Emily hadn't called him back. He wasn't feeling too kindly toward her at the moment, even though she'd helped him with Tina again. He didn't want to argue with her, either, though, so he shut the office door and sat on the chair in front of her desk.

"You handled that awfully well," she said, folding her hands on top of the blotter.

"You knew she wasn't really sick all along?"

"I suspected it. That's why she was with me instead of in the nurse's office."

"Why didn't you just send her back to class?"

Emily smiled. "I considered it. But I think she's testing you, Hank, trying to find out if she can really trust you to be there when she needs you."

"It might be a little more complicated than that," Hank answered.

"What makes you say that?"

Jeez, he hated getting into this, but knew he had to. When he repeated what Tina had said about her that morning, Emily's eyebrows shot up beneath her bangs and her cheeks flushed a shade darker.

"You think she was matchmaking?"

"I wouldn't put it past her."

"Oh, my," Emily murmured, frowning as if the idea of being romantically linked with him, even in a child's mind, appalled her.

Scowling, Hank rose to his feet and walked to the door. "Yeah, well, don't worry about it. I'll set her straight," he said gruffly.

"Wait a minute, Hank. Are you angry about something?" she asked.

Propping his hands on his hips, he turned to face her. "Should I be?"

Emily pushed back her chair and walked around the desk to stand in front of him. "I don't know. If you are, we should work it out, though, don't you think?"

Hank sighed inwardly at her earnest expression. Then he decided he might as well clear the air. "I stopped off for a beer last night and drove by your house on the way home," he said reluctantly.

"Oh, I see," Emily replied, her tone suddenly brusque. "You saw the sheriff's car."

"That's right. I don't like it when women lie and make up excuses to avoid being with me. If you had a date with Andy, why didn't you just say so?"

Her eyes narrowed with irritation and her chin rose to a challenging angle. "Sheriff Johnson was at my house to investigate some vandalism, not that it's any of your business. However, if you like honesty so much, I'll be happy to admit I didn't want to have coffee with you. I don't think it's a good idea for us to see each other socially."

"Why not? Have I done something to offend you?"

"No, it's simply that I have a certain position in the community to uphold. Given your reputation—"

"Whoa," Hank demanded, taking a step toward her. "Just hold your horses, Emily. Are you trying to say you don't want to go out with me because I'm not respectable enough?"

She backed up a step. "I wouldn't put it quite that bluntly, but yes, that's essentially correct."

Anger fired through his system at an astonishing speed. Hank inhaled a deep breath, but it didn't cool him off much. "What would I have to do to get respectable enough, Ms. Franklin? Go to church every Sunday?"

"There's no need to be sarcastic. But now that you mention it, that might be a good place to start. You could also stop swearing and show up at school functions for Tina."

Hank stared at her for a moment, then laughed and shook his head. "You haven't changed a bit, have you? You're still a repressed, self-righteous little prig," he said, advancing toward her again, enjoying it immensely when she retreated, step for step.

"That's enough, Hank," she said when her backside hit the front of the desk.

"I don't think so, Em," he continued, smiling with devilish delight. "Since I'll probably never be respectable enough to suit you, I'm gonna do something I've wanted to do since you were a skinny little girl with braces."

"What are you—"

He raised one hand to the back of her neck and cut off the rest of her question the way it would give him the most satisfaction. At the first touch of his lips on hers, her spine stiffened up like a fence post. She pushed against his chest, and he slung an arm around her waist, pulling her flush against him.

He knew he should let her go, but that light, citrus scent in her hair filled his head, and she felt so soft and warm in his arms, and she tasted so sweet, he couldn't make himself do it just yet. His desire to dominate and teach her a lesson dissipated. He gentled the kiss and stroked her nape with his fingertips, desperately wanting to coax at least a hint of a response from her.

His heartbeat raced as her resistance slowly faded away. He licked her bottom lip, and for a split second, the tip of her tongue darted out and touched his, as if she couldn't help herself. Then she uttered a soft little moan and pushed at his chest again.

Reluctantly lifting his head, Hank gazed down into her stormy green eyes. His breathing sounded ragged in his own ears, and hers wasn't any quieter. Wondering if she might belt him one, he dropped his hands to his sides and backed off a step.

Her throat worked down a gulp as she silently glared at him. Her fingers curled into fists. Damn, but she was cute when she was all huffy and indignant, he thought, clamping his mouth shut to keep himself from smiling or saying something stupid.

"You're the liar, Hank Dawson," she said in a low, frigid tone. "You never wanted to kiss me."

"You don't think so?" He shrugged, then walked to the door. With one hand on the knob, he looked at her over his left shoulder. "If you'd ever stopped lookin' down your snotty little nose at me and treatin' me like I was an idiot or a degenerate, who knows what I mighta done?"

Drawing herself up tall and proud, she refused to rise to his bait. "That all happened a long time ago, Hank. Despite our differences, we still need to work together for Tina's sake. I hope you'll come back to the parenting class."

He tipped his head to one side and thought about it for a moment. "Naw, I don't think so. I'll read your books and get 'em back to you, but I don't think you've got anything to teach that I'd care to learn."

Chapter Six

Hank's indictment of her character nagged at Emily's conscience during the next two days. Once she got over feeling defensive about what he'd said, she realized he hadn't been speaking entirely from anger, but from hurt feelings, as well. She had been angry herself, of course; actually, she'd been furious that he'd had the nerve to admit to checking up on her like that. But that didn't excuse her complete lack of tact.

Then she'd started wondering if perhaps he hadn't been right about her. *Was* she a repressed, self-righteous prig? She didn't want to believe that. Perhaps her standards for behavior were more stringent than those exercised by the rest of society, but other people always seemed to expect *her* to observe all the proprieties. So why did it feel as if she was too demanding?

Whatever the answer to that question, she couldn't deny that her remarks to Hank had been less than professional. It didn't matter if he had wounded her self-esteem, teased and tormented her back in high school. It didn't matter that he could enrage her without even trying. It didn't matter whether she approved of Hank or he approved of her.

The only thing that mattered was the well-being of the children attending her school. Emily had offended a parent, and in doing so, turned him away from getting the help he needed. She might have enjoyed telling Hank Dawson off, but Tina would ultimately pay the price.

On top of the inevitable guilt she felt on the little girl's behalf, Emily found herself reliving over and over again that kiss Hank had given her. Oh, she'd tried to pretend it hadn't happened, that it hadn't been important, that it hadn't been the most exciting kiss she'd ever received. Unfortunately, she couldn't make herself believe any of those things.

Worse yet, she found herself wanting Hank to kiss her again when he wasn't livid with her. If she were completely honest with herself, she would admit that she'd fantasized going a great deal further than kissing the man. Wouldn't he just die laughing if he knew that?

By Sunday morning, Emily felt more confused than she had in years. She knew she owed Hank an apology, but she didn't have the vaguest idea of how to approach him. Perhaps her father could give her some advice. Since returning to Pinedale, she had made it a habit to attend church with him and afterward, cook dinner at his house for the two of them. She'd ask him over the meal.

She picked him up at the usual time, smiling as he hurried down his front walk toward her car. At sixty-seven, Marc Jackson was fit and full of good humor, and appeared to be enjoying his retirement. Emily had always adored him, and looked forward to the time she spent with him.

They sat in their regular pew near the front of the sanctuary, talking quietly until the organ started to play. Then a commotion in the row behind them drew Emily's attention. She glanced over her shoulder, and nearly gasped out loud when she saw Hank settling onto the hard bench between his grandmother and Tina.

She returned smiles from the little girl and Grandma D, and turned her head back toward the pulpit in what she hoped would appear a casual move. She studied her bulletin and willed her suddenly racing pulse to slow down. When the service started, she breathed a silent sigh of relief, assuming the familiar ritual would help her forget the steady gaze she felt burning between her shoulder blades.

Unfortunately, though the organist played the opening hymn with unusual gusto, the only voice Emily could hear was the deep, rich baritone from the pew behind her. While the minister's sermon coaxed occasional laughter and nods from the rest of congregation, she was too aware of Hank's presence to concentrate on a word of the message. Drat the man. It was as if an alien life force had invaded a comfortable and comforting part of her life.

Hank didn't appear to notice her at all, and participated in the service as if he'd been there every Sunday for the past twenty years. Anxious to get away from him, Emily quickly gathered up her purse and coat after the benediction. She should have known that would be impossible, however, given her father's gregarious nature.

To her surprise—or perhaps *shock* might be a better word—Marc turned around and greeted Hank as he would an old and especially dear friend. The two men shook hands vigorously, grinning at each other with what appeared to be genuine delight.

"It's great to see you again, Hank," her father said. "You've come a long way toward recovery."

"Can't complain, Rev," Hank replied. "What's new with you?"

Marc wrapped his arm around Emily's waist and drew her into the conversation. "My beautiful daughter's come back to Pinedale. You remember Emily, don't you?"

Hank nodded and tipped his hat to her, but his smile didn't reach his eyes. "Hello, Ms. Franklin."

"Hello, Hank."

"Oh, by the way," Rev. Jackson said, "I've been meaning to call and thank you for donating that side of beef to the senior citizens' raffle, Hank. And from what I understand, the youth group had a good time at the skating party you allowed them to have at the Circle D last winter."

"Always glad to help, Rev," Hank replied.

"Are you still ranching with your brother?"

Ignoring Emily, Hank told him about buying the dude ranch. "We'll be movin' in next week. Come on out sometime, and we'll chew the fat."

"I'll do that," Marc Jackson answered. "Feel free to drop by my house when you're in town."

Hank shook his hand again, then said goodbye. While her father went on to visit with other friends and neighbors, Emily watched Hank leave. Goodness, but he looked handsome in that charcoal-gray, Western-cut suit. Judging by the number of women who spoke to him on his way out of the church, she wasn't the only one who thought so, either.

A sharp twinge of regret pierced her heart as she remembered his cool civility when he'd greeted her. After so many years of disliking Hank, it was surprising how much his low opinion of her stung. For heaven's sake, they were both adults now. Surely they could at least be friends.

After the short drive to her father's house, Emily opened his refrigerator and took out the package of chicken breasts he'd bought for their dinner. She seasoned them and slid them into the oven to bake while he changed out of his suit. As she peeled the potatoes, he returned to the kitchen and poured them each a glass of wine.

He set hers on the counter and took his own to the table, chatting with her until she finished making a salad. When she took the chair across from his, he reached over and patted her hand.

"You're awfully quiet today, Emily. Is something troubling you?"

Emily smiled and rested her free hand on top of his. "I can't hide anything from you, can I?"

"Of course not," he replied with an easy smile. "Is it something I can help you with?"

"I don't know. Before I get into that, though, I'd like to know how you and Hank Dawson became such good friends."

Her father's eyes took on a sad, reminiscent expression. "He was in the hospital in Jackson, recovering from his first surgery when your mother was dying. I always tried to visit anyone from Pinedale, whether they were members of the church or not. It's pretty lonely to be so far from home when you're hurt or sick. Hank seemed to appreciate my company, and I learned to appreciate his."

"What on earth did you find to talk about?" Emily asked, intrigued by her father's perceptions.

"Religion, politics, the weather, life in general. You'd be surprised," Marc replied with a laugh. "We didn't agree on much of anything, but we had some great arguments."

"It sounds as if you respect him."

"Oh, I do. He's got interesting ideas, and he was doing a lot of soul-searching then." He paused and sipped his wine. "I thought I noticed some tension between you two this morning. Are you interested in Hank?"

"No, of course not." She chuckled and tucked one side of her hair behind her ear. "I thought lightning might strike the church when he walked in this morning."

The Reverend Marc Jackson sighed and sadly shook his head at her. "You're so like your mother, Emily."

"That doesn't exactly sound like a compliment, Dad," she replied with a frown. "What do you mean?"

"She never really understood what the church was all about, either."

Stunned, Emily gaped at him for a long moment. "How can you say that? Mother taught Sunday school and sang in the choir and—"

"Yes, she did a lot of good work," Marc agreed, "but she never could stop judging people. She had a strict sense of right and wrong, and not much compassion for people who didn't live up to her standards."

"Surely you're not suggesting that it's all right for people to do whatever they want," Emily argued.

"Of course not. But we all fall short from time to time. We all have periods of growth. The church isn't a rest home for saints, Emily. It's a hospital for sinners."

"Dad, believe me, I understand that."

"No, I don't think so. Hank Dawson's had his problems, but he's a good man at heart. Don't write him off because he was wild when he was a kid. You could have gone that direction yourself quite easily. A lot of preachers' kids do."

"That's ridiculous. I never wanted to do anything to disappoint you or Mother."

"And we appreciated that, honey, more than you'll ever know. But we tried to give you a lot of support here at home. Maybe Hank didn't get that from his family. You've studied enough psychology to know people usually have reasons for acting the way they do."

"Come on, the Dawsons are a wonderful family. What possible reasons could Hank have had to act like such a jerk?"

"If you really want to know, ask Hank," her father replied. "But if you'll just think about it, I imagine you can figure most of it out on your own."

Perplexed, Emily frowned at him. "Why are you defending him to me? What difference does my opinion of Hank make?"

Marc drummed his fingertips on the table before answering slowly, as if he were choosing his words carefully. "I think someone like Hank would be good for you, Emily. In fact, I wouldn't mind having him for a son-in-law."

"I don't believe this," Emily yelped. "First Margaret, now you. And what on earth do you mean, he'd be good for me?"

"He knows how to have fun."

"And I don't?"

"You've always been so devoted to duty, I'm not sure you ever learned how. Hank could teach you how to lighten up and not take life quite so seriously."

To her consternation, Emily's eyes burned with tears and her throat closed up, making speech impossible. She felt as if her father had betrayed her, as if, despite all the times she'd been a "good girl" when she hadn't wanted to, he liked Hank more than he did her. He reached across the table and pressed his handkerchief into her hands.

"Sweetheart, I didn't mean to hurt you. But I care about you, and I'm afraid you're missing out on too many of the good parts of life."

"Like what?"

"Like a home and a husband and children."

"I've already had a husband. Remember? I failed miserably."

"It wasn't just you, Emily," he said softly. "You and Roger both failed. But that doesn't mean you can never succeed."

Emily gulped, wiped her eyes and blew her nose. "Will you tell me something, Daddy? And be completely honest with me?"

"Sure."

"Am I a repressed, self-righteous prig?"

"Oh, dear," he said with a startled laugh. "Has someone called you that recently?"

She nodded. "Your friend, Hank."

"Do you mind telling me what happened between the two of you?"

"I was planning to tell you about it and ask for your advice, after dinner," she said, giving him a wry grin.

Marc got up and refilled their wineglasses while she related the story. By the time she'd finished, his eyes sparkled with mirth. Emily saw how hard he was struggling to hold back a smile.

"Oh, go ahead and laugh. I know it sounds ridiculous, but it didn't seem very funny at the time."

"I'm sure it didn't. What do you plan to do about it?"

"I'll have to apologize to him, of course. But you haven't answered my question yet, Dad."

"About being a self-righteous prig?" He thought about that for a moment, then shook his head. "No, Emily, I don't think so. You're not paranoid, either. A friend of mine once told me that churches and public schools are the little man's political arena. People like Vi and Keith can cause a lot of trouble for you."

"Why would they want to, though, Dad? I'm doing a good job."

"They can't affect national issues, but they like to think they can control things closer to home. If they can get a minister or a principal or a teacher fired, they feel powerful."

"That sounds terrific."

Marc shrugged. "When you have a career like yours in a small town like this, it's a sad fact of life. But you can't allow a few cranks to bully you, Emily. They'll keep doing it as long as you'll let them."

"I suppose you're right about that," Emily muttered. Then she smiled, handed back her father's handkerchief and kissed the top of his head where his white hair was thinning. "I'll think about it. And I promise I'll talk to Hank as soon as I can find the courage."

Chapter Seven

Late the next Saturday morning, Hank left Tina hanging up clothes in her new bedroom, then went back downstairs to finish setting out mousetraps in the pantry and kitchen cupboards. The old lodge was structurally sound, but it needed an awful lot of work to make it livable, if not comfortable. Grandma D and Dani had offered to help clean it up, but fool that he was, he'd refused.

Still, glancing around the big, homey kitchen, he didn't honestly regret the decision. This project belonged to him and Tina, and nobody else. If it succeeded, it would be their accomplishment. In the meantime, they were learning how to live and work together.

The sound of a car door slamming outside drew him to the living room. He wasn't expecting anybody, and he didn't have time for a chat. It better not be Sam coming to check up on him again.

He peeked out the windows and cursed under his breath. It wasn't Sam walking up the overgrown path to the lodge, but now he wished it was. What the hell did *she* want? To insult him again?

No, wait a minute. Emily had something in her hands that looked as though it might be a plate of cookies, and even from this distance, he could see apprehension in her expression. Interesting.

Well, whatever she wanted, let her sweat, he thought, crossing his arms over his chest while he waited for her to climb the front steps. Her knock on the door came later than it should have, and he grinned as he pictured her standing on the other side, trying to work up the nerve to talk to him. Pausing to put on a stern expression, he took his sweet time about answering her summons when he finally heard it.

"This is a surprise," he said, letting his tone of voice tell her he didn't consider it a pleasant one.

"Good morning, Hank," she said with a hesitant smile.

"You're a long way from home, Ms. Franklin." He leaned one shoulder against the door casing and gave her an insolent once-over. "What can I do for you?"

Her lips tightened and her eyes narrowed with irritation. "You could invite me in," she suggested.

"Yeah. I could. Any reason I should?"

Color flooded her cheeks, but she held her ground. "If you have a moment, I'd like to talk with you."

Enjoying her discomfort, Hank let his gaze drift over her again. He liked what he saw more than he wanted to admit, although she looked so neat and tidy, he wouldn't mind messing her up a little. She wore a brand-new pair of jeans, a pale lavender sweater over a white turtleneck, and an unzipped, light pink jacket. The pristine white sneakers on her feet stood out in stark contrast to the muddy porch.

"I don't think we've got anything left to say to each other," he replied, almost laughing out loud when a spark of temper flashed in her eyes again.

Mouth pursed, she studied him for a long moment. "I'm sorry you feel that way," she said, shoving the plate into his belly and turning away. "Enjoy your new home. Please tell Tina I said hello."

Hank juggled the plate for a second, then reached out with one hand and snagged her arm before she could take another step. "Hold on there a minute, Emily. What did you really come here for?"

She shot him a defiant glance over her shoulder. "I wanted to apologize, but—"

He held up the cookies in his other hand. "You mean this is a peace offering?"

"It *was*. Even repressed, self-righteous prigs can admit when they're wrong. Sometimes."

"Is this one of those times?"

"It *was*."

"Well, then, thank you," he said. "Won't you come in?"

Emily resisted his tug on her arm. Then Tina appeared at the top of the stairs and hollered her name in delight. A warm, welcoming smile spread across Emily's face, softening her strong jawline and suddenly making her look younger.

Hank's breath locked in his chest, and he hardly noticed when his daughter slid down the banister, ignoring his warning not to do that until he'd made sure it was safe. Good Lord, if the woman ever looked at him that way, he'd never be able to keep his hands off her. Damn. He almost wished he hadn't been so hard on her.

"Wanna come see my new room, Ms. Franklin?" the little girl asked, dancing from one foot to the other in excitement.

Emily sent Hank a questioning look, asking his permission to enter the lodge. He shrugged as if he didn't care whether she did or not, and stepped out of her way.

She moved past him and held out one hand to the child. "I'd love to see it, Tina."

Hank watched them walk across the room together, his gaze welded to the gentle swing of Emily's hips as she climbed the stairs. In his opinion, there weren't many women who looked all that great in jeans. Emily was one of the lucky few.

Realizing his thoughts were headed down a dead-end road, Hank shook his head and took the cookies out to the kitchen. After removing the plastic wrap from the plate, he poured himself a mug of coffee and sampled Emily's baking. Not bad for oatmeal. Not as rich as one of Dani's chocolate goodies, but then, Emily was probably a health nut.

He sighed, wishing the dang woman didn't confuse him so much; one minute he liked her a lot, the next minute strangling seemed too good for her. He was flattered that she'd driven all the way out here to apologize, but he wasn't sure what it meant. Had she done it because of him? Or because of Tina? Did it really matter?

A moment later, he heard the two females giggling and gabbing as they made their way back down the stairs. He smiled at the note of pride in Tina's voice as she gave her principal the grand tour. Then he decided it didn't matter why Emily had come. Anyone who could make his daughter that happy just by showing up couldn't be all bad.

When they entered the kitchen, Tina spied the cookie in Hank's hand and charged across the room to grab one.

"Whoa," Hank said, moving the plate out of her reach. "Not 'til after lunch."

"That's not fair," the little girl argued, putting her hands on her hips. "*You're* havin' one, Dad."

"Yeah, but I always eat the stuff that's good for me, too. You don't."

"But I'm hungry *now*," Tina whined, giving him a pathetic look that would have undone him a few weeks ago.

"Well, it's almost noon. Why don't we fix lunch?"

"Can Ms. Franklin eat with us?"

Hank glanced at Emily, then shrugged. "If she likes peanut butter-and-jelly sandwiches, it's fine by me."

"Do you, Ms. Franklin?" Tina asked, her eyes begging.

"I love them," Emily replied.

The affectionate smile she gave Tina made Hank's breath catch again and added to his confusion. If Emily could be that sweet, why was she always so prickly and ready to fight around him? Did she really hate him that much?

"The rule of our house is that everybody makes his own," Hank told her gruffly, already regretting the invitation.

Tina climbed onto the counter, opened a cupboard and got down the giant-size jar of peanut butter while Hank took bread and jelly out of the refrigerator. Without waiting for directions, Emily found the stack of paper plates he'd been using until he could get the dishwasher fixed.

Of course, the first thing Tina did was tear a big hole in her bread when she tried to spread the peanut butter. And, of course, the second thing the kid did was cuss a blue streak. To Hank's surprise, instead of scolding Tina, Emily calmly picked up a knife and showed her how to hold it flat instead of digging in with the tip.

She complimented the kid when Tina managed to get it right on the next try, and then taught her how to cut the sandwich into neat triangles. As inconspicuously as possible, Hank followed her step-by-step instructions, too. The resulting sandwich looked a whole lot more appealing than his previous mangled attempts had.

They all sat on one side of the big, round oak table that had come with the lodge. Tina watched Emily constantly, copying the woman's mannerisms at every opportunity, and eating without her usual dawdling. The tension in Hank's gut from having Emily around gradually relaxed, and he found himself enjoying the lively chatter she engaged in with Tina.

As he glanced from woman to child and back again, he realized this was what he'd wanted when he'd proposed to Janice Fairmont. Oh, he and Tina were doing okay by themselves, but the kid was right. It *did* feel more like a real family when an adult woman joined them.

In a few years, when the memory of Janice's betrayal had faded more, he might consider marriage again. Maybe he'd put an ad in a personals magazine the way he'd done for Sam. He could get lucky and find someone as special as Dani.

He wouldn't even think about getting involved with Emily, however. Sure, he was physically attracted to her. And Tina had already nominated her for the job of stepmother. But he couldn't imagine himself living with Emily in any kind of peace for more than an hour, no matter how hard he tried. They were too damn different.

Besides, he'd struck out twice, and he wasn't ready to poke his neck out again. There were a lot of things a woman could teach his daughter that he couldn't, like how to spread peanut butter, for instance. But Tina would just have to make do with him for a while. Lots of kids survived with only one parent. She would, too.

With that thought firmly in mind, Hank took his empty plate to the garbage can and brought the cookies to the table. He excused himself and went out to the pickup for the tools he'd need to fix the wobbly banister. He wouldn't have been able to resist sliding down it when he was a kid, either.

Emily and Tina were clearing the table when he came back inside. Then Emily picked up her coat, dug car keys out of her pocket and said something he didn't quite catch as she ruffled the little girl's bangs.

"You can't leave yet," Tina protested.

Her gaze darted frantically around the room until she spotted her school backpack on the battered desk beneath the wall phone. "I need some help with my homework. I'm still real far behind in everything."

Emily bit her lower lip, then shot a worried glance at Hank. Tina must have guessed the reason for her hesitation. She ran over to him and grabbed his hand, pulling him into the kitchen.

"Tell her it's okay if she stays, Dad. Please?"

"Would you like to stay, Emily?" Hank asked.

"I'd be happy to, but if you have other plans—"

"We don't," Tina said quickly, running for her backpack.

"Is that true?" Emily asked him softly. "I don't want to impose."

He shrugged. "I'm just tryin' to get this place organized. You'll be more help to her than I would."

After giving him a long, searching look, she said, "All right," and joined Tina at the kitchen table.

Hank shored up the banister, then puttered at odd jobs where he could keep an ear on the conversation between his daughter and the principal, hoping he'd be able to pick up a few pointers for helping Tina himself in the future. After an hour and a half of listening to her coach the kid in math, spelling and English, his respect for Emily's teaching skills had increased tenfold.

With gentle teasing and leading questions, she encouraged Tina to figure out the problems herself. If she succeeded, Emily acted as if the kid were an absolute genius. If not, she explained the concept again, or asked different questions to get Tina to look at it from another angle.

No matter how long it took, she never scolded or lost her patience, and Hank could see his daughter's confidence growing by the minute. The kid would have worked straight through 'til supper if Emily had asked her to, but even principals had to go to the bathroom sometime. While Tina showed her beloved Ms. Franklin to the facilities, Hank started a pot of coffee.

"I wish I'd had a few teachers like you," he said when Emily returned. "You were really great with Tina."

"She's a pleasure to work with," she replied. "She's very bright, Hank."

"Unlike her father?" he asked with a wry smile.

"I always thought you were intelligent."

"Oh yeah?" Hank demanded, surprised and flattered by her answer.

"Of course. You simply didn't care about algebra, and I'm afraid I wasn't a very adequate teacher back then. I didn't have the first idea about how to motivate you."

"You did all right. I passed, anyway."

Tina skipped back into the room. Hank poured her a glass of milk and gave her a handful of cookies. Emily gratefully accepted a cup of coffee, and stood at the counter with him while she sipped it.

"Ready to start again, Ms. Franklin?" Tina asked.

"Maybe you'd better give the lady a break," Hank suggested. "Don't you have some reading or something you can do on your own for a while?"

"I guess so. But what'll Ms. Franklin do?"

"She can come for a walk with me and I'll show her the barn and the guest cabins."

He looked at Emily, one eyebrow raised in query. She nodded her consent.

A cool breeze blew from the west when they stepped out the back door a few moments later. Emily turned her face toward the sun, as if to drink in the meager warmth it had to offer.

Hank frowned at her sneakers. "The ground's still pretty soggy in spots. Want a pair of my boots?"

She eyed his big feet, then chuckled and shook her head. "I'll take my chances."

They walked across the barnyard and on up the rutted dirt road to the cabins in a relaxed silence. In amusement, Hank watched Emily skirt the mud puddles, wondering what she'd say if she dirtied those white shoes. She was as meticulous about where her feet landed as she was about everything else she did.

"So tell me," she said, "when are you planning to open for business?"

"All of the buildings except the lodge are in pretty bad shape. I'd like to have four of the cabins ready for the fall hunting season, but I'm gonna do all the renovations myself, so it'll take some time."

The first of the eight log buildings came into view then, and Emily gave him a sympathetic smile when she saw the sagging porch and dangling rain gutters. "I see what you mean, but it's cute, Hank. Does it have indoor plumbing?"

He grimaced. "Barely. That's one of the things I'm gonna have to upgrade. I want to keep a rustic atmosphere, but I want folks to feel like they've come to a first-class operation, too. For the prices I intend to charge, they're gonna want a few creature comforts like decent bathrooms and good beds."

Emily gazed off toward the mountains and heaved a deep sigh of appreciation. "You've got a beautiful setting here, Hank. People from back east will really be impressed."

"That's what I'm hoping," he agreed. "This is the biggest cabin, but they're all pretty much the same."

"May I see the inside?"

"Sure. Watch your step. Some of the boards are loose."

He took her hand to help her onto the porch, and felt his gut tighten. Maybe this wasn't such a good idea, after all. She'd probably think it was a hopeless dump and tell him so. Sam sure as hell had, and Hank had already listened to about as many negative comments as he could stomach.

But when he opened the door for her and ushered her inside, Emily's eyes lit up and she walked around the combination living room-kitchen-dining area, oohing and aahing over the stone fireplace, the bookshelves and the old branding irons nailed to the wall for decoration.

"Oh, can't you just see a family all snuggled in front of a fire for the evening?" she asked. "I'd make sure they had plenty of wood, old paperbacks and board games. And I'd put marshmallows and chocolate bars and graham crackers in the cupboards so they could make s'mores. Maybe some popcorn..." She paused and looked at Hank, then blushed as if she felt embarrassed because she'd gotten so carried away.

"Go ahead, Emily," he coaxed with a smile.

She chuckled and shook her head. "No, I'm sorry. It's none of my business. I'm sure you've got your own plans."

"Yeah, some," he agreed, "but I could use a woman's opinion, and I figure you probably know city folks pretty well. I can keep 'em busy during the daytime, but I've wondered how they'll react to living without a TV. So, go ahead. I think you were on the right track."

"Are you hoping to attract family groups?"

"Mostly. I'm thinkin' about offering one-week and two-week packages where one price pays for all the activities and meals. A couple of the nights they'll be camping, and we'll get somebody out there to play the guitar so they can sing around the camp fire."

"That's a wonderful idea, Hank. You might want to consider offering a slumber party in the lodge for the children, so the parents can have a night alone."

"Oh, Lord, Emily," Hank said with a groan. "I can see how the parents might love that, but it'd drive me nuts."

"It's only an idea. You could hire some high school girls to entertain the children."

"You know," he said, after thinking it over for a moment, "that just might work. All right, then, how would you decorate this place?"

To Hank's delight, that was all it took to set her off and running again. "Well, I'd clean it up, of course, and put gingham curtains at the windows and matching tablecloths, perhaps some Russell or Remington prints on the walls and one of those big, oval rag rugs on the floor."

"Go for the homey effect, huh?"

"Exactly. Lots of families have such hectic schedules, they don't spend much time together. I'd leave several nights open to let them interact by themselves. They probably won't even miss television once they get used to being without it. You might provide children's books, crayons, paper and art supplies for rainy days."

Hank shook his head in admiration, and couldn't resist reaching out to give her shoulder a grateful squeeze. "Thanks, Emily," he said softly.

A confused frown creased her forehead, but she didn't pull away. "For what?"

"For seeing the possibilities instead of the problems."

"Who could help but see the possibilities?" she asked with a surprised laugh.

"You want a list?" He sighed and stuck his hands in his pockets. "Come on, we'd better get back to Tina. No tellin' what she'll get up to if we leave her alone too long."

"All right." Emily preceded him out the door, pausing to take in the view from the porch. Hank stood close beside her, catching that tantalizing orangy scent in her hair again. Then she turned to him, her green eyes wide with concern. "Are you having doubts about this venture, Hank?"

"Some," he admitted. "My brother doesn't seem to think I can pull it off. Grandma D doesn't, either."

"Why not? You've got all the elements for success here, and there are other thriving dude ranches in the area.

Granted, you've got a big job ahead of you, but I don't see any reason why you can't make it.''

He tested the porch railing's stability before resting against it. ''They don't think I'll work hard enough. I guess I've given them plenty of reasons to believe that, but they're wrong. I came pretty close to dyin' when I hurt my leg, and I've had a lot of time over the last eighteen months to think about what I want.''

''What did you decide?''

''That I wanted to settle down and make a real home for me and Tina.''

''You couldn't do that at the Circle D?''

''Nope. Sam took over running it when Dad died, and it'll always be more his place than mine. I need to build something of my own. And this place…well, let's say I have a vision of what it could be.''

''Tell me about it,'' Emily invited.

Although he wouldn't have believed it was possible yesterday, it seemed like the most natural thing in the world to do just that. He helped her get down from the porch, then ushered her back to the road, and as they walked, he pointed out the projects he had planned. She asked questions that never would have occurred to him, about stuff like insurance, and offered suggestions that made him believe she saw his vision almost as clearly as he did.

Her sincere interest and enthusiasm gave his confidence a needed boost. Emily was an intelligent, extremely practical woman, after all. If she thought he could succeed with this business, then maybe he could.

When they reached the point where he could see the lodge, he decided he wanted to clear up a few things with her while they still had some privacy. Touching her elbow, he guided her over to the corral. He rested his forearms along the top rail and hooked the heel of his left boot over the bottom one.

"Emily, I'm curious about something," he said, smiling when she copied his pose. "What made you decide to come out here today?"

"I told you. I wanted to apologize. I realized I'd been awfully insulting, and—"

"But why did you care about that?" he interrupted. "We used to insult each other all the time, and it never seemed to bother you."

"We were kids. I'd like to think we've matured enough to treat each other with more respect. I didn't mean to sound so self-righteous."

"That really got you, didn't it?"

She shrugged. "It made me do a lot of thinking. I hate to admit it, but I guess I am too judgmental sometimes."

Hank took off his hat with one hand and smoothed down his hair with the other. Since lunch, he'd come to see Emily in a different light. Looking at her now, it was almost like meeting an attractive stranger for the first time.

"So, uh, where do we go from here?" he asked.

"You mean, in terms of our relationship?"

"Yeah."

She gave him a long, searching look, then studied her fingernails with great interest. "Well, I'm sure we'll see each other fairly often because of Tina."

"Forget Tina for a minute. I'm talkin' about you and me. You wanta be friends, or what?"

She looked up at him again, her smile filled with rueful honesty. "I don't know. Do you think that's possible?"

"We can try." He laughed and shook his head. "This is weird, Em. You and me talkin' about bein' friends, I mean."

"We've never gotten along very well," she agreed, a touch of wistfulness in her voice.

"Why do you suppose we didn't?"

"There were lots of reasons." She shrugged and looked off into the distance. "I know I was jealous of you."

"What? You're kiddin'."

"Absolutely not. You were always so popular, and it seemed to me that you were having all the fun I couldn't have. Being the preacher's kid, the new girl in school and a year younger than everyone else in my class, I never really fit in at school or anywhere else, except at church."

"Was it really that bad bein' the preacher's kid?"

She shrugged again. "Sometimes. My parents didn't bother me nearly as much as other people did." She hesitated, as if searching for the right words. "I always felt as if I was living in a goldfish bowl, and everyone was waiting for me to do something they wouldn't approve of."

"Is that why you got so huffy when I told you I'd driven by your house?"

Emily nodded. "I hate that feeling of being watched. And now, here I am, in the same position because of my job. It wasn't so bad in Cheyenne, because a lot of people didn't know who I was."

"I don't imagine you've done much that would shock people, anyway, Emily."

"Well, I'm not exactly a party animal," she conceded with a chuckle, "although, I did have my moments when I was in college. But it doesn't take much to shock some people, either, Hank. Or start them gossiping."

"I think you worry about that too much."

"Probably. Unfortunately, it's a lifelong habit, and I'm not certain I'll ever be able to break it." She shot him a wry grin. "All right, now it's your turn, Hank. Why didn't you like me back in high school?"

"I think it was because I knew you didn't approve of me," he said slowly. "Lots of folks didn't, but it really bugged me coming from you."

"Why was that?"

"It was a defensive thing, mostly. I was into rebellion in a big way, because my dad was always naggin' me. Jeez, from the day I hit school, about all I ever heard was, 'Why can't you be more like your brother?' "

"I take it he was a hard act to follow."

Hank rolled his eyes in disgust. "He was a straight A student like you, president of his class, captain of the football and basketball teams, the girls loved him—you name it. The guy was so damn—sorry, Emily—dang close to perfect, I wanted to hate him."

"But you didn't?"

"You don't know Sam, do you?"

"Not really. He'd graduated before we moved to Pinedale. The few times I've dealt with him about Tina, he's seemed very pleasant."

"Trust me, you can't hate the guy. He's as solid as they come, and he's just naturally nice, but he's not a wimp, either. He helped me whenever he could with Dad."

"How did I fit into all of this?" Emily asked.

"I'm gettin' to that. The truth is, I actually kinda liked you."

"Oh, please, Hank. You despised me."

"No, really, Em, I didn't. At first, I thought you were a lot like Sam because of your grades. I'll admit that irritated me. On the other hand, my teachers were convinced I didn't have any brains at all, but even when you fussed at me, you acted like you at least thought I had one."

He smiled at the memory, then shook his head. "Probably not a very good one, mind you, but a brain, anyhow."

"Why didn't you use it, and show me and everyone else we were wrong about you?"

"Because you were so dang smart, I felt intimidated."

"By *me?*"

"Yeah. You scared the whey out of me. I knew I couldn't keep up with you, so I acted like I didn't care enough to try. That's why guys pick on smart girls, ya know. It's all a bunch of macho bluster. If I could get your goat, then you weren't really superior.''

Emily tossed back her head and laughed, a clear ringing sound that made Hank itch to kiss her. He settled for laughing with her, instead. When they both quieted down, he nudged her with his elbow.

"Didn't you ever know that, Franklin?"

"I guess I did," she answered, wiping her eyes with her fingertips, "but I never expected you to admit it."

"Don't count on it happening again anytime soon."

"Oh, I won't. But thank you for doing it this once." She sighed and let a brief silence stretch out before asking, "So, um, do you want to try being friends, Hank?"

He pulled the brim of his hat down to shade his eyes while he considered his answer. When Emily let down her guard and just talked to him like this, he felt a powerful attraction toward her that had a whole lot more to do with sex than with friendship. But it wouldn't hurt to give friendship a try, would it?

"Yeah," he said slowly. "Why not?"

Tina stuck her head out the back door at that moment and hollered, "What're you guys doin' out there, Dad?"

"Just talkin', honey," he shouted back. "We'll be right in."

Emily turned toward the house. Hank walked along beside her, draping his arm around her shoulders. He laughed at the dubious glance she shot him and gave her a quick hug.

"Relax, Em," he said. "Friends do this kind of stuff."

To his surprise and immense satisfaction, Emily placed her arm about his waist and shyly hugged him back.

Chapter Eight

Hank returned to the parenting class the next Wednesday night. Despite their tentative agreement to be friends, Emily hadn't known what to expect when she ran into him again. For that matter, she still didn't. She was awfully glad to see him, however, and when he lingered after everyone else had gone, she told him so.

"Hey, I'm not cuttin' off my nose to spite my face," he said with a wry smile. "I need to learn this stuff, and you're a good teacher."

"Thank you." Emily leaned against the table behind her and crossed one foot over the other. "How are things going with Tina?"

Hank stuck his hands in his jeans pockets and shifted his weight to his right leg. "Aw, you know, some days are better than others, but I think we're doin' okay. She's still not caught up with her homework, though. I was wonderin' if I could hire you to come out and help her again next Saturday."

"No. You can't hire me," she said, frowning at him deliberately.

His hopeful smile dropped. "C'mon, Em. She works harder for you than she does for me." He sighed and rolled his eyes in frustration. "Besides, she really hates it when I try to correct her."

"Well, you still can't hire me." Emily allowed a teasing grin to escape. "But I'd be happy to help her as a friend. You know, Hank, friends do this kind of stuff."

He tipped back his head and laughed, a deep, rumbly sound that came out of his broad chest, sending a flash of warmth through her midsection. At the same time, gooseflesh erupted on her forearms. Lord, but he was gorgeous when his eyes lighted with laughter and his mouth quirked up at the corners.

"Got me, that time," he admitted, chalking up two points in the air.

"Good. I'm trying to improve my sense of humor."

"You've made a good start." He studied her with a thoughtful expression for a second. "What brought this on?"

She shrugged, wishing she hadn't said that. "My dad told me you know how to have fun. He, um, implied that I don't."

"That hurt your feelings, didn't it?" he said softly.

"A little. I know I've always been too . . . serious."

"Maybe we could work out a trade, seein' as how we're friends, and all. You teach Tina what she needs to know, and I'll teach you how to have fun." He stuck out his big hand.

"Deal?"

"Deal." She shook his hand, liking, more than she wanted to, the way his callused palm felt against hers. She withdrew as soon as good manners would allow. "I'd better get home."

They strolled through the school building, turning out lights and locking up. When they reached the parking lot, Hank opened the pickup's door and turned to face her.

"Why don't you come out about nine and plan to stay the whole day? You can work with Tina in the morning, and I'll give you your first lesson in the afternoon."

"All right. I'll see you then."

"Oh, and Emily?"

"What?"

"Wear something grubby."

She rested one hand on her hip. "Why would I want to do that?"

"Because," he answered, leaning down to her eye level, "sometimes to have fun, you've gotta be willing to get dirty."

"I don't know about this, Hank," she said, her eyes narrowing with suspicion.

"Trust me." He moved closer and grasped her chin with one hand. "You'll love it." Then he dropped a soft, sweet kiss on her mouth that made her heart race despite the brevity and gentleness of the contact.

Before Emily could object, he climbed into his truck and started the engine. She rapped on the window. He rolled it down, grinning at her with all the innocence of a naughty little boy.

"I don't think friends are supposed to do that kind of stuff, Hank," she scolded, fighting to hold back an answering smile.

"Depends on how good o' friends, they are, Em."

He drove away chuckling, leaving Emily to start the short walk home with ambivalent emotions. Her lips tingled, she could still feel the imprint of his fingers on either side of her chin and, darn it, she wanted him to kiss her again. Not as a joke. Not as a way to tease her. But as if he meant business.

She walked faster and inhaled a deep breath, hoping to dispel the antsy, restless sensations simmering in her bloodstream. It was one thing to develop a friendship with Hank Dawson. It was something else entirely to contemplate having an affair with him, which, God help her, was exactly what she was doing.

"Don't be crazy, Emily," she muttered, banging her briefcase against the side of her knee. "You've been alone a long time. It was just a simple little kiss. No big deal."

That little kiss hovered in her mind for the rest of the week, however. On Saturday morning, she took Ivan for a run, then showered and dressed, continually reminding herself that this was supposed to be a *platonic* friendship. Hank probably didn't want more than that, either. He simply knew how to get her goat, and enjoyed doing so.

When she arrived at the ranch, a pajama-clad Tina answered her knock at the front door.

"Hi, Ms. Franklin. Do you like pancakes? Dad's makin' some."

"I love them, Tina," Emily answered, stepping inside.

She glanced around the big, airy living room and choked back a startled laugh. A mountain of unfolded laundry nearly hid the chair beside the fireplace. Rumpled newspapers and dirty dishes covered the coffee table. One end of an empty beer can winked at her from under the sofa skirt. A Monopoly game lay in the middle of the carpet, and a nude Barbie doll reclined on top of the television, which was blaring a cartoon theme song.

"I know it's a mess, but don't pass out on me, Em. Saturday's my housework day," Hank said from the kitchen doorway. "Sorry we're not quite all together yet. We overslept."

Emily turned to greet him, and her mouth went dry. Lord, he was half naked. The thick, dark hair on his head stood up in odd places, as if he'd just crawled out of bed.

His eyes held a sleepy, welcoming expression that made her wonder what it would be like to wake up next to him in the morning. A heavy growth of beard stubble darkened his rugged jaw.

From there, her gaze traveled slowly over his broad shoulders and hairy chest to the waistband of his jeans, then on down his long legs to his big feet, which were every bit as bare as his torso.

Oh, my, she thought, jerking her gaze back up to his face, *a hunk calendar in the flesh.* He propped one elbow against the door casing, drawing her attention to the bulging muscles in his arm.

"Want some coffee?" he asked, smiling as if he could read her thoughts.

To her intense self-disgust, Emily had to clear her throat before she could answer. Her voice had an odd, breathless quality when it finally decided to work. "Yes, please."

She followed him into the kitchen, nearly tripping over her own feet because she was trying so desperately not to look at his naked back. When she glanced at him again, he reached into a cupboard for a ceramic mug, treating her to a front-row view of smooth skin rippling over hard muscles.

"Cream and sugar?" he asked, making a three-quarter turn toward her.

Emily shook her head and accepted the cup from him. Clutching it as if he might suddenly try to take it away from her, she retreated to the table and gulped the hot liquid, scalding her tongue in the process.

He licked the tip of his finger and tested the griddle for readiness. "Why don'tcha take your coat off, Em? Unless you're cold?"

"Oh, um, no," she murmured, feeling extremely foolish. "It's nice and warm in here."

In fact, warm was a serious understatement. She searched her brain for a casual topic of conversation, but couldn't come up with one to save her soul. Her silence didn't appear to bother Hank. He poured a circle of batter as big as a dinner plate onto the griddle, then rummaged in the refrigerator and brought a stack of small plastic bowls to the counter.

Whistling through his teeth, he popped the lids off and carried maple syrup and margarine to the table. He moved with an easy, almost lazy masculine grace that raised Emily's temperature another five degrees. She told herself she wished he'd go put on a shirt, but couldn't deny herself the pleasure of watching him. If he could read her mind now, he wouldn't call her repressed.

He flipped the pancake over and hollered for Tina. The little girl came running and slid onto the chair beside Emily's, grumbling, "Hurry up, Dad. I'm starvin'."

"Hang on there, shorty. I'm doin' the best I can."

Hank transferred the pancake onto a plate, then fished some fruit out of the plastic bowls and carefully arranged it on Tina's breakfast. He set the plate in front of his daughter with a flourish, winking at Emily when the little girl stared at it in delight. Emily leaned over to see what he'd done.

Two eyebrows made out of peach slices curved over a pair of purple grapes for eyes. A fat strawberry had become a nose, pear halves at the sides were ears, and a half circle of raisins at the bottom formed a crooked smile.

"Great art, huh?" he asked, puffing his chest out with exaggerated pride.

Pursing her lips, she studied his creation with a critical eye. "Interesting use of texture and color," she said. "It also looks like a sneaky way to get someone to eat *f-r-u-i-t.*"

"Hush," he whispered, the corners of his eyes crinkled up with laughter. "Grandma D told me my mom used to do the same thing with Sam. Want me to make you one?"

Emily laughed at his hopeful expression. "No thanks, I've already eaten. Feel free to make one for yourself, though. You really should set a good example."

"That's right, I should."

Of course, Hank being Hank, he turned his pancake into a monster face. He clowned his way through the rest of the meal, keeping Emily and Tina entertained. By the time he finally shooed Tina upstairs to get dressed, Emily's sides ached from laughing. She got up to help him clear the table, but he pushed her back into the chair and refilled her coffee cup.

"Save your strength for the kid," he advised.

"Where do you want us to work?"

"Right there at the table. When Tina comes back, I'll go do the bathrooms and muck out the living room. By the time I'm ready for the kitchen, you can move to the coffee table."

Tina came back into the room five minutes later, her backpack slung over one shoulder, a brush, comb and elastic band in her other hand. "Will you braid my hair, Ms. Franklin? Dad's are sloppy and they always come out."

"I heard that," Hank said indignantly. "Ya know, if you wouldn't wiggle all over the place—"

"Would you like a lesson?" Emily interrupted, turning the little girl around when she saw a combative scowl starting to form on Tina's face.

"Yeah."

Hank loomed over Emily's right shoulder, watching the process with the intensity of an intern observing a famous surgeon. His body heat penetrated her clothing, making her painfully aware of his nearness. His breath ruffled the fine hairs that had escaped her ponytail at the back of her neck. A musky, masculine scent filled her head, impairing her ability to concentrate.

"Here. You try it, Hank," she said when her hands fumbled for the third time.

She dropped Tina's hair and scrambled off the chair. Hank shot her a puzzled glance, but obediently changed places with her. Standing behind him was even worse. Now his body heat penetrated the front of her sweatshirt. Her breasts swelled inside her bra, as if begging her to lean forward so they could rub against his smooth, warm skin. His thick, glossy hair brushed the side of her face, tempting her to smooth it down and run her fingers through it. She was definitely losing her mind.

"Like this?" he asked, turning his head toward her.

Their lips were on an equal level. Her eyes met his. The same sensual awareness that was tormenting her glittered in his coffee-colored gaze. Her lungs refused to function. So did her brain. She couldn't think of anything but how much she wanted to kiss him.

"Hurry up, Dad," Tina grumbled. She whipped her head around as if to see what was taking so long, jerking her hair out of his hold.

Emily straightened up, quietly sucking in air like a beached trout. Hank cursed under his breath. A muscle twitching at the side of his jaw, he gathered up the long, silky locks and divided them into three sections.

Taking comfort from the knowledge she wasn't the only one suffering, Emily leaned forward to watch him again. Unfortunately, Hank's fingers started fumbling as hers had done earlier. There was nothing else to do but reach around him and demonstrate the technique again.

"Get it really tight here at the start," she said, doing her best to ignore the heat surging through her at the unavoidable contact of her breasts against his shoulder. "Keep it as tight as you can all the way to the end. See?"

"Yeah." His throat worked down a swallow and his voice sounded even huskier than hers. She didn't dare risk even a glance at his lap. "I'll get it this time."

He succeeded on the next try, thank God. Emily stepped away and crossed her arms over her chest. Tina turned toward the table and unzipped her backpack, the sound loud as a ruler slammed onto a desk in the heavy silence between the two adults.

With a muttered, "I've gotta get to work," Hank left the room. Emily grabbed her mug and carried it to the sink, giving herself precious seconds to regain her composure. By the time she joined Tina over an open math book, her pulse had slowed to normal speed. She managed to pay attention long enough to get the little girl started on her assignment.

The instant Tina set pencil to paper, however, Emily's ears strained to locate Hank. When his footsteps thudded directly overhead, her heart beat a little faster. When the shower started running and continued to do so for twenty minutes, she imagined him standing under the water in the nude. Then she imagined herself holding out a bar of soap to him, offering to wash his back and anyplace else he desired.

It was a disconcerting experience, to say the least, especially for someone like Emily, who was used to controlling her thoughts and emotions. If she *had* to have these feelings, why in heaven's name couldn't she feel them for someone...safer? For the sake of her job, almost any other man in town would be a better choice than Hank.

You thought Roger was a safe bet and look what happened, an inner voice reminded her. *How much worse could it be with Hank? At least he excites you. He always has.*

Emily heaved a disgruntled sigh and shook her head, flushing when Tina looked up at her, her eyes alight with curiosity.

"Is something wrong, Ms. Franklin?"

"No, honey. I was just thinking. Go ahead and finish that page."

The little girl shrugged and went back to work. Desperately needing a distraction, Emily told her student to call if she needed help, and walked over to the sink. If Hank wanted to complain about her loading his dishwasher, that was his problem.

The activity gradually eased her tension. After she'd finished the dishes, it seemed natural to move on to scrubbing the stove, the front of the refrigerator and the countertops. When she couldn't find anything else to scrub, she found a broom in the pantry closet and went after the crumbs on the floor.

Hank appeared in the doorway as she put the dustpan away. He'd obviously showered and shaved, and the form-fitting black T-shirt he wore with an equally tight pair of faded jeans threatened to upset her equilibrium all over again. He glanced around the room, his eyes narrowing as he noted everything she'd done. Emily gave him a guilty grin.

"What can I say, Dawson? I'm a compulsive cleaner. I couldn't just sit there all morning."

A smile stretched slowly across his face. "I'll forgive you this time, I guess."

"You're too generous," she said, her tone dry.

"Yeah, that's me. Mr. Generous. Truth is, I really hate doing this stuff. I appreciate the help."

Before Emily could reply, a loud knock sounded on the back door and a tall, auburn-haired woman let herself in, calling, "Anybody home?"

"Aunt Becky! You're back!" Tina shouted, bolting out of her chair.

The woman dropped a large paper sack on the counter and scooped the little girl into her arms. Hugging her close, she whirled Tina around in a circle. Laughing breathlessly, she held the child slightly away, checking her over with maternal affection.

"Good grief, kid, you've grown three inches since I've been gone." She hugged the little girl again. "Oh, I've missed you so much!"

Tina gave her aunt's neck a fierce squeeze. "I missed you, too. Where's Jonathan?"

"Home with your Uncle Pete. I was hopin' you'd come have a girls' day with me. We'll go into Pinedale for lunch and do some shopping."

"Just you and me?"

"Yup. If it's okay with your dad, you can come home with me and spend the night, too. Would you like that?"

Tina turned wide, pleading eyes on Hank. "Can I, Dad? Please?"

"What about your schoolwork?" he asked. "It seems kinda rude for you to leave when Ms. Franklin came all the way out here to help you."

"I've already finished my math and English," Tina argued. "All I've got left is reading, and I don't need any help with that. I promise I'll do it tomorrow."

Hank shot Emily a what-the-heck-should-I-do? look.

"She's worked hard this morning," Emily said, smiling at the anxious little girl. "We were just about ready to quit for the day, anyway."

"Pretty please, Dad?"

"All right. Go pack your stuff, honey," he answered.

Becky set Tina on her feet, then grabbed her arm before she could take off. "Whoa, there. Don't you want the present I brought you from our trip?"

"Yeah. Where is it?"

Becky dug two gift-wrapped boxes out of the bag. She handed one to Tina and tossed the other one to Hank. Tina opened hers in ten seconds, sending a flurry of paper and ribbon onto the floor. Hank wasn't far behind her.

"Hey, look at this neat sweatshirt, Dad," Tina said, holding it up in front of her. "It matches Aunt Becky's."

"Go put it on, and we can be twins," Becky suggested. "And don't forget to pack your toothbrush," she called as Tina ran out of the room.

"You're supposed to make her say thank you, sis," Hank grumbled, leaning over to kiss Becky's cheek. "Welcome home."

She playfully punched his arm. "Well, how do you like yours, Hank?"

He held up the Washington Redskins sweatshirt she'd brought him and eyed it with distaste. "This was Pete's idea, right? He knows I'm a Broncos fan."

Becky gave him an I'll-never-tell shrug, then offered her hand to Emily. "It's nice to meet you again, Ms. Franklin. I hope you'll excuse our bad manners. We haven't seen each other for a month."

Chuckling, Emily returned the handshake. "No problem, Mrs. Sinclair. It's nice to see you again."

"Well, I'm sorry if I interrupted you. What's this about helping Tina? She usually does real well in school."

"I'll tell you all about it later, Beck," Hank said. "She got behind, and Emily's helping her catch up."

One eyebrow raised in a thoughtful pose, Becky studied her brother. Emily could well imagine her thoughts. *Oh, so it's Emily, is it? Hmm. What's going on here?*

Then Becky smiled and started talking about her recent trip and her infant son. When Tina returned, she bustled the kid out the door in a hurry, promising to bring her back the next day. After all that cheerful chitchat, the lodge suddenly seemed awfully big and awfully quiet.

Excruciatingly aware that she was alone with Hank, Emily found herself trying to chatter and fill the silence. Unfortunately, she'd never been very good at small talk, and Hank didn't help her one bit. He leaned back against the refrigerator, stuck his thumbs in his jeans pockets and crossed one foot over the other, a smirk lurking behind his bland expression. Drat the man. He was enjoying her discomfort.

The kitchen walls suddenly seemed to contract, and her lusty fantasies of Hank in the shower reappeared in her mind—full-blown, and in living color. Her mouth closed with an audible snap, but she refused to lower her gaze. They stared at each other for a long, breathless moment.

"Well, Em? Whaddaya wanta do now?" he drawled, blatantly undressing her with his eyes.

"I, um, thought you had something planned."

"Yeah. But somehow, fixin' the porch at cabin number one has kinda lost its appeal."

"That was your idea of fun?"

"Not anymore."

Emily shivered at the gritty note in his voice. Outside of her marriage, her experience with men was extremely limited. If even a third of the stories she'd heard in the girls' locker room at Pinedale High about Hank's prowess were true, she was in trouble. Big, big trouble. God only knew what he'd learned in the past twenty years.

"Perhaps I should go," she said.

"Why would you want to do that?"

"You know why, Hank. Our definitions of friendship appear to be quite . . . different."

"I wouldn't say that." He straightened away from the refrigerator and crossed the distance between them in two long strides. Then he tucked her hair behind her ear, his rough fingertips caressing the sensitive skin at the side of her neck. "I'd say our minds are toolin' down the same track, honey. Don't be afraid of what you're feelin'. I'm feelin' it, too."

She gulped and tried to step back, but the sink was in her way. "I'm not afraid," she lied.

His mouth curved up on one side, telling her he didn't believe her for a second. "That's good." His voice softened to a husky whisper. He stroked her cheek with the backs of his knuckles, his touch so gentle, his dark eyes so sincere, she had to shut her eyes against them or melt into a puddle at his feet. "That's real good, Em. 'Cause I think maybe we were meant to be more than friends."

"We're not really even friends yet, Hank. I'm not ready for anything more."

He lifted her chin with his index finger, coaxing her to look at him. "Hey, there's no rush. All this sizzlin' chemistry's kinda thrown me for a loop, too."

"It has?"

"Damn right. I didn't want to feel attracted to you any more than you wanted to feel that way about me. But we're both feelin' it, and it's stupid to try to pretend like we don't."

Realizing he was right, she nodded slowly. "So, um, how do you think we should proceed?"

"Well, I don't know about you," he drawled, his eyes glinting with laughter, "but I think we oughtta get the heck out of this empty house and go pound on some boards for a while. Relieve some of this tension, you know?"

Laughing, Emily shoved at his chest with both hands. "Now, I get it, Dawson. You're just trying to get some free labor."

"Whatever works, Franklin. Whatever works."

Chapter Nine

Driving out to cabin number one, Hank smiled to himself at the sight of Emily bundled up in one of his old denim jackets. She'd said she didn't care if her own coat got dirty, but he hadn't thought it was heavy enough to keep her warm. Though there were only ten days of April left, the air at this elevation was still downright cold.

Besides, his jacket covered her almost all the way to her knees. He hoped it would help him keep his mind on work and his hands off Emily. He was glad they'd admitted they were attracted to each other, and he intended to give her more time to get used to the idea before he did anything about it.

But man, oh man, it wouldn't be easy to behave himself if he had to see her cute little fanny swishin' around in those jeans all afternoon. She'd sworn up and down that the outfit she had on was as grubby as her wardrobe got. He suspected that was true, but it didn't cool his libido any.

Emily looked mighty pretty in her skirts and suits. In a sweatshirt and jeans, however, she was pure dynamite. She just looked softer and more...touchable in casual clothes. God knew, he *did* love to touch her and watch her big green eyes get all wary and confused—as though it excited her, but she didn't think it should, somehow.

You're a jerk, Dawson, he told himself. *And if you don't stop thinkin' about her like a damn lecher, you're gonna blow it and scare her off.*

The cabin came into view. Hank backed the pickup as close to the building as he could. She helped him unload the lumber and tools from the truck bed. Then, in typical Emily fashion, she insisted that he explain what he planned to do, step by step, so she could organize the equipment properly.

Hank figured it was a royal waste of time, but he obliged her. This was supposed to be a lesson in having fun for her, and he knew it would drive her batty to jump right into the project the way he'd rather have done.

An hour later, he concluded her methods weren't half bad. When he needed a crowbar, a hammer or a certain size of nail, he didn't have to hunt around. With Emily measuring and sawing planks to replace the ones that had rotted, the boards always fitted slick as you please the first time. She seemed to be enjoying herself, too, even though they were both working up a sweat.

He peeled off his coat and tossed it aside, then wished he hadn't when she followed suit. He tried not to notice when she bent over to pick up her pencil and yardstick. He really did. Unfortunately, his eyes had a will of their own, and they liked lookin' at her behind. When he hammered his thumb the second time, he decided he'd better find a distraction but quick.

"Mind if I ask you a personal question?" he said. She straightened up and smiled at him. "That depends on how personal it is."

"Well, you know, I told you about Tina's mom, and Janice. I've been wonderin' what happened to your marriage, Em. Feel like tellin' me about it?"

She looked off toward the mountains to the west, but not before he saw the flash of hurt in her eyes.

"Hey, it's all right if you'd rather not," he said, when her continued silence became uncomfortable. "I mean, I'm curious, but if it's too painful for you—"

"It's not that, Hank," she said, cutting him off. "My divorce was final five years ago, and I know it was the right decision for both Roger and me. I'm just not sure how to explain it without sounding as if I feel sorry for myself."

"Why don't you start at the beginning?" he suggested. "Where did you meet good ol' Roger?"

"In a freshman chemistry class at the university."

"Cozied up over the Bunsen burners, huh?"

She grinned at that. "Not exactly. We studied together and eventually started dating. After graduation, we got married. It was all quite... conventional."

"I think you're leavin' out some big chunks of the story, but keep goin'. What didja do after the wedding?"

"I got my first teaching job to support us, and Roger went to dental school. Then we moved to Cheyenne and he went into practice with his father and his older brother."

"Sounds like one big happy family."

Emily shrugged. "It seemed that way, at first. I wanted to have a baby, but Roger said he didn't want that much responsibility yet. I got a teaching job. We built a new house, and I thought everything was fine, until..."

"Until what?" Hank asked quietly.

"He, um, well..." Her voice broke and she blinked hard, as if fighting back tears. "He came home one night, packed a suitcase and told me he was moving in with a barmaid."

"Good Lord, Em, the guy was an idiot."

She shook her head vehemently. "No, Hank, he wasn't an idiot, or a jerk, or any of the other nasty labels I tried to

IT'S FUN! IT'S FREE!
AND IT COULD MAKE YOU A
MILLIONAIRE

If you've ever played scratch-off lottery tickets, you should be familiar with how our games work. On each of the first four tickets (numbered 1 to 4 in the upper right) there are Pink Metallic Strips to scratch off.

Using a coin, do just that—carefully scratch the PINK strips to reveal how much each ticket could be worth if it is a winning ticket. Tickets could be worth from $100.00 to $1,000,000.00 in lifetime money.

Note, also, that each of your 4 tickets has a unique sweepstakes Lucky Number . . . and that's 4 chances for a **BIG WIN!**

FREE BOOKS!

At the same time you play your tickets for big prizes, you are invited to play ticket #5 for the chance to get one or more free books from Silhouette®. We give away free books to introduce readers to the benefits of the Silhouette Reader Service™.

Accepting the free book(s) places you under no obligation to buy anything! You may keep your free book(s) and return the accompanying statement marked ''cancel.'' But if we don't hear from you, then every month, we'll deliver 6 of the newest Silhouette Special Edition® novels right to your door. You'll pay the low subscriber price of just $2.96* each—a saving of 43¢ apiece off the cover price! And there's no charge for shipping and handling! You may cancel at any time.

Of course, you may play ''THE BIG WIN'' without requesting any free book(s) by scratching tickets #1 through #4 only. But remember, that first shipment of one or more books is FREE!

PLUS A FREE GIFT!

One more thing, when you accept the free book(s) on ticket #5, you are also entitled to play ticket #6, which is GOOD FOR A GREAT GIFT! Like the book(s), this gift is totally free and yours to keep as thanks for giving our Reader Service a try!

So scratch off the PINK STRIPS on all your BIG WIN tickets and send for everything today! You've got nothing to lose and everything to gain!

Here are your BIG WIN Game Tickets, worth from $100.00 to $1,000,000.00 each. Scratch off the PINK METALLIC STRIP on each of your Sweepstakes tickets to see what you could win and mail your entry right away. (SEE OFFICIAL RULES IN BACK OF BOOK FOR DETAILS!)

This could be your lucky day - GOOD LUCK!

TICKET 1

Scratch PINK METALLIC STRIP to reveal potential value of this ticket if it is a winning ticket. Return all game tickets intact.

LUCKY NUMBER

1D 534455

TICKET 2
Scratch PINK METALLIC STRIP to reveal potential value of this ticket if it is a winning ticket. Return all game tickets intact.

LUCKY NUMBER

4M 521983

TICKET 3

Scratch PINK METALLIC STRIP to reveal potential value of this ticket if it is a winning ticket. Return all game tickets intact.

LUCKY NUMBER

7D 575659

TICKET 4
Scratch PINK METALLIC STRIP to reveal potential value of this ticket if it is a winning ticket. Return all game tickets intact.

LUCKY NUMBER

22 515043

TICKET 5

FREE BOOKS

We're giving away brand new books to selected individuals. Scratch PINK METALLIC STRIP for number of free books you will receive.

AUTHORIZATION CODE

130107-742

TICKET 6

FREE GIFT

We have an outstanding added gift for you if you are accepting our free books. Scratch PINK METALLIC STRIP to reveal gift.

AUTHORIZATION CODE

130107-742

YES! Enter my Lucky Numbers in THE BIG WIN Sweepstakes and when winners are selected, tell me if I've won any prize. If PINK METALLIC STRIP is scratched off on ticket #5, I will also receive one or more FREE Silhouette Special Edition® novels along with the FREE GIFT on ticket #6, as explained on the opposite page.

(U-SIL-SE-04/92) 235 CIS ADPX

NAME _____

ADDRESS _____ APT. _____

CITY_____ STATE _____ ZIP _____

Offer limited to one per household and not valid to current Silhouette Special Edition subscribers.
© 1991 HARLEQUIN ENTERPRISES LIMITED.

**Carefully detach card along dotted lines and mail today!
Play _all_ your BIG WIN tickets and get everything you're
entitled to—including FREE BOOKS and a FREE GIFT!**

ALTERNATE MEANS OF ENTRY: Print your name and address on a 3″ × 5″
piece of plain paper and send to: Silhouette Reader Service,
3010 Walden Ave., P.O. Box 1867, Buffalo, NY 14269-1867

pin on him for a long time. I was too focused on my career and continuing my education to give him the kind of attention he needed. He said I bored him to death. I probably did.''

''Don't you think you're bein' a mite hard on yourself?''

''No,'' she answered, producing a lopsided smile. ''You didn't disagree with me when I said I've always been too serious. For heaven's sake, Hank, I'm thirty-seven years old, and I'm here right now so you can try to teach me how to have fun. If that's not the definition of a boring person, I'd like to hear a better one.''

Hank dropped his hammer and walked around the pile of lumber at Emily's feet. Grabbing her shoulders when she would have turned away from him, he gave her a gentle shake. ''C'mon, Emily, you're not *that* bad. You just need to lighten up a little. I've never thought you were boring. Infuriating and stubborn as hell, yes, but not boring.''

''Stop being nice or I'll cry all over you.''

''I've had women cry on me before.''

''Well, I don't want to,'' she grumbled. ''I cried enough over Roger to last me another twenty years.''

He eyed her doubtfully for a moment, wondering if she wouldn't be better off letting go, whether she wanted to or not. Still, he had to admit, she'd already told him more than he'd expected. He knew from firsthand experience how humiliating it was to admit your spouse had rejected you.

Wrinkling her nose at him, she shooed him away with both hands. ''Get back to work, Dawson. I'm fine. End of story.''

''Yes, ma'am,'' he drawled, squeezing her shoulders before releasing her. ''Whatever you say, Ms. Franklin.''

''And don't get smart, either.''

''Would I do that?''

''Of course, you would.''

They traded good-natured barbs for a while, then traded jobs because Emily claimed her sawing arm had worn out. Hank refrained from pointing out that her sawing arm would be the same one she'd use to swing the hammer, figuring she was sick of measuring and sawing, but was too polite to say so.

She started pounding away with more enthusiasm than skill. Hank didn't mind. Since the ruckus she raised made conversation difficult, he turned his thoughts back to the story she'd told him.

Good ol' Roger had done quite a number on her, all right. Hell, the creep might as well have ripped her guts out with a pitchfork. Hank had been torn up when Christine had left him, but he suspected he'd gotten off easy compared to what Emily had gone through.

Deep down inside, he'd never really believed his marriage would last. He and Christine had shared a lot of laughs, traveling the rodeo circuit. When she'd turned up pregnant, he'd married her. It had seemed like the decent thing to do, but he couldn't honestly say he was crazy in love with her.

Emily would have been different, though. She wouldn't have taken those wedding vows without fully expecting to spend the rest of her life with the guy. He'd bet both the dude ranch and the Circle D on that.

Yeah, she'd have had great big ol' stars in her eyes and babies on her brain. If that damn fool would've given her the kids she'd wanted, Hank doubted she'd have all those fancy diplomas hanging on her office wall. It wouldn't surprise him a bit if she had planned to stay home, happy as a horse in an oat bin, wantin' to be a mom.

She'd be a helluva good one, too, whether she worked an outside job or not. He'd seen that after five minutes of watching her with Tina. The woman didn't just know a lot about kids, she loved bein' with 'em, even when they acted like polecats.

Hank glanced at her and chuckled. Her ponytail looked straggly. Her face was dirty and flushed. She'd finally smudged those white sneakers but good. Best of all, there was a world of childish glee in her eyes as she pounded away on those nails. He hoped like hell she was pretending to smash in good ol' Roger's face.

Yeah, Em could be stuffy and finicky and rigid, like her mom had been. She probably wouldn't be the easiest woman in the world to live with. But easy women didn't stick around when life got bumpy. If he ever got up the nerve to get married again, he'd want a quality woman. Like Emily.

Her dad was an okay kind of guy, and he'd had his share of influence on her, too. Hank didn't think she needed lessons in having fun as much as she needed opportunities to have it and somebody to have it with. Well, he could provide that. And he would.

"Hey, Franklin," he shouted.

She looked up at him, hammer paused in midair. "What?"

"I've been thinkin' over here."

"Oh yeah? Pretty hard work, huh?"

"Knock it off," he said, trying for a stern teacher's voice. "I've got an assignment for you."

Sitting back on her heels, she lowered the hammer and gave him her complete attention. Damned if she didn't look about eight years old. "What is it?"

"Whenever you're out here at the ranch, I want you to stop thinkin' about what you *should* do, and concentrate on what you *want* to do instead."

"Is that supposed to help me lighten up?"

"Yeah. The way I've got it figured, you've worked hard to please everybody else all your life. It's time you started thinkin' about what'll please *you*. I don't want to hear any *should*s come out of your mouth. As far as you're concerned, it's a dirty word."

"What if I slip up? Are you going to give me detention, Mr. Dawson?"

Hank liked that sassy grin she was givin' him. In fact, he loved it. He made a big show of considering her question, then shook his head. "Nope. But you'll owe me a kiss every time you say it."

"That's an interesting teaching method. I suppose we could try it."

"Good. We're startin' right now."

"Yes, Mr. Dawson."

"Knock off that Mr. Dawson stuff, too. Treat me too much like a teacher, and I'm liable to break out in hives."

She gave him a droll look and went back to pounding. They finished the porch an hour later and drove back to the lodge. Needing to get off his bum leg, Hank grabbed a couple of beers from the refrigerator and handed one to Emily. She accepted it without comment, refusing the glass he offered.

He sat at one end of the kitchen table, elevating his leg on an empty chair. Emily plunked herself down across from him, yanking the rubber band out of her ponytail.

"Does your leg bother you a lot?" she asked after taking a long drink.

"Only if I'm on it too long. Whaddaya want for supper? I can do spaghetti or frozen pizza."

"Oh, I really shouldn't—"

"That's *one*," Hank said with a grin.

She rolled her eyes and huffed at him. "I suppose you want me to pay up now?"

"Nah. I think I'll save up a whole string of 'em."

"That's not fair."

"So what? I'm the teacher, and the teacher gets to make up the rules."

She took another hefty swig from her beer can and set the drink down with a bang. "I didn't agree to that. You can't save up any more than four at a time, or the deal's off."

Hank shrugged his acceptance. By the time he'd kissed her four times, he'd make damn sure she lost count. Remembering she wasn't much of a drinker, he thought about telling her to slow down with the beer, then decided against it. He wouldn't let her get drunk, but he'd sure get a charge out of seeing her tiddly.

"Back to the question, Franklin, and answer it honestly. What do you *want* to do? Have a great supper here with me, or go home and eat a sandwich all by yourself?"

"All right, I'll stay. But only for supper, and I choose spaghetti."

"Sounds good to me." He polished off his beer and climbed to his feet, smiling to himself when Emily did, too. "Well, come on, then. I'm starvin'. Want another beer?"

"I don't know if I should—"

"That's *two*."

"Oh, fiddlesticks," she muttered, looking disgusted with herself. Then she sighed. "Just give me another beer, Dawson. I'm telling my father you're driving me to drink."

The second beer didn't exactly make her tiddly, but it relaxed her enough that she stopped flinching every time their hands or hips accidentally brushed while they were cooking. She squawked like an enraged hen over some of the more creative ingredients he tossed into the spaghetti sauce. Hank decided her next assignment would include learning how to ignore instructions and break rules.

When they sat down to eat, she took a cautious bite and admitted the sauce wasn't too bad. She told him that, unfortunately, it was spicy enough to take the hide off the roof of your mouth. It had kind of a delayed kick to it, so you didn't really feel the heat until about the third bite. Then, wham—fire city.

Hank drained his water glass in one gulp. It didn't help. He saw Emily's cheeks start to turn red, and ran for the refrigerator. Grabbing the last two beers, he tossed one to

Emily. She caught it, popped the top at the same instant he popped his and they chugalugged together.

By the time they'd finished wiping their streaming eyes, both cans were empty. Hank didn't know about Emily, but he was starting to feel the alcohol. She raised one fist to her mouth in an obvious attempt to be discreet, and ripped out a belch that would have put Gusty Edwards to shame.

The horrified expression on her face was Hank's undoing. Laughter gushed out of him before he could even think about trying to prevent it. Emily glared at him. He couldn't stop. She yelled at him and punched his arm so hard, he knew he'd have a bruise come morning. He still couldn't stop.

Leaning his behind against the refrigerator door, he slid to the floor, clutching his stomach. She stood over him, looking like she wanted to kick him from here to Sunday.

"Now, Em, I know you couldn't help it after drinkin' a beer like that. But you're always such a lady…" He gasped, knowing he was going to lose it again. "And then that l-look on your f-face…"

He reached out and slapped the floor tile with each successive round of hoots, his eyes squinted so he could hardly see a thing. He didn't know whether the ridiculousness of the situation finally hit Emily, or the alcohol had invaded her brain cells, but the next time he paused for air, Hank heard the tail end of a giggle.

Tipping back his head, he forced his eyes open. Her lips were mashed together. Though her arms were clenched tight against her sides, her shoulders vibrated. Her eyes had a desperate, no-I-shouldn't-do-this-but-I'm-going-to-anyway kind of look in them. Another giggle leaked out.

Hank grabbed her hand and yanked, toppling her onto his lap. The air in her lungs whooshed out. Then her gaze met his, and she couldn't fight it any longer. She slid off his lap, her giggles turning into belly laughs, which turned into whooping guffaws. She sagged against him when the storm finally passed.

"I was afraid I was gonna have to slap you in a minute," Hank said, stroking her soft, shiny hair.

She wiped her eyes with the knuckles of one hand and inhaled a shaky breath. "Look who's talking. You were the first one rolling around on the floor. If I'd known it was going to be so entertaining, I'd have burped sooner."

"Don't make me laugh anymore," he begged, chuckling in spite of himself. "Lord, it sounded like you'd stored all that up for years."

"I have. At least at that sort of thing."

"Why? It's a natural reaction, Em."

"Because a teacher shouldn't—"

"That's *three.*"

"Oh, shut up," she grumbled, though there was more amusement than heat in her voice.

"Tsk, tsk. Is that any way for a teacher to talk, Ms. Franklin? And what were you gonna say about teachers?"

She elbowed him in the ribs. "When you're the lone adult in a room with twenty-seven kids, you don't dare laugh at rude noises. They make so many, you can't encourage them."

"You mean, you have to stand there and try to pretend it didn't happen?"

Emily nodded. "You do, if you want to get any teaching done. They even get into ridiculous contests sometimes. You wouldn't believe the remarks they make when the cafeteria serves beans for lunch."

"Is that hard for you? Not laughin', I mean?"

"Not really," she said with a grin. "I pretend my mother's frowning at me, the way she used to do when I misbehaved in church, and the urge to laugh dies fast."

Having experienced Emily's mother's bloodcurdling frowns of disapproval more than once himself, Hank nodded in understanding. The woman could wilt a rosebud at forty yards. They shared a companionable silence for a few minutes. Then Emily sighed and climbed to her feet.

"Come on, Dawson. I'll help you do the dishes, and then I have to go home."

"You can't leave for a while, Em," he said, taking the hand she offered to help him up.

"I can't stay. Ivan and my cats will be hungry."

He picked up a beer can and waved it under her nose. "You've had one too many of these to drive. Ivan'll just have to suffer, unless you wanta risk a DWI charge. That oughtta be great for a principal's image."

She stared at him in consternation. "Oh, dear. I didn't think of that."

After looking at the clock, as if calculating the minutes until she could escape, she snatched both of their plates from the table. "You didn't want to eat any more of this, did you?" she asked on her way to the sink.

Hank's mouth burned at the idea. "No, thanks. I guess you were right about that cayenne pepper."

"If you'd just followed the recipe—"

"It wouldn't have been any fun at all." He carried the pot with the rest of the killer sauce to the garbage can and dumped it. "Don't you ever experiment when you're cookin'?"

"Not unless I'm fairly sure it'll turn out all right."

"Well, we had a good laugh, didn't we?"

Her lips compressed into a tight line. "Yes, and my dog's going to pay for it. Sometimes you have to think about consequences before you have fun."

Hank rested his hand on her shoulder and gently squeezed her rigid muscles. She stepped away from him, as if her nerves were too jumpy to tolerate his touch.

"Aw, come on, Emily, it's not that big a deal. Ivan won't starve to death. Give him an extra dog biscuit with his supper and he'll forget all about it."

She grabbed the dishrag and attacked the stove. Hank bit back a sigh. Damn. They'd had a good time today, and now she was tensed up and irritated as a horse with a too-tight cinch. There had to be a way to salvage the situation.

"You want a sandwich?" he asked.

"I've lost my appetite." She rinsed out the cloth and moved on to the table, scrubbing as if somebody might have to do surgery on it.

He watched her for another second, then snapped his fingers. "Hey, I've got a great idea. Becky bought me tons of movies when I was laid up. Ever seen *Star Wars?*"

"No, but I'm not in the mood for a movie."

That was obvious, Hank thought grimly. She was lookin' for a fight, and he'd be damned if he'd give her one. She probably thought *Star Wars* wasn't "artistic" enough for her, too. Well, tough noogies.

He stomped into the pantry, brought out the popcorn popper and loaded it. While it was doing its job, he melted a stick of butter in the microwave and dug out the biggest bowl he owned. Emily flitted around the kitchen, wiping off this and straightening that, carefully avoiding him.

In fact, she was *so* careful not to touch him, Hank began to wonder if she was all that worried about Ivan. Maybe the issue was really that she'd said the "S" word three times, and she was afraid of what would happen if she did it again.

What he'd first thought were brisk, efficient movements looked more like nervous ones on closer examination. Every time she had to come anywhere near him, her eyes darted around, as if she might be searching for an escape route in case he decided to pounce on her. His anger faded abruptly when he considered the situation from her viewpoint.

Here she was, alone with a guy she didn't know that well on an isolated ranch. It was dark out, and they'd both had

a fair amount to drink. And he *had* teased her a lot about
those kisses. Maybe she deserved to be a little jumpy.

But he couldn't let her leave just yet, and he didn't want
to risk his own driver's license, either. On the other hand,
if she cleaned one more thing, he was gonna go nuts. The
movie was a good idea, after all.

He carried the popcorn into the living room, turned on
plenty of lights and set up the tape. Then he went back to
the kitchen, snatched the dishrag out of her hand and
tossed it at the sink. Ignoring her protests, he got two cans
of Coke out of the fridge and herded her to the sofa.

She huddled at one end, shooting him a scowl when he
plunked her soft drink on the end table beside her. Hank
put the popcorn on the middle cushion, sat at the other end
and hit the remote control. He'd practically memorized this
film, but it was fun to sneak glances at Emily and watch the
magic gradually win her over.

Before long, she had her shoes off and her feet tucked
under her. When he saw her absently dipping into the bowl,
her gaze glued to the screen, Hank's tension eased. Leaning back, he propped his feet on the coffee table and shov-
eled a handful of popcorn into his mouth.

For the next ten minutes, they were both absorbed in the
action. Then their hands hit the bowl at the same time, their
fingers barely brushing. Emily jerked hers away as if he'd
stabbed her with a needle.

Hank swallowed his irritation that time. The third time
it happened, however, he stopped the tape and glared at
her. "Will you relax, for God's sake?"

"I beg your pardon?"

"You've been skitterin' around like you're afraid I'm a
rapist. If I decide to jump your bones, I'll give you fair
warning. Trust me."

"I trust you, Hank."

"Ya coulda fooled me," he grumbled, crossing his arms
over his chest.

"No, really, I *do*."

"Well, *something's* buggin' you. Does the thought of kissin' me make you wanta puke or what?" Her genuine laughter convinced him that wasn't the case. Smiling, he softened his tone. "Talk to me. What's goin' on?"

"It's not you I don't trust," she said slowly, her cheeks turning pink. "I haven't dated many men besides Roger. I'm not sure I'd recognize a fair warning if you gave me one."

"Want me to show you?"

Her gaze dropped to her hands. "I don't know if that would be very wise."

Hank moved the bowl out of the way and slid closer to her. "You don't always have to do the wise thing. I'll admit I'd love to jump your bones, babe, but I'm not some randy kid who can't control himself. Anytime you want me to stop, all you have to do is say so."

She raised her eyes to meet his, earnestly searching for something he couldn't name. He held his breath and waited for her decision. His heart beat faster and he felt himself getting hard. Well, maybe he *was* randy, but he'd keep his promise or die trying.

"All right," she murmured. "Show me, Hank."

Hoping to lighten the mood, he stood, then shook out his arms and hands and pushed back his sleeves like a pianist approaching a concert grand. Emily rewarded him with a soft chuckle. He gave her a snooty nod and cleared his throat.

"Okay now, pay attention, Franklin. First thing I'd do is turn off about half these lights," he said, matching actions to his words. "Got that?"

"Yes, sir."

He crossed the room to the stereo system and selected two of his favorite compact discs. "Then I'd get a little soft music goin', and if you weren't tryin' to sober up, I'd bring out a bottle of wine."

"Just like in the movies, Hank?"

"Hey, I never claimed to be original." He walked back to the sofa and sat beside her. "But I reckon just about anything that would get a woman nice and comfortable oughtta work just as well. So watch out for stuff like that."

"Oh, I will," she said dryly.

He draped his arm over the back of the sofa behind her and scooted closer until their hips touched. Then he reached over, picked up her hand and laid it palm-down on his thigh, lacing his fingers over the tops of hers.

"Now, this is kind of a sneaky move, here," he explained. "It looks like you're just holdin' hands, and the woman gets a false sense of security. What you're really doin', is gettin' her used to touchin' some kinda intimate places."

It was Emily's turn to clear her throat. "Yes, I can see that. What would you do next?"

"Well, we'd talk for a while, and I'd stroke her hand a little. Then, I'd start playin' in her hair with this hand over here," he said, indicating the arm he'd stretched behind her head.

He twined one of her blond locks around his index finger, sliding it slowly across his skin. "If she didn't complain, I'd let my other fingers brush her neck and behind her ear, like this."

"That's, um, certainly effective," she said, her voice barely above a husky whisper.

"Yeah," he muttered, "works on men, too." All this touching and seeing her eyes turn a darker shade of green was torturing him. He sucked in a ragged breath and continued his lecture.

"Now, if you wanta move on to a kiss, all you've gotta do is nudge her head a little, so she's facin' you. And then, you just lean down and do it."

She raised one finger to his lips before he could demonstrate that point. "This doesn't quite fit my picture of jumping bones. Isn't this more like a seduction?"

He nibbled her fingertip. "Well, there's jumpin', and then there's *jumpin'*, Emily. If a guy's got any class at all, he won't just throw a woman down and start pawin' at her. I've always thought coaxin' and wooin' was fun."

"Oh, really?"

"Mmm-hmm." He flicked her finger with the tip of his tongue and smiled when she shivered in response. "Women are naturally wary critters. If you wait 'til they're ready, to kiss 'em, they're a whole lot more cooperative."

Her eyelashes lowered in pure invitation. "Do you think I'm ready?"

"What do you think, Em?"

"Maybe you should quit talking and find out."

She was ready, all right. Good thing, too, because he'd damn near run out of patience. At the first tentative touch of their lips, she trembled. He tipped his head to one side and stroked her lower lip with his tongue.

Uttering a soft whimper, she opened her mouth to him and flowed into his arms as if she'd always belonged there. Her hands crept to his shoulders. Then her fingers slid into his hair, brushing his ears, stroking the back of his neck.

His heart slammed against his rib cage. Blood rushed into his groin. He felt hot all over, as if he'd swallowed the whole can of cayenne pepper. God, but he wanted her, more than he'd ever wanted any woman in his life.

He hadn't expected this—not with reserved, cautious, conventional Emily. Sure, he'd begun to see her in a different light, discovered there was a lot more to her than most folks saw. He'd thought they would enjoy each other, neck a little, maybe pet a little, if he got damn lucky. But he'd never imagined her honest, uninhibited response to his kisses would torch off this powder keg, this…whatever the heck it was between them.

He lost track of what he did and what she did, and where who was touching whom. Making out with Emily was like shooting the rapids on the Snake River in a rubber raft— one belly-whompin' rush of excitement after another. He couldn't get enough of tasting her, of smelling her own unique, feminine scent, of feeling her breasts rubbing against his chest, of cupping those luscious breasts in his palms.

Lord, he ached to get closer and closer, and she wasn't doing anything to slow him down. No, she was kissing him with equal hunger, touching him with equal need, making the same, greedy, gasping little noises he was. If they didn't quit soon, he'd have her flat on her back and show her just how little class he had.

Feeling the last bits of his control starting to shred, he captured her hands and held them between their bodies. "Emily, darlin'," he whispered, between kisses, "we've gotta stop."

"What if I don't want to?" she whispered back, going for the side of his neck.

He groaned, wishing she hadn't said that. It had been so long since he'd been intimate with a woman, the very last thing he wanted to do was stop. But this wasn't just any woman in his arms. It was Emily. Sweet, vulnerable Emily, who wasn't ready for this, even if she thought she was. She would hate him and herself in the morning if he took her up on her invitation.

Raising his shoulder to his ear, he blocked her progress. "Em, don't," he said, more forcefully than he'd intended.

She blinked in confusion. "What's the matter?"

"Nothin', hon." Despite his body's raging protests, he smiled and gently tucked her hair behind her right ear. "We were just gettin' a little out of hand, is all."

"Oh. I see." Color faded abruptly from her face. She pulled her hands from his and moved as far away from him as she could get and still remain on the sofa.

Perplexed, Hank reached out and grasped her shoulder. "What is it you think you see?"

"That I've made a fool of myself." She checked her watch, then stood and straightened her clothing. "I've really got to go now, Hank. Thanks for your hospitality."

"Wait a minute," he muttered, struggling to get his feet under him.

Her posture rigid, she walked to the kitchen. Hank's left leg cramped up on him, forcing him to hobble after her. "Whaddaya mean, you made a fool of yourself?"

"Don't worry, I got your message. You won't have to fight me off again." She picked up her coat and purse.

He grabbed her arm as she tried to brush past him on her way back into the living room. "Fight you off? Good Lord, Emily, did you think I was rejecting you? That I didn't *want* you?"

"*Please,* Hank. I'm embarrassed enough."

"For a smart lady, you're awful damn dumb sometimes." He took her hand and pressed her palm against the fly of his jeans. "Does that *feel* like I didn't want you?"

Her mouth formed a little O of surprise, whether at his crude action or the strength of his arousal, Hank couldn't say. He was so frustrated at the moment, he didn't much care, either. He grasped her chin with his other hand and forced her to meet his eyes.

"You got the wrong message. I was tryin' to be noble and give you a chance to be sure of what you were doin'. Any time you want to finish what we started in there, I'll be more than happy to oblige, honey."

Color rushed back into her face with a vengeance. "May I have my hand back now?" she asked in a choked voice.

"I kinda like it where it is," Hank told her with a grin. "Are you plannin' to slap me?"

"No, I don't think so."

"Aw, hell, c'mere." He released her hand and pulled her into his arms for a bear hug. He rocked her back and forth until she finally stopped resisting him. ''Don't be embarrassed, Em. And don't get yourself all upset over it, either. We're both single, healthy adults and we didn't do anything wrong.''

''I know.''

Holding her at arm's length, so he could see her eyes, he stroked her cheek with his knuckles. ''Will you come back next Saturday? I promise Tina will be here. And you can bring Ivan. She'll love playin' with him.''

''I . . . I'll, um, have to think about it.''

''You do that.'' He hugged her again, then walked her to the front door. ''I'm gonna be sittin' by the phone, worryin' like an old mother hen, until you call and let me know you got home safe. Promise you'll do that?''

She gave him a tremulous smile. ''I promise.''

Hank stood in the doorway until her taillights disappeared. Then he went back inside, his footsteps echoing on the hardwood floor in the entryway. He tried to picture the living room the way it would be when he finally opened for business—full of tourists, laughing and swapping lies about their fishing trips and trail rides.

But all he could see was a vision of Emily's face, just before she'd realized he was calling a halt to their lovemaking. His gut tightened in a painful knot, and a cloud of loneliness drifted into the big, empty lodge, oppressive as the air just before a thunderstorm. Damn. He wanted . . .

Snorting in disgust, he plunked himself down on the sofa. Emily was a wonderful, sexy lady, but she was too complicated for the likes of him. She wasn't the kind of woman to have an affair, and he couldn't offer her anything more. Hell, he shouldn't have invited her to come back to the ranch. But why should he worry about it?

Emily wouldn't come back. If he knew her at all, she'd avoid him like a nest of rattlers. They'd most likely see each other at the parenting class, and just kinda let the relationship fizzle out. He'd be relieved when that happened. At least, he oughtta be.

So why the hell did he feel so empty now that she'd gone? And why the hell didn't that damn phone ring?

Chapter Ten

The next Saturday morning, Emily agonized ad nauseam over whether to accept Hank's invitation to visit the ranch again. He'd come to class on Wednesday night and acted as if nothing unusual had happened between them. His behavior had eased her embarrassment at seeing him again, and had angered her at the same time.

She'd been reeling all week. Had he honestly been so unaffected by their... necking session? That was an awfully adolescent term for the explosive sensations she'd experienced, but she couldn't think of a better one.

To be honest, she couldn't seem to *think* at all, at least not rationally. No, all she could do was *feel*. She bounced from one emotion to another, in no particular order, until she felt so off balance, so unable to concentrate, she wanted to scream with frustration. She'd actually tried that, much to her surprise and chagrin, but it hadn't helped.

Her relationship with Roger had developed gradually, progressing from acquaintance to friendship during their freshman year, friendship to casual dating during their sophomore year and so on. With Hank, she couldn't predict or plan or control anything. Did even God know what the crazy man would do or say next? It was like trying to keep up with a demented frog.

Emily laughed and shook her head. The truth was, she'd been just as bored with Roger at the end of their marriage as he'd been with her. The truth was, she found Hank's unpredictability exciting, and... and, all right, she'd admit it, *fun.* The truth was, she wanted to explore a relationship with him more than she'd wanted anything in years. Perhaps in her entire life.

If she could only get past the fear that reared its hideous head every time she got to this point in her reasoning process. Unfortunately, it was alive and growing—almost overwhelming. Daily, sometimes hourly, it whispered in her ear, *"You'd have to be insane to risk your heart to a man with a nickname like Heartbreak Hank."*

But he didn't *seem* like a heartbreaker when she was with him. Though he could be rough and even crude at times, he could also be caring, compassionate and surprisingly sensitive. When she'd been in his arms, sharing those searing kisses and caresses, she'd felt cherished, even while he'd been showing her an entirely new dimension to her sexuality.

On the other hand, what if she dug up the courage to continue the relationship, and he eventually found her as inadequate, in bed and out of it, as Roger had?

Emily threw up her hands in disgust and muttered a word that would have sent her mother running for a bar of soap. Ivan whined and laid his head on her knee, his soulful eyes saying, "Don't be sad. *I* love you." She ruffled his fur, then slid to her knees and hugged him.

"Thanks, pal," she said with a chuckle. "Okay, you make the decision. Should we go see Hank and Tina?"

He barked and danced around in a circle, his toenails tapping on the tile floor.

"I take it that's a yes?"

He barked again.

"All right, get your leash. But it's on your head, if I end up in a mess."

That didn't worry Ivan. He bounded into the car as if he knew he'd have a kid to play with. As it turned out, they all played with him, and the day passed with astonishing rapidity.

Without allowing herself to think too much about it, Emily accepted another invitation for the following weekend, and eventually the one after that, as well.

On the third Friday in May, she worked in her office after everyone else had gone home. With the school year rapidly drawing to a close, she needed to finish the annual staff evaluation forms as well as what seemed like a million other forms. She was determined to catch up with the paperwork tonight, so as not to miss a single minute of what had become her "Saturdays with the Dawsons."

Noting Harold Matheson's name on the next file in the stack, she groaned. It was difficult to be objective about a teacher whose mother continually plagued her. In fact, Vi had phoned Emily just yesterday to inform her that people were talking about the way Hank Dawson hung around to talk to her after the parenting class she was teaching.

Hadn't Vi, out of the goodness of her heart, warned Emily to stay away from that womanizer? As tactfully as possible, Emily had told the woman to mind her own business, and terminated the conversation. The evaluation she was going to give Harold would be like throwing gasoline on a campfire.

After teaching for fifteen years, any enthusiasm or creative spark Vi's beloved son had ever possessed had long since died. Despite four separate visits from Emily—to make absolutely certain she wasn't simply biased against him because of his mother—and countless suggestions for improvement, Harold gave every indication of planning to coast until his retirement. Since he had tenure, there was little Emily could do to remedy the situation without extensive documentation.

She reviewed the notes she had taken while visiting his classroom, then sighed and started to write. The fifth graders in Harold's class were paying the price for his burnout with mind-numbing boredom and increasingly serious behavior problems. Many of them would enter middle school the next year completely turned off to learning, making the middle school teachers' jobs more difficult.

Emily couldn't afford to worry about the trouble an honest evaluation would provoke; her first concern would always be the children. Next year, she would continue to document Harold's deficiencies. If his performance didn't improve, he would be gone.

By the time she'd finished the last page, her hand was cramped and her head ached. She got up to make another pot of coffee, then started when the phone rang. Who on earth would call the school at seven o'clock on a Friday night? She picked up the receiver, but before she could speak, a raspy male voice came over the line.

"You're workin' awful late tonight, Ms. Franklin."

An uneasy sensation invaded the pit of her stomach. The fine hairs at the back of her neck tingled. "May I ask who's calling?" she said, forcing a calm note into her voice.

"It don't matter. I'm surprised you're still at the school, though."

She tightened her grip on the handset. "If you'll tell me your name and state your problem, I'll be happy to try to help you, sir. Otherwise, I'm afraid I'll have to hang up."

"No need to get snotty. Just tell me whether Hank Dawson's as big a stud as all the gals say he is."

"I don't have to listen to—"

"You'd damn well better listen, Ms. Franklin," the man said, sneering her name, "and you'd better stay away from Dawson's ranch, too. We don't want any sluts workin' with our kids."

Emily slammed the receiver onto its cradle, wrapped her arms across the front of her waist and waited for the trembling to stop. And to think she'd been worried about an obscene phone call. Of course, the call *had* been obscene, though not quite in the way she'd feared.

An ordinary heavy breather wouldn't have scared her. But her caller hadn't sounded like a disgruntled student disguising his voice. He'd sounded mature, and as if he were enjoying himself tremendously.

Should she consider his last remark a threat? From the vicious tone his voice had suddenly taken at the end, definitely. Could the caller have been Lawrence Paxon? Possibly. She inhaled a deep breath, wondering if she should call the sheriff.

Emily had almost convinced herself that wouldn't be necessary, when another thought occurred to her. How had the man known she was working late at the school? Since she always walked to work, her car wasn't in the parking lot. A person would have had to come right up to the front doors in order to see the light on in her office.

But he *had* known. He'd started talking before she'd identified herself, confident she was on the other end of the line. And how had he known about her trips to Hank's ranch? Good Lord, was he following her? Watching her house?

She dialed the sheriff's office. Andy Johnson arrived ten minutes later. Emily let him in and explained what had happened. He checked around outside the building, but didn't find anything. His expression grim, he took the chair opposite Emily's desk.

"Tell me exactly what he said again," Andy requested, taking notes while Emily recounted the conversation verbatim. "Are you sure you didn't recognize his voice?"

She shook her head. "I don't think so. What really bothers me is that he's tracking my movements. I've only been to Hank's ranch five times. Other than my father, I've never told anyone I was going there. I can't imagine Hank would, either."

A broad grin stretched across Andy's face. "You didn't have to. How many other ranches do you pass on the way to Hank's place?"

Emily's face heated. "People really are talking about us? Simply because I've driven out there a few times?"

"It's been a boring spring," Andy told her with a shrug. "Your parenting class got a lot of folks excited, and it's focused more attention on you."

"Does everyone assume we're having an affair?"

His eyebrows shot up in mock surprise. "You mean, you're not? Ol' Hank must be slippin'."

"I don't find this amusing, Sheriff."

"I can't blame you for that, but don't let it get you down. You're both single. If you and Hank enjoy each other's company, it's nobody's business but yours."

"If only that were true," she muttered.

"It's just one of the joys of small-town living." Andy climbed to his feet. "Come on. I'll give you a ride home."

"You'd better not, or everyone will think I'm having an affair with you, too," Emily grumbled.

"This is official business. I want to check out your house and make sure you don't have an uninvited guest waiting for you."

She shot the sheriff a sharp look. "Do you think this man is dangerous?"

"Hard to say. If he's the same one who tossed that rock through your window, he could be. Don't work here alone again. If you need to stay late or come in on the weekends, bring your dog along.''

Emily nodded, then picked up her purse and briefcase and accompanied the sheriff out to his patrol car. He drove the few blocks, parked and led her into the house, which he proceeded to search.

When he finished, he cautioned her again. "Be careful, Emily. And don't hesitate to call if anything scares you.''

"All right. Thanks for your help, Andy.''

She stood on her front step, watching him drive away. As she turned to go back inside, she saw the curtains at the front windows on the house across the street twitch. So, Dorothy Stiegel was keeping tabs on her, too.

Gritting her teeth so hard they hurt, Emily slammed her front door. Ivan barked at the sudden noise. When he decided nothing was wrong, he went to his basket and brought out his leash, wagging his tail hopefully at her.

In her present state of mind, a long hard run sounded wonderful. She'd never been afraid to go jogging after dark in Pinedale before, but after Andy's warnings, she hesitated. What if her caller was out there? Did he know their usual route?

Infuriated to realize she was allowing some creep to control her actions, Emily stormed into her bedroom and yanked on her sweats. She put on a jacket, got Ivan and left the house. To hell with the guy, and anyone else who didn't have anything better to do than talk about her. If they'd already tried and convicted her of having an affair with Hank, she might as well go ahead and have one.

She took a different route, just in case, and the exercise gradually sapped her anger, clearing her mind for more rational thoughts. There was little she could do to defend herself against gossip. As long as nobody had proof she was doing something immoral or illegal, however, her job should reasonably be safe.

She returned to her house and got Ivan a fresh bowl of water, then stepped into the shower, continuing to mull over the situation. What would her life be like without Hank and Tina? Too drab, too quiet, too empty.

Unlike most people, Emily had always looked forward to Monday mornings, because that was when the most interesting part of the week began. Weekends were simply a time to catch up on paperwork and household chores and give her pets some extra attention. All of that had changed since she'd started driving out to the Happy Trails Ranch.

Just thinking of the brainstorming session that had produced the name made her chuckle. They'd all sat around the kitchen table, tossing out wacky suggestions—Dudes Unlimited, Greenhorn's Delight and Emily's personal favorite, Hank's Happy Hideaway.

They never did anything particularly spectacular, but whether they worked on a renovation project or took a walk or were forced indoors by a thunderstorm, she had fun. Hank could turn digging post holes into a memorable event. He always had a story or a new joke to tell. He teased her unmercifully.

He didn't just add spice to her life. He added cayenne pepper, she thought with a chuckle.

While some of his methods for coping with his daughter struck Emily as being a bit unorthodox, she couldn't deny they were working. Who cared if the kid only ate vegetables five days a week and stayed up until midnight on Fridays, as long as she received so much love and undivided attention? Tina obviously didn't.

Emily loved watching the child blossom, loved being included in the Dawsons' adventures, loved watching the Happy Trails Ranch changing from a dream into a reality. Since the night Tina had been gone, both Hank and Emily had backed away from sexual involvement and worked on developing their friendship instead.

The attraction between them hadn't disappeared, of course. Far from it. But since they had taken the time to know each other better, the prospect of making love with Hank intrigued her more than it worried her. In fact, she frequently fantasized about it in vivid detail.

She turned off the water and reached for a towel. Rubbing it over her arms and breasts, she found herself remembering what it had felt like when Hank had touched her there. Soon. She wanted to experience those sensations again soon.

Perhaps she'd start saying the word *should* more often. Furthermore, she wouldn't flaunt her relationship with Hank before the community, but she wouldn't give it up, either. Pinedale's busybodies could just stick that in their collective ear.

"Shake a leg, Tina," Hank ordered, carrying a load of dirty plates, cups and glasses from the living room into the kitchen. "Finish your breakfast so you can pick up your toys and stuff before Ms. Franklin gets here."

"Aw, Dad." She lifted a spoonful of oatmeal above her head and flipped it over, letting the cereal plop back into the bowl in a splash of milk. "Why do we always have to clean house when Ms. Franklin comes?"

"She likes things neat and tidy, honey," he said. "You don't want her to think we're slobs, do you?"

"She wouldn't care," Tina argued as he hurried back to the living room.

"Well, I do," Hank retorted, fishing a pair of dirty socks out from under the sofa. He stacked up the week's worth of newspapers, grabbed a pile of junk mail and hauled them all out to the trash can on the porch.

"Aunt Becky never makes me do stuff like that," Tina grumbled. "She does it for me."

"Well, I'm not Aunt Becky. Now, quit playin' in your oatmeal and get a move on, or I'll make you go to bed at eight o'clock every night for the rest of your life."

Heaving a martyred sigh, the little girl carried her dishes to the sink and trudged from the room. Hank smiled and shook his head. He stuffed the dishwasher as full as he could, then filled the sink to take care of the overflow.

Raising a kid by yourself did funny things to a guy, he decided, plunging his hands into the hot, soapy water. If he'd been living alone, he wouldn't have cared how awful the house looked. In fact, Grandma D had literally made him swear on the family Bible that he'd clean the kitchen and bathrooms at least once a week before she'd let him move Tina to the lodge.

She hadn't needed to do that, of course. He didn't want Tina to live in squalor any more than Grandma did. He didn't want the kid to grow up thinkin' there'd always be somebody around to pick up after her, either. That was how *he'd* gotten to be such a slob in the first place.

He glanced over his shoulder at the room behind him and grimaced. Lord, how did women keep their sanity? No matter how much housework he did, there always seemed to be more that needed doing. He'd just mopped this damn floor on Wednesday, and it already looked cruddy. The stove was pretty crusty, too, and he'd either have to break down and do laundry or buy Tina some more underwear.

It was enough to make a man downright cranky. He was getting better at it, though. He'd never be a great housekeeper, but they didn't live like hogs. And first thing on Monday morning, he was gonna buy some no-wax tile for this kitchen, with a pattern that wouldn't show every dang speck of dirt the way this one did.

Keeping a close eye on the clock, Hank finished the dishes and wiped down the counters and the table. Emily usually showed up between ten and ten-thirty. It still surprised him how much he looked forward to her weekly visits, but then, Emily had surprised him a lot lately.

For one thing, in the past months, she'd become the best friend that he'd ever had. She'd been supportive and enthusiastic about the dude ranch from the beginning. And she didn't expect to be entertained or treated like a guest. In fact, she honestly seemed to enjoy helping with whatever project he'd planned for the day, even if all she could do was hand him tools or keep Tina out of his hair for a little while.

He hadn't known how to act with her after the night they'd watched *Star Wars*. He'd finally decided to treat her the same way he would Becky, and that had worked okay so far. The only problem was he didn't feel very brotherly toward her. Every time he saw her, he felt even less brotherly, and he wasn't sure how much longer he could handle this platonic stuff.

On the other hand, he sure didn't want to scare Emily off. Her friendship meant too much to him and to Tina. He didn't want to hurt her, either. But it wasn't easy waiting for her to give him some sign she wanted more.

The minute she walked in the door, his damn hormones jumped up and stood at attention. He was probably just bein' fanciful, but it seemed to him that Emily got a little sweeter, a little softer, a little prettier from one Saturday to the next. He wished she hadn't gotten so darn good at not saying "should."

"She's here! She's here!" Tina hollered from the living room.

Anticipation kicking through his system, he drained the sink and rinsed the soap off his hands. Then he shook the water off, smoothed down his hair with damp fingers and headed out the front door to greet Emily. Tina welcomed her with a fierce hug and crowed with delight when Ivan jumped out of the car, a ball in his mouth. Hank couldn't help laughing at the big, ugly mutt.

Emily looked up at him, her smile hesitant. "I hope you don't mind that I brought him again," she said, gesturing toward the dog. "He looked so pitiful when I tried to put him in the backyard, I couldn't bring myself to leave him."

"No problem," Hank replied, admiring the way her Cheyenne Frontier Days T-shirt outlined her breasts.

Tina tugged at the ball. Refusing to let it go, Ivan dodged away and charged across the lawn with the little girl in hot pursuit. Emily reached back into the car and pulled out a covered cake pan.

That was something else Hank appreciated about her—she never came empty-handed. It was a small, thoughtful gesture, the kind of thing the women in his family were always doin'. But having her home-baked goodies around made the lodge seem more like a home.

"Dad, make him give me the ball so I can throw it," Tina called.

Emily laughed and handed the pan over to Hank. "I'm afraid he still hasn't figured that out yet, Tina."

"Hey, we both love these," he said, peeking under the lid. "Thanks."

"You're welcome."

Was her smile a little warmer than usual? Or was it just a trick of the sunshine? She shot a quick look at Tina, then tossed her hair back over her shoulder, exposing the smooth length of her neck before glancing back at him. Her gaze landed square on his mouth, then it slowly moved up to meet his. Hank felt his temperature climb a few degrees, and told himself if he didn't know better, he'd think Emily was trying to flirt with him.

He took the bar cookies she'd brought to the kitchen, then hurried back outside and stood a little closer to Emily than he usually did. She didn't move away. Interesting. They all played with the dog for over an hour. When Ivan finally flopped on his belly in exhaustion, Tina ran into the lodge to get him a bowl of water.

Hank and Emily collapsed on the grass with the panting animal between them, enjoying one of the first truly warm days they'd had all spring. Laughing, as if for the sheer joy of it, Emily rolled onto her side facing Hank and propped her head up with her hand.

"I think I'm getting old," she said.

"Bite your tongue, lady. You're younger than I am, and I refuse to be old." Hank buried one hand in Ivan's thick fur and let his gaze roam from Emily's tousled hair to her sneakers. "Besides, you look pretty darn good to me."

"Oh yeah?"

"Yeah. With that blond hair of yours, the gray ones hardly show at all."

She sat up, yanked out a fistful of grass and threw it at him. "I don't have any gray hair."

Her playful challenge provided exactly the opening he'd been waiting for. Walking around Ivan on his knees, Hank sat behind her, his legs stretched out on either side of hers.

"Quit that," she ordered, laughing and trying to swat his hands away from her head. "What do you think you're doing?"

"Lookin' for gray hairs, whaddaya think? Now stop that wigglin', or I'll know you're a liar, Franklin."

He plowed his fingertips into her hair. Combing through the strands and holding them up to the light, he studied them with the serious concentration of a scientist. Lord, it was so soft and shiny, he wanted to bury his face in it, too. Emily gradually relaxed and leaned back against his chest.

His jeans suddenly felt tight. If her little fanny had been flush against him, she'd have known in a hurry this little game was just another excuse to touch her. She turned her head and smiled at him, and his hands froze in midair. Why, the little devil. She knew exactly what was goin' on.

"Find any?" she asked.

He cleared his throat. "Not yet. You've sure got a lot of hair, though. We could be here a while."

She chuckled and shook her head, making her hair slide over his hands in a silken caress. His fingers moved more slowly, more deliberately, rubbing her scalp, brushing the baby-soft skin at her nape, stroking her temples. She closed her eyes and tipped her face toward the sun, obviously enjoying his attentions.

An insistent throbbing started in his groin. He cupped the sides of her head, coaxing her to turn and face him. Her eyes met his without flinching. Her lips parted, her tongue skated across the lower one in a gesture that was both nervous and provocative at the same time.

Before he could explore her silent communication any further, however, the lodge's back door slammed. Tina charged across the grass, splashing water over the sides of the bowl she carried.

"Whatcha doin', Dad? Lookin' for ticks?"

Emily sputtered with laughter and climbed to her feet. Reluctantly releasing her, Hank followed suit.

"Well, ladies, we'd better get some work done."

"Aw, Dad," Tina complained. "That's all we ever do."

"You don't have to help," he replied. "You can play with Ivan if you'd rather."

"What're you gonna do?"

"Remember those old horseshoes we brought back from the Circle D? I found some more in the barn here, and I'm gonna start building a fence for the front yard with 'em."

"How're you gonna do that?"

"Weld 'em together. I hoped you and Ms. Franklin could figure out a design for me."

"Okay. I'll help."

Hank exchanged amused glances with Emily at Tina's eager acceptance, the approval in the woman's eyes warming him straight through to his bones. Lord, he was gettin' hard again. He turned away and headed for the barn, woman, child and dog at his heels.

For the rest of the morning and afternoon, they cleaned horseshoes, hauled them to the yard in a wheelbarrow and laid them on the grass. As the hours passed, Hank became convinced that he hadn't imagined a change in Emily's attitude toward him.

She could hardly look at him without smiling. She maintained eye contact with him for longer periods of time. When they were down on their knees, arranging the horseshoes into different patterns, their shoulders and hips brushed constantly, and it sure as heck wasn't all his doing.

"Whaddaya say we go out to dinner tonight?" he suggested when Tina and Ivan wandered off to their own pursuits. "I'm sick of cookin'."

"I'd be glad to cook," Emily offered quickly.

"Nah, you've done enough work for one day."

"I don't mind, Hank. I'd rather stay here."

There was something a little too insistent in her voice. Hank studied her for a moment. "I haven't been into town in over a week, Em. I'd really like a night out for a change."

She bit her lower lip and glanced off toward the barn. "It's not a good time for me to do that, Hank."

"Why not?"

"Evidently someone has noticed my driving out here every weekend. There's been some gossip about us, and—"

"Well, this sounds familiar," he muttered. "Are you sayin' you don't want to be seen in public with me because of some gossip? Or is it because you're still not sure I'm respectable enough?"

"Don't be ridiculous."

"I'm not. But you are. You can't let other people run your life for you."

"If I was going to do that, I wouldn't have come at all today," she argued, her eyes sparking with anger. "All I'm asking is that we be discreet for a little while."

"Discreet?" Hank snorted in disgust. "That's just a polite word for sneakin' around so nobody'll see us together."

"You don't understand."

"Damn right, I don't. I'm too old for these games."

"There are people who want to have me fired, Hank."

"And there's a lot of folks who think you're doin' a great job, too. I heard plenty of that at the parenting classes. Besides, what could anybody say about us going out to dinner?"

"I don't know, and I don't want to find out."

Hank pulled off his hat and slapped it on the ground in frustration. "Dammit, Emily, I thought we were friends. I thought we were gonna have something really special together."

The anger faded from her eyes. "I've wanted that, too, Hank," she said earnestly, laying her hand on his wrist. "We can still make it special."

"Not if we have to hide like a couple of criminals."

"Now you're being melodramatic."

He shook his head, then sighed and pulled away from her touch. "I don't think so. And I just can't do this. We either have a relationship out in the open, or we don't have one."

"Is that your final word on the matter?"

"Yeah. What's yours?"

Emily pushed herself to her feet and looked down at him. "I'll have to think about it."

"You do that. I'll be waitin' to hear from you."

Chapter Eleven

"Why did Ms. Franklin have to leave so soon?" Tina asked, standing beside Hank as he watched the trail of dust left by Emily's car settle to the ground.

"I guess she had somethin' else to do," he said. He bit back a disgruntled sigh, then took Tina's hand and walked toward the lodge.

"I'm hungry, Dad."

"Yeah, me, too. Wanta go out for supper?"

"I'd rather go to Aunt Becky's." She shot her father a sly grin. "I bet she'd invite us over if you called her."

"She might," Hank agreed with a chuckle.

The idea appealed to him. He needed to discuss a few things with his sister, and almost anything would be better than sitting around waiting for the phone to ring. Not that he expected it to anytime soon.

He doubted Emily would respond well to the ultimatum he'd just given her. He'd known that the minute the words had popped out of his mouth, but he hadn't been willing to change his stance.

"Tell ya what," he said to his daughter when they reached the back door, "you get cleaned up while I talk to Aunt Becky. If she says no, we'll grab a burger in town."

While Tina ran upstairs, he dialed his sister's number. Receiving an invitation proved as easy as Tina had suggested, and they were on the road fifteen minutes later. Holding his four-and-a-half-month-old son in one arm, Peter Sinclair welcomed them with a broad smile.

"Get tired of your miserable cooking, Hank?"

"Might say that, Doc," Hank replied. "Jeez, that kid of yours is gonna be a moose."

"No kidding. Wait'll you see all the new tricks he's learned. He's going to be hell on wheels when he starts crawling and walking."

Jonathan reached for the bow in Tina's ponytail. She grabbed his hand and wrinkled her nose at him. He giggled, waved his other arm and made frog kicks with both legs. Peter carried him to a blanket spread on the living room carpet and laid him on his tummy.

Becky came out of the kitchen to greet her brother and niece, promising supper would be ready in ten minutes. Tina sat cross-legged on the floor in front of Jonathan, handing him toys and talking to him. Hank shot the bull with Peter, enjoying the casual atmosphere of his sister's home.

The chicken-and-rice dish Becky served tasted wonderful. Tina must be as sick of his cooking as he was, Hank noted with amusement. The kid ate everything on her plate and asked for seconds before he'd finished his first helping.

After strawberry shortcake for dessert, Peter took Jonathan and Tina back to the living room, and Hank helped Becky clean the kitchen. She teased him about his improved "woman's work" skills, then insisted he sit down at the table and visit with her when they'd finished the dishes.

"How's Tina doing in school now?" she asked, setting a cup of coffee in front of him.

"Fine. Her teacher's plannin' to pass her to third grade, anyhow."

Her eyes filled with regret. "Lord, I'm sorry I interfered in your relationship with her."

"You've got nothing to be sorry about," Hank said sternly. "Tina would have been in a world of hurt without you. I can't thank you enough for the great job you did with her. Don't you ever apologize for that again."

"All right, don't blow a gasket. How're you two getting along?"

Hank shrugged. "We're learnin'. She can be a stubborn little wretch, when she puts her mind to it."

"She comes by that honestly," Becky said with a grin. "How do you like livin' off the Circle D?"

"It seemed pretty strange at first," Hank said. "If one of us breaks a dish or spills milk, there's nobody but me to clean it up. I like not havin' to check out everything I want to do with Sam, though."

Becky nodded in understanding, then unfastened the first button on her blouse when a lusty infant's cry came from the living room. Peter appeared in the doorway a moment later, carrying a red-faced, squalling Jonathan.

"Sorry to interrupt," he said, "but somebody's hungry and I don't have the right equipment to help him."

Becky took the baby, soothing him while she undid the next two buttons. "It's okay, sweetheart. Mama's right here. Don't be so impatient."

Hank felt his neck and ears get hot when he figured out what his sister planned to do. He was curious because Christine had refused to breast-feed Tina, but he doubted Becky would want him for an audience. "Uh, why don't you call me when you're done?"

"Why, Hank, you're embarrassed." Becky chuckled and smiled at Pete. "Honey, will you please get me a blanket?"

"I'm not embarrassed," Hank protested when his brother-in-law left the room, hooting with laughter. "I just thought you might be."

"Maybe I should," she answered, positioning Jonathan at her breast. "But it's such a natural part of my life now, I don't think about it unless we're out in public."

"Go ahead, before the little dude starves to death."

The second she rubbed her nipple against his tiny mouth, Jonathan stopped crying. Becky's face took on a sweet, maternal glow. Pete came back with a blanket and draped it over her shoulder. Jonathan immediately yanked it off and went right on nursing, making both of his parents laugh.

Hank envied them at that moment. There was a world of love and joy in their eyes as they looked at each other. He looked away and cleared his throat.

"Tina challenged me to a computer game," Pete said. "I'll see you guys later."

Stroking Jonathan's bald little head, Becky turned her attention back to Hank. "Where were we? Oh yeah. Need any help over at your place? When I came to get Tina a few weeks ago, I noticed your fences are in bad shape."

"Nope. I want to do this on my own."

"I'll be going to horse shows all summer. Want me to keep an eye out for some good saddle stock and pack mules?"

Now *there* was an offer he wouldn't pass up. His sister knew good horseflesh when she saw it. "Will you charge me what you'd charge anyone else?"

"Aw, c'mon, Hank. We don't need the money, and you're gonna need all the cash you can get your hands on."

"I mean it. You treat me like any other customer, or it's no dice."

She scowled at him, then nodded. "All right. But if you need some money down the line, will you let us help? It can be a loan if you want."

"You think I can't make it on my own, don't you? Just like Sam and Grandma."

"For God's sake, don't be a pigheaded idiot. If a loan means the difference between your bein' able to hire enough help and workin' yourself into an early grave, then, dammit, I want to do it, because I'm your sister."

"Calm down, Beck," Hank answered with a grin. "You're gonna give Jonathan indigestion."

She lifted the baby to her shoulder and patted his back until he burped. When she had him settled at her other breast, she scowled at Hank again. "Do we have a deal?"

"Yeah. Thanks."

"You're welcome." She leaned back and fixed a speculative gaze on him. "Tina tells me Ms. Franklin's been spending some time with you two. Anything going on there I should know about?"

"Like what, for instance?"

"Well, Tina seems taken with her. I wondered if you might be, too."

"Emily's all right, I guess," he said, keeping his tone casual. "She's been a lot of help with Tina."

"You knew her pretty well in high school, didn't you?"

"Uh-huh."

"And you took a class from her?"

"Uh-huh. So?"

"So, are you interested in her or not?"

"Sorta."

Becky huffed at him. "What's that supposed to mean?"

"It means it's complicated and confusing." He sighed, then gave in and told her about his argument with Emily. "I'll be damned if I'll put up with that nonsense. I mean, I pay my bills, and I don't get drunk or fight in bars anymore. Why should anybody care if she goes out with me?"

"You *do* have quite a reputation as a ladies' man, brother dear."

"Ancient history. I was faithful to Jan when we were engaged, and I haven't dated anybody else since. Hell, that's over two years now."

"You were laid up most of that time, Hank. You've changed a lot, but the folks in Pinedale probably haven't realized it yet. Any idea who's giving Emily a hard time?"

"She never mentioned any names."

"Well, you can't blame her for trying to protect her job. She's not really askin' for all that much."

Hank snorted in disgust. "It seems like a helluva lot to me. Ya know what? Christine wanted the excitement on the circuit I could give her. Jan wanted money. I'm sick of tryin' to figure out what women want from me. From now on, they can either play it my way or lump it."

"Do you love Emily?" she asked quietly.

"I don't know. I think I could. But I'd hafta know Tina and I are more important to her than her damned job."

"Relationships take some compromise, Hank. I almost lost Pete because I wasn't willing—"

"I know, but I've gotta draw the line somewhere. I'm through with tryin' to live up to somebody else's standards. If Emily can't handle that, too bad."

"Give it some time. She might surprise you."

"Yeah, she might. But don't expect a big romance."

"Okay."

Hank didn't buy that innocent expression on her face for a second. Nuts. Becky had been his accomplice in getting Sam married off to Dani. She'd probably start in on him next, especially since he'd spilled his guts about Emily.

"We'd better get goin'. Thanks for supper, sis."

Tina was half asleep by the time Hank got her home. He tucked her in bed, opened a Coke and settled into his recliner with a tired sigh. His leg informed him he'd punished it too much today. He massaged it with his left hand and used the remote control to turn on the television.

When nothing caught his interest, he switched it off and picked up the book on small-business management he'd checked out of the library. His brain refused to make sense of the words on the page. Muttering a curse, he laid it aside.

His conversation with Becky replayed itself in his mind, returning again and again to the question guaranteed to torment him the most—"Do you love Emily?"

He didn't want to, that was for damn sure. He was already trying to make a lot of changes in his life, and the last thing he needed was more emotional upheaval. If he had any smarts at all, he'd call Emily up and end the relationship right now, before things got any more complicated.

But the thought of not seeing her again left an ache the size of Yellowstone Park in his chest. She'd gotten under his skin, kind of like the chaff that imbedded itself in his clothes during haying season. They both irritated the hell out of him and were impossible to stop thinking about.

The phone rang. Unable to believe his ears, Hank sat there like an idiot until it rang a second time. Then he lunged to his feet and ran for the kitchen. His bum leg nearly buckled, forcing him to hobble.

"Don't hang up, dammit," he muttered. Grabbing the receiver at last, he gulped in a deep breath and prayed it was Emily. "Hello."

Her low, soft voice soothed his nerves better than a shot of whiskey. "Hank? It's Emily. I was, um, wondering if you'd like to have dinner with me tomorrow. At my house."

"Just me? Or do you want Tina to come, too?"

"Just you. Of course, if you can't get a sitter on such short notice, Tina would be more than welcome."

"Can I park my truck in front of your house?"

"Yes."

"All right. I'll be there. What time?"

"Sixish?"

"Sounds good. I'm glad you called, Em."

"I'll see you tomorrow," she said. "Good night, Hank."

He held on to the receiver long after she severed the connection. When he realized what he was doing, he laughed at himself and hung up. "Well, I'll be damned," he muttered, shaking his head. "I've got a date with the Worm."

At five minutes to six the next day, Emily checked the table for what must have been the twentieth time. Of course, nothing had changed, except that her nerves were a bit more shredded than they'd been the last time she'd checked the place settings. She sighed and tucked her hair behind her ears, firmly telling herself she was going to stop acting like a coward.

She'd searched her soul for hours after leaving the Happy Trails Ranch yesterday, and had come to the conclusion that Hank had been right. She *was* letting other people run her life. She'd always feared disapproval and worked hard to maintain a spotless reputation.

That attitude had kept her out of trouble, but it hadn't brought her much happiness. She didn't want to sit on life's sidelines and watch other people have all the fun and excitement anymore. She was a grown woman, and it *was* time she started pleasing herself.

Being with Hank pleased her. That was all that mattered. She wouldn't insult him again by trying to hide her relationship with him.

"Brave words, Emily," she murmured, jumping when a pickup door slammed outside.

She smoothed damp palms down the sides of her lavender dress, and forced herself to walk slowly to the front door. The sight that greeted her when she opened it pushed all her niggling doubts about the wisdom of what she was doing completely out of her mind.

Wearing a grin as wide as his truck, the same charcoal-gray suit he'd worn to church, a white shirt with a maroon tie and shiny dress boots, Hank Dawson strolled up her sidewalk. His black Stetson pulled low over his forehead, he carried a bottle of wine in one hand and a bouquet of flowers in the other. He looked wonderfully, unbearably sexy.

"Afternoon, Ms. Franklin," he said, his eyes dancing with unholy glee as he climbed the last step.

Sputtering with laughter, Emily grabbed his arm and yanked him inside. He handed her the flowers and the wine bottle with exaggerated politeness, then removed his hat. She thanked him, ushered him into her living room and excused herself to put the daisies in water.

The sound of him tussling with Ivan made her chuckle as she hunted for a vase. Honestly. The man was an absolute wretch to make an entrance like that. The telephone lines were no doubt humming all over town.

When she returned to the living room, he pushed Ivan away and sat up straight. Accepting the glass of wine she offered him, he studied her while she seated herself in the overstuffed chair that matched the sofa.

"Nice weather we're havin'," he drawled, his appreciative gaze roaming from her head to her white sandals.

So, he wanted to play games, did he? She could outdignify him any day. Emily smiled and crossed one knee over the other. "Yes, it's been very pleasant. Where is Tina?"

"She's staying the night with my brother and his wife."

"How nice. I hope she'll enjoy that."

He glanced around the room as if he'd never been there before. "You've got a nice place here, Ms. Franklin."

Emily had had quite enough of this. After setting her wineglass on the coffee table, she crossed the room. Standing in front of him with her hands on her hips, she leaned down and scowled directly into his face.

"All right, buster, what have you done with him?"

His lips twitched, but he maintained a bland expression. "Excuse me, ma'am?"

"Don't play innocent with me. You're not Hank. Bring him back immediately."

"Who do you think I am?"

"I don't know," she said, her voice dark with suspicion. "An alien impostor, perhaps?"

He raised one fist to his mouth and cleared his throat. "What's wrong with my disguise?"

"Everything." She threw her hands up beside her head, then reached out and ruffled his hair. "This is far too neatly combed to belong to the *real* Hank Dawson.

"And this." She untied his tie and unbuttoned the top two buttons of his shirt. "He wouldn't put up with that, unless he had no choice whatsoever. Of course, the *real* Hank wouldn't sit here on a warm day with a suit coat on, either."

He obligingly took off the offending garment and handed it to her. She folded it and draped it neatly over the back of the sofa. Then she studied him again.

His shoulders were shaking. His face looked as if he might choke if he didn't laugh soon. She dragged an ottoman toward his feet, then lifted his left boot onto it.

"That's much better. The *real* Hank likes to kick back and relax. You *should* have known that."

A big hand flashed out, wrapped around her waist and toppled her onto his lap. Strong arms surrounded her. A pair of hard lips covered hers in a fierce, demanding kiss that stole her breath and went on and on and on.

"Was *that* real enough for you, Em?" he asked when he finally let her up for air.

She batted her eyelashes at him and affected her best Scarlett O'Hara simper. "Why, Hank, darlin'! You're back!"

Laughter roared out of him in great, lusty shouts. His arms hugged her waist. She laid her head against his shoulder, giggling helplessly. There wasn't another human being on the planet who would have taken such delight in playing along with her. In fact, she didn't know another soul with whom she felt free enough to act this silly.

She turned and looked up into his dark, shining eyes, and suddenly knew she'd fallen in love with this man. A sweet, hot glow started in the pit of her stomach and radiated through the rest of her body. She touched his face with her fingertips, tracing the contours of his features.

"Hank?" she murmured, watching his pupils dilate with heightened awareness.

"What, Em?"

"Should, should, should, should, should."

He raised an eyebrow at her. "Oh yeah?"

"Yeah."

Sliding her hands up the back of his neck, she pulled him down to her. His mouth wasn't hard this time, but warm and mobile, responsive to her slightest caress. She tickled his bottom lip with the tip of her tongue. Moaning, he granted her access. He tasted of wine and a hint of toothpaste and a darker, richer flavor she couldn't identify, and couldn't get enough of, either.

Sampling it again and again, she stroked his thick, glossy hair, his temples, the place behind his left ear that made him shiver. She kissed his eyebrows and his cheekbones and his chin, loving the different textures she discovered.

His hands leisurely explored her back and shoulders, as if simply touching her gave him incredible pleasure. She tipped her head back, wanting him to kiss her neck. He obliged her, then went on to her collarbones and her shoulders, his breath warm through the fabric of her dress.

Wild, delicious feelings mushroomed inside her, making her ache to touch him without the barriers of clothing. She fumbled at the rest of the buttons on his shirt and slid her hands inside. His chest was hard and liberally dusted with black hair that tickled her palms. He inhaled a deep, shuddering breath, then trapped her hands against his skin.

"You're gettin' into risky territory, Emily. Are you sure you want this?" he said, his voice strained and husky.

She gazed into his eyes and saw the same needs and desires that were driving her. "Yes. I want you, Hank."

"Oh, babe, I want you, too."

He closed his eyes and rested his forehead against her breasts, as if gathering his strength. She kissed the top of his head, holding him to her, sensing this might be the proverbial calm before the storm. Anticipation surged when he looked at her again.

"I'd love to carry you to your bed," he said, nibbling at her lips, "but I'm afraid my leg might give out."

She jumped off his lap, surprised at how shaky her knees had become. "Good Lord, Hank, I didn't even think about your leg. Did I hurt you?"

"I wasn't thinkin' about it, either," he said with a devilish grin. He pushed himself to his feet and adjusted the front of his trousers. Wrapping an arm around her waist, he nudged her toward the hallway.

An attack of shyness hit her when they entered her bedroom. This was her true sanctuary from the world. She'd indulged every feminine impulse she possessed in decorating it. Standing amid all the eyelet lace, ruffles and delicate flowers adorning her bed and covering the window, Hank suddenly seemed big and dark, even a bit... dangerous.

He gazed at the furnishings for a moment, then turned to her with a tender smile. "It's pretty, Em. Almost as pretty as you."

"Thank you," she whispered.

"You're not scared of me, are ya?" he asked, cupping the side of her face with his hand. "We don't have to do this."

"I just feel a little awkward and nervous," she admitted, turning her head to kiss his palm.

"You think I don't?" He chuckled, no doubt at the skeptical expression in her eyes. "Hey, I haven't done this since before I got hurt. I'm not even sure all my parts'll still work."

She glanced at the bulge straining against the front of his pants. "I don't think that's going to be a problem."

Laughing out loud, he pulled her into a hug. "I guess we can always hope for the best." Then he held her at arm's length and studied her with a wicked, speculative gleam in his eyes. "Hmm. I wonder . . ."

"What do you wonder?"

"If your underwear's as sexy as your bedroom."

"I'll never tell."

"I guess I'll just have to find out for myself, then, won't I?"

He reached around and slowly lowered the zipper at the back of her dress. The air felt cool against her hot skin, making her shiver. He smiled at that. Grasping the edges of the lavender fabric, he slid it forward and down until the bodice fell to her waist. She pulled her arms free of the sleeves, then pushed the garment over her hips and stepped out of it when it hit the floor.

"Sweet heaven," he muttered, staring at her pale pink teddy with unabashed delight.

She reached for his belt buckle. "Now it's my turn."

"You've been wonderin' about *my* underwear?" He fished his wallet out of his hip pocket and tossed it on the nightstand.

"Would that surprise you?"

"After seein' you in that little number, honey, I don't think anything you did would surprise me." When she unfastened the metal hook above his zipper, he stopped her. "Hold on. Let me take my boots off first."

He sat on the side of the bed, his gaze never leaving her while he accomplished the task. Then he removed his socks and shirt, and drew her to him as if he couldn't wait another second to touch her again.

Skimming his hands up her sides, he nuzzled her midriff. "Lord, babe, you feel so good, and you smell so good."

So did he, she thought, caressing his upper arms and shoulders. And he had such a broad, strong back.... She quivered at the sensations caused by his fingers stroking up her thighs, releasing her stockings from their garters.

"You have gorgeous legs, Em," he said, his breathing more ragged as he brushed her stockings down to her knees and beyond. "Did I ever tell you that?"

She shook her head because she couldn't find her voice.

"I didn't? Well, shame on me."

He kissed a path between her breasts, making her heartbeat race a little faster with every touch. His hands closed over her bottom and squeezed it gently before following the curve of her hips to her waist.

"I like your sassy little fanny, too. It about drove me crazy that day we worked on the cabin porch."

He filled his hands with her breasts, massaging the nipples into hardened peaks. Fearing her knees would buckle, she dug the pads of her fingers into the smooth, taut skin of his shoulders. He fiddled with the thin straps holding up the bodice, then snorted in frustration.

"How the heck am I supposed to get you out of this thing without rippin' it off?"

"There are snaps in the, uh, crotch."

"Well now, that's mighty convenient. Lemme see."

Widening her stance slightly, she held her breath while his thumbs slid up her inner thighs. He dispatched with the snaps and raised his head, watching her face when he touched her most intimate flesh. The air rushed out of her lungs in a sigh as shaky as her legs had become.

"Kiss me," he commanded, his voice suddenly rough.

His tongue entered her mouth, stroking in time with his fingers. It was like melting into a hot sea of sensation. She burned, she ached, she needed more of him, all of him. A sheen of perspiration broke out all over her body, and his back and shoulders were slick with sweat beneath her restless hands.

A husky moan came out of his throat as he broke the kiss. "Babe, I don't know if I can be very...patient."

"I don't want you to be patient. I want you now."

He stripped the teddy off over her head, then guided her onto the bed. Lying back against the pillows, she watched him shed the rest of his clothing. The sight of his rampant arousal made her gasp in admiration. He went absolutely still. His gaze darted to meet hers, searching, questioning.

"What is it?" she asked, confused by the sudden uncertainty in his expression.

"I know it's damn ugly," he said, running his hand over the mass of scars on the front of his left thigh, as if he wanted to hide them from her. "If it puts you off..."

She shook her head at him. "I wasn't looking at your leg...."

"Oh." He glanced down at himself, then chuckled and puffed out his chest. "So, whaddaya think?"

"Come here, and maybe I'll tell you," she suggested, crooking her finger at him.

He crawled onto the bed and lay beside her, propping his head on one hand. They looked into each other's eyes. The amusement fled, and the wanting started all over again.

Almost moving in slow motion, he leaned down and kissed her with a tenderness that brought a lump to her throat. Time stretched into a new dimension of sweet, lazy caresses and whispered love words. She'd never known a man could be so utterly gentle.

With his hands and his lips, his teeth and his tongue, he explored her body as if it were infinitely beautiful and precious. He encouraged her to do the same, freeing her from any inhibitions about touching him. It was both earthy and spiritual, exhilarating and more arousing than anything she'd ever experienced.

She whimpered when he pulled away and drew a small packet from his wallet. He soothed her with his voice while he saw to her protection. Then he knelt between her legs and pressed himself against her moist, aching flesh.

Ripples of pleasure raced along her nerve endings and she took him into her body. He thrust into her again and again, in a slow, steady rhythm, and her inner muscles clutched at him, as if to prevent each withdrawal. The tempo increased, faster and harder, pulling her tighter and tighter, until a frenzy of sensations overwhelmed her and she cried out in ecstasy.

He didn't stop. Corded muscles stood out in sharp relief on his neck and arms. His lips pulled away from gritted teeth, he continued the sweet violence. Tension spiraled within her again, quick and hot as a flash fire.

Her fingernails raked his back and buttocks. Her legs clamped around his hips. His tortured breathing echoed hers. Vivid colors danced behind her closed eyelids, and a moment later, his guttural shout of completion triggered her second release.

He collapsed into her arms. She held him close, savoring the thunderous beating of his heart against her breasts, the feel of his heated skin touching the full length of hers. Raising up onto his elbows, he smiled down at her before rolling to his side, bringing her with him.

Heads resting on the same pillow, they talked and giggled and fondled, supremely content to share these moments of bliss. Then Hank stretched like a big lazy cat awakening from a nap in the sunshine.

"I've got a proposition for you, Emily."

She propped herself up on one elbow and twirled a tuft of his chest hair around the index finger of her other hand.

"I'm not completely certain of this," she said thoughtfully, "but I think you were supposed to say that before we made love."

He pinched her fanny. "Shame on you. Not *that* kinda proposition."

"What other kind is there?"

"How'dja like a summer job?"

Emily raised an eyebrow at him, then glanced down at their naked bodies. "What kind of work did you have in mind?"

"Not *that* kind," he retorted with a chuckle. "Although we might consider it as a fringe benefit."

"Are you serious?"

"Yeah. I'm gonna be tied up outside renovatin' the cabins and gettin' the fences replaced. I need somebody to help me keep track of Tina and get my office organized, kinda be my girl Friday. It's the only way I'll be able to spend much time with you for the next couple of months. Interested?"

It sounded better than painting the outside of her house, which was what she had planned. In fact, it sounded wonderful. "I might be." She ran her heel up the back of his leg. "Tell me more about the fringe benefits."

Laughing, he rolled her onto her back and gave her a long, wet kiss, setting her body humming with anticipation again. "I think I'd rather show you."

"Mmm. Please do."

Chapter Twelve

On the last day of school, Emily stood at the front door with Margaret, waving the last of the stragglers off to their summer vacation.

"Free at last, free at last," the secretary muttered, turning back toward the office.

Emily laughed and put her arm around the older woman's shoulders. They marched behind the counter and collapsed at Margaret's desk, savoring the complete silence for a moment. Margaret opened a cooler at her feet, pulled out two cans of diet soda and handed one to Emily.

"Lord, I can't believe it." She toasted Emily with her pop can. "Two more weeks of paperwork, and Hawaii, here I come."

"I can just see you now. Stretched out on the beach in your bikini, a mai tai in one hand and a romance novel in the other." Emily shook her head. "Some people really have it rough."

"What are you going to do? Didn't you say something about painting your house?"

"I did, but I've decided to work for Hank this summer instead."

"Really?" Margaret's smile faded slightly. "I knew you two were dating, of course, but this sounds serious."

"It could be."

"Are you in love with Hank?"

"Yes," Emily admitted with a wistful sigh.

"You haven't told him that yet?"

Emily nodded. "I don't think he's ready to hear it. I'm hoping that will change soon."

"Oh, dear," the secretary murmured, her eyebrows drawing together.

Confused by the woman's reaction, Emily studied her for a moment. "What's going on, Margaret? I thought you'd be happy about this. You told me to give Hank a chance."

Margaret set her pop can on the desk, then patted the back of her hair. "I know I did. And I think Hank's been good for you."

"But," Emily prompted.

"But, I was in The Beauty Nook having my hair done last night, and I heard Esther Bingham and Kay Daniels talking about you and Hank."

"Keith Daniels's wife?"

"That's the one. Our very own school board member. Evidently, Vi Matheson calls other people besides you."

"Well, that's no surprise. She's been complaining about me from the beginning. That hasn't bothered you before."

"You didn't give her any ammunition before, Emily. But she's trying to start a citizens' committee to look into your behavior, and those women seemed to think it was a good idea. Maybe you and Hank should...cool it for a little while."

"I can't do that. If I do, I'll lose Hank."

"If you don't, you might lose your job," Margaret argued. "The kids need you. Think about what this place would be like if Harold Matheson took over. Can you imagine *him* standing up to Larry Paxon? Hah! That man is such a wimp, he can't even stand up to his mother."

Emily sighed and rubbed her temples. "The board didn't hire Harold before."

"That's because you applied. You were so much better qualified, they didn't have any choice. But how many people want to live in a burg like this?"

"Oh, come on. Pinedale has a lot going for it. It's got beautiful scenery and a clean environment, and—"

"And nobody's ever heard of it." Margaret gave her a crooked grin. "Look, I know this will sound selfish, but I don't want to lose you as my boss. After working with you, I could never work for Harold, and I'm too old and cranky to find another job."

"You're not, either. I appreciate your confidence in me, Margaret, but I can't pass up this chance to be with Hank and Tina. He hasn't said it, but I think this is his way to gradually work me into their family. He's opened up a whole new world for me. I love him, and I'm just going to have to take the risk."

Margaret reached across the desk and patted Emily's hand. "All right. I understand."

"I'll be as careful as I can. He wants me to move out to the ranch for the summer, but I've already told him I won't do that."

"Well, that's something, I guess. Park your car in the driveway every night, so everybody'll know you're there."

"Why don't you go home and put your feet up?" Emily suggested. "I'll have a stack of papers two feet high for you to type by Monday morning."

"No way. I wouldn't put it past Vi to have somebody watching the school to see if we leave early. I'm not going to give that witch any help." Margaret flexed her fingers over the computer keyboard and grinned at Emily. ''Bring on the work. I'm ready.''

Hank pounded the last nail into the last shingle of his barn's new roof, then sat back on his heels, looked out over the ranch and smiled with satisfaction. It was only the fifth of July, and the place was really starting to take shape. A lot of the credit for that belonged to the blonde painting the horseshoe fence down there at the side of the lodge.

He chuckled at the picture she made, meticulously dabbing black paint on each individual horseshoe as if it were the ceiling in the Sistine Chapel. Nobody but Emily would even think about doing that job in a pair of white shorts and a pink polo shirt, but he'd bet his favorite saddle she'd walk away without a speck of paint on her. He'd never known anybody could be that neat.

He'd never known anybody who could get as much work done and still keep Tina in line, either. The kid followed her around like a lost puppy and practically worshipped her. Hank was beginning to feel pretty much the same way.

After only three weeks of seeing Emily on a daily basis, he could barely imagine the ranch without her. He was already dreading the first of August when she'd have to go back to work at the school. That thought scared him plenty, but not enough to send her away.

In fact, if things went along as smoothly for the next three weeks as they had for the past three, he just might find himself proposing marriage. The truth was, he'd fallen in love with Emily. He wasn't sure when or how it had happened, but he couldn't deny that it had.

He'd spent hours trying to figure out what it was about her that hit him so hard. It wasn't the sex, although that had been fantastic the few times they'd managed to find the privacy to indulge themselves. And it wasn't the way she handled Tina or the efficient way she'd waded through the nightmare of permits and licenses, reservation systems and pricing, getting brochures printed and finding out about employee issues, like wages and Social Security.

He admired her for all those things, but he didn't love her because of them. He could have hired a baby-sitter and a business manager to do all that stuff. No, his feelings for Emily went a whole lot deeper than that.

Despite all their obvious differences, they *did* have a lot in common. They'd both been hurt by past lovers, and were pretty dang cautious as a result. They both hid their vulnerabilities from the world. He did it with jokes and clowning around. She did it with her brisk, businesslike attitude and proper manners.

It was really the same thing when you got right down to it, though. It was also a helluva lonely way to live. But somehow, with Emily, he didn't feel he had to hide so much.

When they talked, which was a whole lot more often than he'd ever talked with any other woman he'd dated, she really listened to him—as if she thought his opinions were interesting and important. She believed in him in a way nobody else ever had. Considering their past relationship and all her education, he thought that was pretty damn amazing.

Oh, he knew she wasn't perfect. She had plenty of idiosyncrasies that could drive him batty if he let them. But when she smiled at him or kissed him or teased him, which she was doing more and more often these days, her quirks didn't seem to matter. Besides, he wasn't any prize in a lot of ways, either.

Still, he couldn't quite see them married to each other. She was so smart and independent, it didn't seem to him that she was all that interested in marriage. Maybe he couldn't see himself being married again, period. If he'd met Emily again before Janice had betrayed him and his family, it might have been a different story.

Well, he thought, pulling on his short-sleeved chambray shirt and gathering up his tools, there wasn't any hurry. Neither of them was going anywhere. When and if it was right for him to ask Emily to marry him, he'd know it.

In the meantime, Becky had taken Tina to Pinedale to practice her part in the Green River Rendezvous Pageant. It'd be a shame to waste a rare afternoon's privacy by working. He slid to the edge of the roof on his seat, then climbed down the ladder and gave Emily his best wolf whistle.

"Thank you," she called, sending him a laughing glance over her shoulder.

Hank dropped his tool belt by the barn door and ambled over to the horseshoe fence, his open shirt flapping in the hot breeze. Lord, he was gettin' hard just lookin' at those long, bare legs of hers.

"There's some lemonade in that jug over by the tree," she told him.

"Why don't you come have some with me?" he suggested.

"I just had some, and I want to finish this before I stop again," she said, concentrating on her task.

He flicked her ponytail as he passed her on his way to the tree. After gulping down a full glass of the icy liquid, he filled the glass again and walked back over to the fence with it. He couldn't see Emily's legs as well, since she stood on the other side, but he had a fine view of her from the waist up.

"You're makin' good progress," he said, bracing one hand on the top rail.

"Mmm-hmm. It's hard to keep up with you when you work on it every night."

"If you'd stay here every night, I'd have somethin' else to do."

She paused for a moment. "We're not going to argue about that again, are we?"

"Nope. Just statin' a fact. When's Tina comin' back?"

She turned her wrist sideways and glanced at her watch. "Not for another two hours, at least. Wait'll you see the costume Becky's making for her. She'll look like a little Indian princess."

Hank inhaled a deep breath, then rubbed one hand over his sweaty chest. "You'd get done a lot faster if you'd use a bigger brush."

"I like this one fine."

He reached down and pulled a long, fuzzy-topped weed out of the ground. Poking it through the middle of a horseshoe, he tickled the side of Emily's left thigh with it. She swatted at it with her free hand, as if it were a pesky fly, and went right on painting. When he did it again, she looked down in time to catch him.

"Did you want something?" she asked in a tone she might use on an unruly third grader.

He almost laughed out loud at that loaded question. Did he *want* something? Did skunks stink? Did bears hibernate? Did chickens roost? Still, he didn't want to be *too* blatantly lecherous.

He shrugged and gave her an innocent smile. "Oh, no. Just a little company, I guess. It was kinda lonely up there on the roof all by myself."

She grinned and went back to painting. "Maybe you should go check on those boys you hired to work on the fences."

"Nah. I could see 'em when I was up there. They're doin' fine."

"That's good."

She squatted down to get the bottom row of horseshoes. He used his weed on the back of her neck.

"Honestly, Hank, you're as bad as Tina." She huffed in exasperation and glared up at him. "Will you please stop that?"

"I doubt it. Why don't you put that stuff away, Em?"

"You know I can't stand to leave something like this unfinished. Give me twenty minutes."

"What if I don't want to?" he asked, tickling her left earlobe.

Eyes flashing indignantly, she rose to her full height and pointed her paintbrush at him. "Then I might be forced to take drastic measures."

"Oh yeah? Like what?" Hank propped his hands on his hips and waited for the explosion. There wasn't a teacher alive who could ignore that insolent tone of voice.

"Like...like this!" She gave the paintbrush a hard flick, spattering his face and chest with fat, black spots.

"I can't believe you did that," he yelped, wiping his chin with the back of his hand.

Laughing, she dipped the brush into the can at her feet, then raised it to a threatening level. "Well, you know what, Dawson? It was fun. I might have to do it again."

"Don't do it, Emily. I'm warnin' you."

"Oh yeah?"

"Yeah."

"You don't scare me." To prove it, she let him have it again.

When he saw her going back to the can for a third round, Hank reached across the fence, grabbed her under the armpits and lifted her over to his side, mashing the dripping paintbrush between them. The horrified expression on her face told him the exact instant the gloppy stuff soaked through the front of her shirt. It was running down his belly into his navel, but he was a lot more used to that kinda thing than she was.

"Ooooh," she wailed, smacking him on the shoulder. "You wretch!"

He wrapped one arm around her hips and pulled her tightly against him, letting her feel the arousal she would have seen if she'd stopped painting long enough to look at him. Her gaze shot up to meet his, her mouth dropped open. He took full advantage of it, kissing her until her body molded itself to his.

"I just wanted a little attention, Emmie," he murmured, nibbling on her earlobe.

She slid her hands under his open shirt and caressed his back. "You've got it now."

"Wanta go up to my room and talk about your fringe benefits?"

"That would be lovely."

Hank led her inside, never noticing when the paintbrush fell to the ground. He made love to her in the shower, and again in his king-size bed, but it wasn't enough. He didn't think he'd ever get enough of hearing her excited little cries, of seeing her face contort with the pleasure he gave her, of feeling his body become a part of hers.

As he stood at the horseshoe fence and watched her drive away later that evening, he felt abandoned, bereft and more than a little angry. He wondered how she really felt about him. She gave herself to him so completely in bed, he wanted to think she loved him.

She'd never said it, though. If she loved him, how could she go off and leave him every night? Well, maybe she didn't. Maybe he was just a fling to her—an adventure off the straight and narrow path that was so important to her. Maybe she saw helping him and Tina as her good deed for the summer.

"Yeah, and maybe you're just feelin' sorry for yourself, Dawson," he muttered. "Maybe you're too damn cynical about women for your own good."

Sighing in disgust, he shot a wry smile at the unpainted portion of the fence, shoved his hands into his pockets and walked back to the lodge.

After a restless night of trying to sleep on sheets that still smelled like Emily, he awoke the next morning feeling grumpy all over. The phone rang before he'd had his first cup of coffee, but the sound of Emily's strained voice cleared the cobwebs of sleep from his brain in a hurry.

"What's wrong, babe?" he asked once the initial greetings were out of the way.

"I'm going to be late this morning," she said, obviously struggling for control of her emotions. "I've had some, uh, car trouble."

"I'll drop Tina off at Becky's and be there in half an hour."

"That's not necessary, Hank. I can take care of it."

He didn't doubt that she could, but dammit, she didn't have to, and he wasn't gonna let her. He knew his way around engines as well as the next guy, and it'd make him feel good to be able to do something to help her for a change.

"I'll be there," he repeated, and hung up the receiver.

When he drove onto her street and saw the sheriff's car in front of her house and a group of neighbors gathered to the left of her driveway, his gut knotted. He parked behind the patrol car and hurried across the lawn. His first sight of Emily's little blue sedan stunned him.

All four tires had been slashed, the radio antenna dangled at an improbable angle and the word *slut* had been spray-painted across the trunk and both sides in a gross, neon orange color. Jeez, no wonder she'd been so upset.

Rage blurred his vision, and it took him a moment to realize Emily wasn't anywhere in the crowd. He ran to her front door and let himself in without knocking. Her father stepped out of the kitchen when Hank called her name.

"She's in here, Hank. Andy's going over her statement with her," he said, offering his hand in greeting.

More worried than ever, Hank shook Marc Jackson's hand. "Is she all right?"

Marc nodded. "I think so. She's distressed over Ivan, of course, but she's pretty tough."

"Where *is* Ivan?" Hank asked, realizing he hadn't had to fight off the dog's affections when he'd walked in the door.

"At the vet's. Doc Shumaker says he'll make it, but—"

"Wait a minute. You've lost me. What the hell happened here, Rev?"

"As I understand it, Ivan must have heard the man who vandalized Emily's car and started barking around four o'clock this morning. When she opened the door to see what was disturbing him, Ivan knocked her down, got out and attacked. The man stabbed him twice and drove off in a green pickup."

"Good God," Hank muttered.

"Exactly," her father agreed with a grim smile. "Emily didn't get the whole license number, but she did see enough to be positive it was local."

"Does Andy have any idea who it was?"

Marc shrugged. "Probably the same man who's been harassing her since last spring."

"Say *what?*"

"She didn't tell you, either?" Her father sighed and shook his head. "Well, that's my Emily. Independent to her toenails. I doubt she'd have called me this morning to take Ivan to the vet if her car had been drivable."

"What else has this guy done to her?" Hank demanded.

"Obscene phone calls. Rocks through her windows. That sort of thing."

An aching hollow spot opened up in the pit of Hank's stomach, rapidly expanding to fill his chest. Raised voices distracted him before he had time to analyze it, however.

"No, Andy," Emily shouted. "I will *not* let that jerk drive me out of my own home."

"Will you be reasonable?" the sheriff shouted back. "You're not safe here without Ivan. He might come after you instead of your car next time."

Hank marched into the kitchen. "What's the problem?"

Emily sat across the table from Andy, Attila curled up on her lap. Her hands were clenched in the cat's fur, her face pale and tense. Both she and the sheriff looked up at the sound of his voice, and Hank cursed inwardly when he saw that her eyes were red from crying.

Andy shot him a look that clearly said, "Talk some sense into her, will ya?" "Your girlfriend's turned stubborn on me. I want her to stay someplace else for a few days, but she won't do it."

Hank crossed the room and squatted on his heels beside Emily's chair. "Hey, babe, listen to the guy," he said, gently smoothing a lock of hair behind her right ear. "Come stay with me and Tina. We'll take good care of you."

"I can't, Hank. There's going to be enough gossip about this as it is."

"I don't give a damn about gossip. Whoever did that to your car's not rational. Andy's right. You could be in danger."

"I'm not going to bring it to your house or to my father's," she insisted, squeezing Attila's fur so hard, he yowled and jumped to the floor. "And I refuse to let him think he's intimidated me."

Andy rolled his eyes at the ceiling, as if he'd heard all this before. Then he climbed to his feet and stuck his notebook and pen into his shirt pocket. "Well, you guys hash this out. I've got a pretty good idea who I'm goin' after. Maybe I can clear this up before dark."

Hank nodded, then turned his attention back to Emily. She met his gaze with a defiant glare that warned him to back off. He walked around the table, lowered himself onto the chair the sheriff had just vacated and waited for her to speak.

"It won't do any good to pressure me, Hank. I won't change my mind."

"You're not thinkin' straight, Em. For God's sake, let me help you."

"You can't. You're part of the problem."

"What do you mean?"

She sighed, then looked down and started picking cat hair off her jeans. "The creep thinks I'm a slut because I've been seeing you."

"He *said* that?"

"Several times."

"Why in the hell didn't you say something?" Hank demanded.

"I thought it was all just hot air. Principals get obscene phone calls all the time, Hank. I reported them to Andy, and as far as I was concerned, that was the end of it."

"You dad said he's thrown rocks through your windows."

"He only did that once," she said with a shrug. "It was the night of the first parenting class. I think I mentioned it to you the next day."

Remembering that, Hank nodded. "You still should have told me about this, Emily," he insisted. "Did you think I wouldn't care?"

"Of course not. But you couldn't do anything about it, so why should I bother you with it?"

"Because we're supposed to be friends. And if he was buggin' you because of me, I had a right to know."

Emily shook her head at him. "I'm a big girl, Hank. I make my own decisions and take care of my own problems."

"Dammit, now listen—"

"No. We've been dating and I work for you, but you're not my husband. You don't have any right to tell me what to do, or expect me to tell you everything that's going on in my life. I don't need you to take care of me."

Hank pushed back his chair and stood. "Fine. Have it your way, Emily. Let me know when you're ready to come back to work."

He stormed through her living room, barely acknowledging her father on his way out the front door. He climbed into his truck and sat there, willing himself to calm down. Staring at her forlorn, damaged car, he recognized that hollow ache in his gut for what it was—a replay of the shock he'd felt when he'd discovered Jan's betrayal.

That didn't make sense to him at first, but gradually the similarities became clear. Janice hadn't told him her parents needed money because she hadn't believed he loved her enough to want to help. Emily hadn't told him about her enemy because she hadn't believed he *could* help.

He wasn't sure which thought hurt worse. God, was he so inadequate, women didn't think he could even lend emotional support when they had a big problem? Well, fine and dandy. From now on, he wouldn't even try.

Chapter Thirteen

On the basis of Emily's description of the green pickup, Andy Johnson obtained a search warrant and drove out to Lawrence Paxon's ranch Saturday afternoon. He found Paxon suffering from untreated dog bites on his face and hands, and he found a hunting knife wrapped in a blood-stained shirt, tucked under a pile of hay in the barn. Andy arrested the man and hauled him to the county jail.

Emily phoned Hank with the news and apologized for being so cranky with him that morning. Since her father insisted on loaning her his car until her sedan received a new set of tires and a coat of paint, she returned to the Happy Trails Ranch on Monday. Hank and Tina welcomed her back, and on the surface everything seemed perfectly normal.

Over the next two weeks, however, Emily began to sense that Hank was distancing himself from her. He worked longer hours, most of them out with his fencing crew, or up at cabins three and four. When he came in for meals, he was quiet, responding with shrugs and grunts to her questions about his renovation projects. It was as if his endless supply of jokes and stories had suddenly run dry.

At first, Emily chalked up his change in attitude to physical exhaustion and temperatures in the nineties. But by the middle of the second week, when he didn't even crack a grin at her use of the word *should,* she knew something was wrong. She missed his teasing and his naughty innuendos. Looking back, she realized his good-night kisses had become brief, almost perfunctory, and he didn't stand out in the yard and watch her drive away anymore, either.

Since he steadfastly brushed off her expressions of concern, she had no idea of how to go about solving the problem, whatever it was. On Friday, hoping a change of scene would help, she suggested they drive to Jackson for dinner and a movie.

To her relief, Hank agreed to her plan, and Tina was delighted with the prospect of spending the night at the Circle D. Surely she could get a decent conversation going with the man while she had him trapped in the pickup with her for seventy-seven miles. He hummed along with his favorite tape for the first half hour, and his mood seemed so much better, Emily decided not to push her luck.

Chatting about inconsequential things for the rest of the trip, they arrived in Jackson Hole by late afternoon. As usual in the summer months, the streets were jammed with cars, trucks and motor homes, and the sidewalks swarmed with tourists. After twenty minutes of cruising the downtown area, Hank found a parking spot, and eagerly swept Emily into the cheerful chaos.

They window-shopped, toured a couple of art galleries and dressed up in vintage clothes at an old-time photo shop, Emily as a dance-hall girl and Hank as a gunslinger. He looked so dangerously sexy in the resulting photograph,

Emily became excruciatingly aware that they hadn't made love in an awfully long time.

Hank must have come to the same conclusion. When they left the studio, he wrapped his arm around her waist and kept it there, as if he'd suddenly remembered he enjoyed touching her. After watching the shoot-out, staged nightly on the town square, they strolled toward the Cadillac Grille for dinner.

As they passed the saloon next door, Emily looked up at the sign out front. "I've heard about this place, but I've never been in it. Do you mind if we peek inside?"

Halting abruptly, Hank stared at her in disbelief. "You've never been in the Million Dollar Cowboy Bar on a Friday night?"

She shook her head. "I guess none of my dates ever thought I'd fit in."

"Well, your education's been sadly lackin', Ms. Franklin," he drawled with a broad, wicked grin. "We're gonna have to fix that, but you'll need some different duds, and we're gonna have to find a motel room so we don't have to worry about drivin' home."

He marched her past the restaurant and on up Cache Street to the Buckskin Mercantile. Ignoring her protests that it was silly to buy clothes she'd probably never wear again, Hank sicced an eager salesclerk on her. He told the woman Emily wanted to be a cowgirl, then hunted through hand-tooled leather belts and women's Stetson hats while Emily tried on jeans and shirts.

When she stepped out of the dressing room, and his gaze slid over her in heated approval, Emily decided she might wear this outfit on a regular basis, after all. Hank whipped out a credit card before she'd struggled into her second boot. She tried to insist on paying for her own clothes, but the sudden anger in his eyes stopped her.

"Consider this a bonus," he said, barely moving his lips. "You've done more than enough for me and Tina. Let me do something for you just this once, okay?"

"Okay," she murmured, confused by his hostile reaction. "Thank you."

"You're welcome." He plunked the hat he'd selected onto her head and chuckled, his anger fleeing as quickly as it had ignited. "Ya look great, Em."

Winking at the clerk, who'd been listening with avid interest, he offered his arm to Emily. She placed her hand in the crook of his elbow and allowed him to escort her from the store. They'd barely taken two steps back down Cache Street, when they came face-to-face with Vi Matheson and Dorothy Stiegel.

Sinking her fingernails into Hank's arm, Emily forced a polite smile onto her face. He shot her a questioning glance and tipped his hat to the women.

"I suppose you're here for a little Friday-night fun, Ms. Franklin?" Vi asked after the initial greetings were completed, enough acid behind her friendly question to melt the sidewalk.

Emily nodded. She glanced at the shopping bags the women carried. "As a matter of fact, it looks as if we've been to a lot of the same places you have."

Vi sniffed, but Dorothy Stiegel butted in before the other woman could reply. "Oh, isn't it fun to shop in Jackson? I just love watching the tourists. We're going to the rodeo with Vi's sister in a little while."

"We won't keep you, then, ladies," Hank said, stepping to one side and taking Emily with him. He tipped his hat again. "Be seein' ya."

Feeling Vi's vindictive gaze slicing into her spine, Emily held her head up and strolled along beside Hank. When she finally risked a look over her shoulder, the two women had disappeared from sight.

"I think we'd better forget about the Million Dollar Cowboy Bar and go back to Pinedale," she said.

"I thought you'd gotten over worryin' about what other people think."

Hank's mild tone didn't fool Emily. The muscles in his arm tensed beneath her fingers, and his eyes held an intent, watchful expression.

"I have, Hank. But Vi Matheson has been making trouble for me since the day I was hired, and—"

"Aw, who'd listen to that old biddy? Besides, she can't prove anything. What's she gonna do, follow us to our motel with a camera?"

"She might," Emily grumbled, slapping his arm when he hooted at her. "Oh, all right. I'll stay. But it'll be all your fault if I get in trouble over this."

"You won't," Hank assured her. "Let's find a motel room before they're all gone. Then we'll forget about everything but havin' a good time."

Hank did his best to fulfill that promise. He'd hated holding himself apart from Emily. When she'd suggested this trip, he'd figured it would be a good way to get close to her again. She'd hurt his feelings over that mess with Larry Paxon, but he didn't think she'd meant to.

After all, she hadn't told her dad about her problems with the guy, so maybe he shouldn't take it personally that she hadn't told him, either. If there was still a little voice in the back of his head yelling, *Yeah, but you were supposed to be friends and lovers. What else will she hide from you in the future?* he was ready to tell it to shut the hell up.

While he'd been punishing her with his withdrawal, he'd punished himself, too. But enough of that nonsense. From here on out, he'd take it one day at a time. However long his relationship with Emily lasted, he intended to enjoy it as much as he could.

By the time they finished registering at the Antler Motel, walking back to the restaurant and finishing their buffalo tenderloin entrées, he wanted to forget about partying and head straight for their room. Emily looked so darn cute in her cowgirl getup though, he knew he wouldn't do it. An evening of laughs wouldn't hurt either of them.

Leaving the 1940s Art Deco atmosphere of the Cadillac Grille one minute, and walking into the Million Dollar Cowboy Bar the next, was like being transported to a different time and place. When they stepped inside, Emily's mouth dropped open and her eyes widened in amazement.

Thousands of silver dollars, encased in acrylic, covered the tops of two bars stretching for yards and yards down both sides of the first room. Regular bar stools wouldn't do for this western establishment. Instead, each bar sported a row of saddles mounted on steel posts, so a cowboy would always feel right at home. Pool tables covered the territory in the middle.

The dim lightning in the second room revealed a sea of cocktail tables, a dance floor and a stage at the far end, where a band was tuning up. There were huge paintings of western scenes on most of the walls. Tourists in every kind of summer wear imaginable mingled with local residents, enjoying the friendly atmosphere.

Putting his hand on the back of Emily's waist, Hank guided her to a table under a wagon-wheel chandelier. He ordered them each a beer from the barmaid, who laughed when Emily muttered, "This looks like a movie set."

"Clint Eastwood thought it did, too," the young woman told her. "He filmed a scene from one of those ape movies in here. I can never remember which one."

"I don't know what to look at first, the people or the paintings or all this...stuff," Emily complained, swiveling her head from side to side.

Hank laid his arm on the back of her chair and squeezed her shoulder. "Take your time. We'll stay as long as you want. Didja see the wolf goin' after the Rocky Mountain sheep in the glass case?''

"No. Where is it?"

She started to rise, but Hank grabbed a belt loop on the side of her jeans and yanked her back down. "Wait'll our drinks come, and I'll go with you. That is, unless you want lover boy over there hittin' on you. I don't think I'm up to fightin' him, Em. Not even for you."

After shooting him a questioning frown, she turned her head in the direction he indicated with his thumb. Her eyes bugged out so far, he was afraid her contacts might pop onto the table. The guy had to weigh over three hundred pounds. Judging from the length of his legs, Hank figured he probably stood six foot seven or eight.

He sat backward on the saddle at the end of the bar on the north side of the room, an empty shot glass in one hand, his other hand scratching his chest through his long beard and the laces on his filthy buckskin shirt. His buckskin britches and moccasins weren't any cleaner. His black hair hung past his beefy shoulders in matted clumps, and when he smiled drunkenly at Emily, one of his front teeth was missing.

Shuddering, she turned back to Hank, her eyes pleading. "Tell me he's not real."

"Oh, he's real, all right," Hank said with a chuckle. "And he must have a thing for blondes."

When their drinks arrived, Hank escorted Emily around the room, enjoying her dry comments about the artwork, stuffed animals and the rest of the clientele. He was more than a little relieved to notice her amorous new friend had left by the time they returned to their table. Then the band started cranking out a string of country-and-western songs.

He coaxed Emily onto the dance floor, and for the next three hours, they danced and drank, laughed and danced some more. Any doubts about her ability to let go and have fun vanished into the cloud of cigarette smoke gathering around the ceiling. Given enough beer and the right encouragement, she had a downright bawdy sense of humor.

By midnight, his bum leg couldn't handle any more dancing, and his libido couldn't handle any more of Emily's rubbing against him during slow songs. When he asked if she was ready to leave, she tipped her head back and looked up at him with a sweet, sexy smile that made the throbbing in his groin worse.

Taking her hand, he led her out into the cool night air. The streets were still busy with bar-hopping tourists. Music blared from a variety of open doors. Neither of them talked much as they walked back to the motel. Neither of them noticed the car with three older women following at a discreet distance, either.

Anticipation of the pleasures ahead made his hands unsteady. Emily let out a jaw-cracking yawn and leaned against him as he fumbled the key into the lock. He kissed the tip of her nose, chuckling when she wrinkled it at him.

"Don't even *think* about fallin' asleep on me now, woman," he said, giving her a one-armed hug.

"You'd better get that door open soon, cowboy," she retorted. "I'm fading fast."

The lock finally gave. He pushed the door open with his shoulder, pulling her off balance. They swayed on the threshold, giggling and clinging to each other. Then the laughter died, and she tipped her face up for a kiss.

He crushed her against him, taking her mouth the way he ached to take the rest of her luscious body. Lord, he must have been completely bonkers to deny himself the taste and feel of her for so damn long. Shaking with need, he nudged her inside and kicked the door shut with the heel of his boot.

Darkness enveloped them. Without taking his lips from hers, he fumbled behind him for a light switch, then sidestepped her past the bathroom into the bedroom. Her fingers popped the pearl snaps down the front of his shirt and slid inside, raking through his chest hair, shredding what little restraint he had left.

Grasping her shoulders with both hands, he sat her at the foot of the king-size bed and pulled off her boots. Then he yanked off his own and tossed the protection he'd bought in the men's room onto the bedspread. She scooted to the middle of the bed and lay back against the pillows, welcoming him with open arms.

"I want you, Emmie," he groaned, pressing her into the mattress with his greater weight.

She slid her hands into his back pockets and ground her pelvis against his fly. "I want you, too, Hank. Don't make me wait."

"That's the nicest thing anybody's said to me all day."

Articles of clothing sailed through the air in a feverish rain, landing on the floor, the television, the lamp shades. He kissed his way down the center of her body, detouring to rediscover the fullness of her breasts. She clasped the sides of his head, guiding him, her nipples hardening beneath his eager mouth.

Wanting her to burn as hot as he was, he moved lower, dipping his tongue into her navel, then lower still. Her legs trembled when he parted them. He soothed her with caresses, then nuzzled the thatch of blond curls and kissed the moist, tender flesh between her thighs. She flinched at the first touch of his lips and tongue, as if she wasn't used to such intimacy.

He continued his ministrations, whispering assurances, loving the sweet, womanly taste and smell of her. Her heels dug into the bedding; her breathing came in quick, shallow gasps. He slid one finger inside her, his groin tightening painfully when he felt the tremors signaling the start of her release.

Raising onto his knees, he ripped open one of the packets he'd tossed on the bed and protected her. Then he entered her body, shutting his eyes against the intense, searing pleasure racing through his nervous system. Her legs wrapped around his waist. Her hips lifted to meet each thrust; her soft cries of delight urged him on and on, into a rough, reckless ride, more exhilarating than the wildest rodeo bronc had ever given him.

It was happening too fast. He wanted to hold on to the sensations, the closeness, the fires she touched deep inside him. Her eyelids fluttered, then opened when he called her name in anguish. She felt it, too; he could see it in her eyes. Awed wonder spread over her face as she reached the peak, and with a final, powerful lunge, he followed her into completion.

He collapsed on top of her. Her arms closed around him, as if to shelter him from the violent shudders ripping through him. He rolled onto his side, turning her to face him.

"It's never been like this for me," she whispered, smoothing his hair from his forehead.

Bringing her hand to his mouth, he kissed each finger and pressed her palm to his chest. "Me, either. You do strange and wonderful things to me, Em."

"I'm glad."

"Mmm. Me, too."

She nudged him onto his back, then snuggled close and rested her head on his shoulder with an exhausted sigh. Hank pulled the sheet up over them, and settled his head on the pillow for a little snooze. Emily rubbed her cheek against him like a contented kitten.

Just before the mists of sleep could close in around him, he heard her murmur, "I love you, Hank."

His heart lurched and his eyelids flew open. Had she really said what he thought she had? If she had, did she mean it? Nah. It was too easy to say those words in the glowing aftermath of sex. Besides, she'd had too much beer for anyone to take anything she said seriously.

She opened one eye and tipped her head back to look at him. "Did you hear me?"

"Yeah." He kissed the side of her forehead. "Go to sleep, baby."

A moment later, he felt soft, even puffs of air ruffle his chest hair, and knew she'd slipped off to dreamland. He tried to blank his mind, willed his body to relax, but it seemed like a helluva long time before he joined her.

Emily awoke the next morning to bright sunshine streaming through a gap in the drapes and a heavy arm tossed over her waist. Needing to use the bathroom, she carefully freed herself and grinned when Hank didn't move so much as a finger. He'd worn himself out making love to her again and again during the night. Poor baby.

Studying him closely, she decided that was a poor choice of words. Hank was no baby; even sound asleep, he didn't exactly look boyish. A dark crop of stubble covered his chin. The lines carved around his nose and mouth by maturity and exposure to the sun were more noticeable when his gorgeous eyes weren't open to distract her attention.

No, he was all man, and she desperately wished he belonged to her. A hollow ache started in her abdomen that had nothing to do with hunger. She hadn't intended to tell Hank she loved him.

Once the words had come out of her mouth, however, she'd hoped he would respond in kind. He hadn't, of course, and she'd told herself the words didn't matter. She knew he cared for her; he showed his affection in a dozen different ways. She would much rather have him tell her to go to sleep than lie about his feelings to make her happy.

Still, even with that little pep talk, disappointment accompanied her into the bathroom. She showered and dressed, then used the makeup kit in her purse. When she entered the bedroom again, she found Hank propped up on the pillows, his hands clasped behind his head.

"What are you doin' with all those clothes on, woman?"
He patted the spot beside him and gave her a lazy, wicked
smile. "C'mon over here and give me a good-mornin'
kiss."

Emily laughed. "No way, Dawson. It's almost checkout
time and I'm hungry."

"I'm hungry, too."

"I'm talking about food. Pancakes, sausage, eggs." She
dug a brush and a ponytail holder out of her purse and
turned to the mirror above the dresser.

Hank heaved a sigh that would have done any martyr
proud, then tossed back the covers and climbed out of bed.
Emily stole a surreptitious peek at his physique as he
stretched his arms over his head. Oh my. He *did* look awfully... hungry, at that.

Their eyes met in the mirror. Approaching her, he flexed
his biceps as a bodybuilder would. "All this could have
been yours, Franklin."

More tempted than she wanted to admit, Emily turned
her head and looked at him over her shoulder. He swooped
down and kissed the tip of her nose. Then he patted her
fanny and strutted into the bathroom. Chuckling, she resumed brushing her hair.

After a hearty breakfast at the Village Inn, they took off
for Pinedale. Hank insisted that she sit next to him with her
hand on his thigh. She sat back to enjoy the ride, feeling
like a besotted teenager and loving every minute of it.

They were deep in a discussion over the merits of install-
ing a pool table at the lodge, when a car pulled out from
behind the pickup to pass. Emily glanced through Hank's
window, and felt as if the bottom of her stomach had suddenly plummeted to the toes of her new boots. She'd seen
that light green sedan many times, parked across the street
from her house, in Dorothy Stiegel's driveway.

The woman in the passenger seat was Vi Matheson. She turned toward the pickup, her gaze meeting Emily's. Then the car sped up and swerved back into the right lane, leaving Emily with a fleeting impression that there had been triumph in the smile on Vi's thin lips.

Chapter Fourteen

By the end of the next week, Emily had pushed her worries about Vi Matheson to the farthest corner of her mind. Her favorite project at the ranch had been to help Tina decorate her bedroom. The wallpaper strips, bedspread and curtains the little girl had chosen finally arrived on Tuesday. They'd had to hurry to get the painting done before the carpet layer came on Thursday.

When the man left, they hauled the furniture back into the room, made up Tina's bed and hung the curtains. Then Emily helped the little girl sort through her dresser and closet, laying aside the clothes she'd outgrown. Heaving an adult-sounding sigh of relief, Tina flopped down in the middle of the floor and gazed around her new domain.

"It looks great, Mom," she pronounced with a broad grin.

Emily shot her a surprised glance, and a look of chagrin crossed the child's face.

"Oops. I didn't mean to call you that, Ms. Franklin."

Sitting on the side of the bed, Emily patted the space beside her. "Come up here and we'll talk about it."

"I don't know why I said that," Tina said, following Emily's suggestion. "It just kinda slipped out."

"It's all right, Tina. I'm flattered you thought of me that way. You miss having a mother, don't you?"

The little girl nodded and looked down at her shoelaces. "Uh-huh. I don't remember my real mom. Aunt Becky was kinda like one, but she was always real busy. It's been nice havin' you here all the time."

"I've enjoyed it, too." Emily crooked a finger under Tina's chin, coaxing the child to look at her. "I'd be extremely proud to have you for a daughter, Tina."

"You would?" Tina's eyes sparkled with excitement. "Why don't you marry my dad, then? That'd make you my stepmother, an' I could still call you Mom, couldn't I?"

"Yes, you could if it happened," Emily said cautiously, "but I don't think you should count on that, honey. Your father and I are very close friends, but we've never talked about marriage."

"Well, that's easy to fix. Just tell him you wanta get married to him. Or I'll tell him if you want me to."

"No, Tina. Please don't say anything to your father."

"Why not? You guys are always huggin' and smoochin' when you think I'm not lookin'. Don't you love him?"

Emily sighed and shook her head in frustration. Things always looked so simple from a child's point of view. "Yes, I love him very much. But it's more complicated than you think. You see, I'm not certain he loves me the same way."

"Can't you ask him?"

"I'd rather wait until he's ready to tell me himself."

The little girl's eyes misted with tears. "But this is your last week. After tomorrow, you'll go back to work at the school, an' I won't hardly ever get to see you or Ivan."

"Maybe not as often, but you'll still see us," Emily assured her. "We'll come out on weekends, and once school starts, you'll see me every day."

"It won't be the same." Tina stomped across the room. Folding her arms over her chest, she stared out the window. "Then you'll just be my principal again."

"Am I such a mean old principal?"

"No, but I'd rather have you for a mom," Tina grumbled.

If she were completely honest, Emily knew that if she had to make a choice, she'd rather be Tina's mom than her principal, too. However, Hank's reaction to her confession of love had told her quite plainly that he wasn't ready to talk about a commitment. If she tried to push him for one at this point, she wouldn't be surprised if he ended their relationship.

"I'm sorry, Tina," she said softly. "Right now that's the best I can do."

"You could ask him if you really wanted to," Tina muttered, her voice thick with emotion.

Emily studied that proud, rigid little back, and decided continuing this conversation would only upset the child more. A lump forming in her throat, she quietly left the room and went downstairs to start lunch.

How could you have been so blind? her conscience demanded. *Anyone with half a brain would have known Tina would become attached to the first woman who paid attention to her.*

"I didn't mean to hurt Tina," she whispered.

No, of course not. But she'll be hurt even more if you don't talk to Hank.

"All right, all right. I'll talk to him."

The man in question walked through the back door a moment later, his eyes lighting up at the sight of her. He crossed the kitchen in three long strides and dropped a quick, hot kiss on her lips.

"Mmm, sweet," he murmured, snatching the pickle she'd just laid beside his sandwich. Winking at her, he popped it into his mouth and went to the sink to wash his hands. "I saw the carpet guy leavin'. You gals need any help?"

"No, we're all finished, thanks." Emily took a deep breath for courage. "Hank, we need—"

The phone cut her off. Hank tossed down the towel he'd been using to dry his hands and grabbed the receiver.

"Oh, hi, Beck. You did? How many? That's great." He nodded enthusiastically at something his sister said. "Yeah. We'll be over right after lunch to look at 'em."

Tina wandered into the room in time to catch the tail end of the conversation. "Who was that, Dad?"

"Your Aunt Becky. She just got back from that horse show in Casper. Sounds like she found us some good ones."

"Can I go look at 'em with you?"

"Sure, shortcakes." He picked her up and hugged her. "In fact, she said she's got a surprise waitin' for you."

"She did?"

"Yup. So you'd better get busy on your lunch, or we'll never find out what it is." He set her down, turned her toward the sink and gave her a gentle push. "Wash those grubby little paws, first."

He walked over to the counter and took the plate Emily handed him. "What were you gonna say, Em?"

She shot a glance at Tina. "I'll tell you later."

"Okay. You're gonna come with us this afternoon?"

Emily wanted to, but she thought it would be better to give Tina some time away from her. "Not this time," she said, softening her refusal with a smile. "I still have some things to clear up here."

"Aw, can't it wait, honey?"

"I have to go back to my real job next week," she reminded him. *And back to my real life, too.*

He gave her a long, searching look, as if he sensed the troubled emotions behind her brisk tone. Frowning, he sighed, then muttered, "All right. Whatever you want."

Emily and Tina joined him at the table a moment later. Evidently, the prospect of receiving a surprise from her aunt had erased their previous conversation from Tina's mind. She practically gobbled down her sandwich. Emily barely managed to choke down two bites, while Hank related the information Becky had given him over the phone.

When the Dawsons left, Emily sat at the table, trying to understand the feeling of grief gnawing inside her. She finally realized something Tina had said was at the core of her distress—*It won't be the same.*

The past six weeks had been a wonderful time for her. Something almost . . . magical had happened. Between all the hard work, laughter and shared meals, the three of them had come awfully close to becoming a family.

And Tina was right—it wouldn't be the same. Perhaps it would never be the same again. Hank would take over running the business office she'd set up for him. He'd probably hire a housekeeper. He simply wouldn't . . . need her anymore, at least, not the way he did now.

Tina wouldn't, either. Once school started and she got used to the routine, she would be fine. Emily would become "just" her principal again, just another friendly adult.

A tear rolled down Emily's face. She dashed it away with the back of her hand, then carried a load of dishes to the sink, muttering, "Stop it. Feeling sorry for yourself won't change anything, and it's not as if Hank will never love you. He still might. Someday."

After finishing the dishes, she forced herself to go into the office and recheck the files she'd set up. Of course, everything was in perfect order, which left her with nothing to do. On impulse, perhaps out of a need to get in touch with her "real" life, she picked up the phone and dialed Margaret Sheridan's number.

"Hi, Margaret. This is Emily. Are you ready to come back to work on Monday?"

"Oh, Emily, I'm glad you called," the secretary said fervently. "I was planning to phone you this evening."

"What's up?"

"I don't know for sure, but Vi Matheson's been contacting every member of the school board and half the town. Everywhere I've gone for the last two days, people have stopped me to ask if it's true you spent a night in Jackson with Hank."

"Lord." Emily rubbed her forehead, hoping to quell the pain threatening to start there.

"Well, *is* it true?"

"I'm not going to answer that, Margaret."

"I don't blame you. But Vi claims she can prove it. There's not any chance of that, is there?"

"I don't know. I suppose it's possible. Do you think people will really care that much?"

"Oh, who knows?" Margaret sighed. "I know a lot of folks felt bad about what Larry Paxon did to your car and your dog, but since the judge just put him on probation, I think some of them wonder what that was really all about."

"Doesn't everybody know he's supposed to be getting psychiatric care as one of the provisions of his probation?"

"Nobody seems to be mentioning that. I'm afraid this might turn pretty nasty."

"What do you mean?"

"Vi's been hinting that Larry got a raw deal. Like, maybe he had a right to be so indignant about your behavior. He's never been arrested for anything else."

"Only because his wife's too scared to charge him with assault and battery," Emily retorted.

"I just thought you should know about this, Emily," Margaret replied quietly. "I'm on your side."

"I know. I'm sorry if I've been short with you."

"Hey, don't worry about it. I understand."

"I, uh, I have to go now, Margaret," Emily said, fearing her voice would break if she talked any longer.

"I'll be here if you need to talk later."

Too agitated to stay inside, Emily stormed out the back door and called her dog. She didn't have her jogging clothes with her, but the shorts, T-shirt and sneakers she had on were close enough. Setting a furious pace to match her mood, she ran across the barnyard and veered off onto the road leading to the guest cabins, Ivan at her side.

They passed cabin numbers one and two without slowing down. The sun scorched her head, and the hot, dry air tortured her lungs, but she barely noticed it. Her feet pounded up puffs of dust as the road climbed higher, narrowing to a rutted path as they passed cabin three.

She wanted to run forever. Away from the vicious gossip threatening to destroy her career. Away from the isolation and loneliness that had followed her since she'd first discovered she was going to be judged by different standards than other people. Away from the man and the little girl who could so easily break her heart.

Ivan whined at cabin number six. Emily glanced down, grimacing when she saw how tired he looked. The big dog would run with her until he collapsed. He'd made a good recovery from Lawrence Paxon's attack, but running in this heat was harder on him than it was on her.

She slowed to a walk and kept going until her muscles had cooled enough to prevent cramping. Then she retraced her steps and sat on the porch at cabin six. Panting heavily, Ivan flopped down at her feet. She petted him in apology, and gazed out at the view.

The building sat against the side of a steep hill, affording glimpses of two of the other cabins, the lodge and the barn below. The jagged peaks of the Wind River Mountains scraped the sky to the east. Their ancient, awe-inspiring bulk reminded her that in the greater scheme of things, human lives and problems had about as much permanent impact as the changing of a traffic light.

Her heartbeat gradually resumed its normal pace. Her anger drained away, exposing the fear beneath it. Running wouldn't solve anything. Neither would hoping her problems would go away on their own. Still, she felt too besieged and uncertain to take any sort of action.

If only she could have more time with Hank, perhaps they would grow close enough to cope with this situation more easily. If only other people would leave them alone. If only there wasn't a child involved.

"If only you had a magic wand," Emily muttered, pushing herself to her feet.

Ivan looked up at her, his head tipped to one side. She grinned at his quizzical expression and patted her thigh.

"Come on, boy. I need some advice. I think I know just the man to get it from."

She walked back to the lodge, left a note for Hank, then loaded Ivan into her car and drove back to town. She found her father puttering in the vegetable garden behind his house. Ivan charged across the lawn and licked his face. Marc laid his hoe on the grass with a surprised laugh, turning to Emily with a smile.

"Well, hi there. Have I forgotten a date?"

Emily shook her head. "No. Can't a girl drop in on her dad if she wants to?"

"Of course she can." He crossed the space between them and kissed her cheek. "I'll even treat her to a glass of sun tea."

"That's the best offer I've had all day."

Wrapping her arm around his waist, she walked into the house with him. She set the sugar bowl on the table and sliced a lemon while her father put ice in their glasses and poured the tea.

"Would you rather sit on the patio?" he asked. "Or do we need more privacy?"

"You know what I'm here for, don't you?"

"I've heard...rumors." He carried the glasses to the table and pulled out a chair for her. "Come on, honey. Sit down and tell your old dad all your troubles."

"You don't mind?"

"Of course not. I'm delighted you came to me. I don't know what I can do to help, but I'll be glad to listen."

She sipped her tea, then began to tell him about Hank, Tina and Vi Matheson. He encouraged her with an occasional nod or a question. When she'd finished, he smoothed his white hair down at the back of his head and crossed one leg over the other. Then he looked at her for a long moment, his eyes filled with sympathy.

"You know what you have to do, Emily."

"Talk to Hank?"

Marc nodded. "I don't understand why you're so hesitant to tell him what's going on. He's not an unreasonable man, and he's helped put you in an untenable position."

"I'm afraid he'll think I'm trying to make him feel obligated to marry me. I don't want that."

"You *do* want to marry him, don't you?"

"Yes. But not because of Tina or my career. I want him to love me, Dad."

"It sounds to me as if he already does, Emily."

"I think he does, too. But if he's not ready to admit it, he's going to feel manipulated."

"He might. But he needs to know what Tina said, and you need to know how he feels about you. It's not manipulation to tell someone the truth."

"Dad, you don't understand. Hank's...wary about women, with good reason. He really doesn't care if people gossip about him. He never has. He'll think I'm blowing this mess with Vi completely out of proportion."

"What would it take to convince him you're not?"

"I don't know. I suppose if the school board fired me, he'd have to believe me."

Her father sighed and shook his head. "That's not fair to you, honey. You've worked awfully hard to get this job. I'd hate to see you lose it because of Hank's attitude."

"I'm not sure my job's worth all this hassle anymore."

"You don't mean that."

"Yes, I do, Dad." She shoved back her chair and paced from the table to the stove and back. "I'd never really thought about it much before I got involved with Hank, but I'm tired of having to watch everything I say and do. I'm sick of having other people deciding how I should live my life. Where do they get off?"

"It comes with the territory, Emily."

"Then I'm sick of the territory! This past six weeks, I've been really... happy with Hank and Tina. Why should I give that up?"

"You love education, too," he pointed out. "You've spent years studying how to help children learn. They can't help but benefit from your expertise. It would be such a waste—"

"But I *love* Hank and Tina, Dad. What about *my* life and *my* happiness? Don't they matter?"

"Of course they do," he said quietly. "Look, maybe you're getting upset prematurely. The school board could tell Mrs. Matheson they're not interested in her charges."

"You don't believe that's going to happen any more than I do." She dropped back into her chair and propped her elbows on the table. "Especially since she's getting everybody involved."

"Then call the state principal's association and talk to their lawyer. You don't have to make it easy for them."

Emily considered his suggestion for a moment. "I might do that, although I'd probably be better off resigning."

"And give Vi the satisfaction of knowing she intimidated you into backing down without a fight?"

"No way."

Chuckling at her emphatic reply, he reached across the table and patted her hand. "Atta girl. In the meantime, you'd better talk to Hank."

"All right. I'll do it tomorrow. But I'm only going to tell him about Tina."

"You might as well tell him about your other problem, too. He'll hear about it sooner or later."

"Maybe I'll get lucky, and it'll be later," she said with a wry grin. "Like, after he's declared his undying love and proposed to me."

He scowled at her, then shrugged. "Well, you know him better than I do. But will you think about something?"

"Sure. What is it?"

"How much is your relationship with Hank really worth, if you can't be completely honest with him?"

Chapter Fifteen

Her father's question haunted Emily late into the night. She awoke the next morning, tired, but determined to convince Hank to listen to her. She sincerely doubted she would receive the declaration of undying love and proposal of marriage she had mentioned to her father. It seemed to her, however, that the least he could do was give her some indication of his feelings for her.

After all, he and Tina were not the only ones in the relationship with needs to be considered. She had done what he wanted since they'd become lovers. Now it was time to find out if he cared enough about her to be willing to make some compromises for the sake of her career.

Despite what she'd said the day before, she *did* love working in education. She found the dual challenge of motivating teachers and providing a safe, nurturing environment in which children could learn, the most exciting and rewarding thing she'd ever done. It would be almost impossible to find another principalship if she were dismissed from this one on a morals charge.

Of course, she could do other things to earn a living. Most of those other things would force her to leave Pinedale, however, which would mean losing Hank and Tina through geography. She would rather have waited a few more weeks for this discussion, but Tina and Vi weren't going to allow her that luxury. No, she had to talk to Hank today.

Unfortunately, when she drove into the ranch yard, she found two horse trailers parked to one side and a Dawson family reunion taking place around the corral. Tina raced over to welcome Emily and Ivan.

"Ms. Franklin, Ms. Franklin! Come see our new horses! We got eight of 'em and one of 'em's mine!"

"That's wonderful," Emily replied with a smile.

The little girl danced from one foot to the other while Emily put Ivan's leash on. Then she grabbed Emily's hand and practically dragged her over to the group of people standing along the fence. Everyone greeted her warmly, and went back to admiring the horses. Hank and Becky waved to her from inside the enclosure. Tina scrambled up to sit on the top rail of the fence.

"Hey, Dad! Bring Midnight over so Ms. Franklin can see her."

Hank singled out a black mare with white stockings on her front feet and led her over to meet Emily. His gaze skimmed over her, a slow, sexy smile spreading across his mouth.

"I missed you last night," he said softly. "Where'd you run off to?"

"I went to see my dad."

"How's he doin'?"

"Just fine." She eyed the horse Tina was hugging. "Isn't that an awfully big horse for a little girl?"

He smiled and stroked Midnight's glossy neck. "Nah. She's so gentle, Jonathan could ride her if he could hold on. Becky did a great job pickin' out this bunch."

Sam interrupted their conversation with a question about the cabins. Hank answered him, then turned back to Emily.

"Can you believe the whole clan showed up like this?" he asked, his eyes glinting with amusement. "You'd think they'd never seen horses before."

"They're probably curious about what you've been doing all summer."

He chuckled. "I think they're even more curious about what *you've* been doin'. Tina talks about you all the time, you know. They're all checkin' you out to see if you're gonna be part of the family."

Emily's heart beat faster at that remark. Hank didn't appear to be particularly upset by his family's interest in their relationship. Perhaps he was more ready to talk about it than she'd thought.

"That's an interesting concept," she said, her tone cautiously neutral.

He shrugged as if it didn't matter, she thought, wincing inwardly. Then he changed the subject.

"We're gonna turn the horses into the pasture in a few minutes, but Grandma D's lookin' a little tuckered. Would you mind takin' her up to the lodge? Tell her you need some help in the kitchen or she won't go."

"All right. Will your family be staying for lunch?"

"Oh, I reckon. They're all gonna want the grand tour, anyway. There's a pack of hamburger patties in the freezer and some buns. See what else you can find to go with 'em."

Irritation replaced the disappointment she'd felt a moment earlier. Why, the big jerk. He'd dismissed the possibility of marriage in one breath and expected her to perform wifely duties with the next. They were definitely going to have a talk before this day ended.

Grandma D accepted her invitation to go inside, demanding they take baby Jonathan along with them. Peter pried his son's hands out of his hair and handed him to the elderly woman. After setting up a playpen beside the kitchen table, Peter kissed Grandma D's cheek and went back outside. She sat on one of the chairs.

"Mercy, it's hot out there," she said, taking off the baby's hat.

Emily brought her a glass of iced tea. Grandma D took a long drink and smiled up at her in appreciation.

"If you'll hold this little rascal for a minute," she said, pushing Jonathan into Emily's arms without waiting for an answer, "I'll get his diaper bag and see if I can find his toys and apple juice."

The little boy looked up at Emily with round, curious eyes the same color as Tina's. He flashed her a big smile, showing off his four teeth, and gurgled at her when she smiled back at him. Chuckling, she sat on the chair Grandma D had vacated, turning him to face her. They had a lovely conversation until the elderly woman returned.

When Jonathan caught sight of his bottle, he squawked and waved both arms at it. Grandma D gave it to him, insisting that Emily should sit still and hold him. Emily cuddled his sturdy little body close, inhaling his talcum powder smell. Oh, what she wouldn't give to have a sweet baby like him.

Grandma D got out the hamburger patties and buns, and put eggs and potatoes on to cook for potato salad. She chattered about the weather, Hank's dude ranch and how nice Tina's new room looked. Before Emily quite knew what had happened, she found herself telling Grandma D about why she'd returned to Pinedale and how her relationship with Hank had developed.

Pushing her big, red glasses farther up onto the bridge of her nose, Grandma D nodded at Jonathan, who was now fast asleep in Emily's arms. "You're awful good with little ones. Ya oughtta have some of your own."

"I'd like to," Emily admitted with a wistful sigh, gently smoothing down the baby's flyaway hair. "I know they're a lot of work, but they're so much fun, too."

"I hear ya. They just sorta soak up love like sponges and give it right back." Grandma D paused, as if choosing her next words carefully. "I want to thank you for helpin' Tina so much."

"She's a delightful little girl, Grandma D."

"Well, she wasn't for a long time, there. Lord, how I've worried about that kid. Hank, too. But they're both doin' fine, thanks to you."

"Hank just needed to learn to trust his instincts with Tina."

"Yeah, but it seems like it was easier for him to take advice from you than from anybody in the family. We're all grateful to ya."

Since Emily didn't know what to say to that remark, she smiled and got up to lay Jonathan in his playpen. Then she walked over to the work counter to see what she could do to help. Grandma D handed her a knife, and the two women stripped the skins from the boiled potatoes in a companionable silence until the old lady spoke again.

"You plannin' to marry Hank?"

"I would if he asked me."

Grandma D snorted and shook her head. "That boy can be dumber than a fence post. He gives you any trouble, you just come to me. I'll set him straight in a hurry."

Emily believed her. "I appreciate the offer, but—"

"Yeah, I know. Mind your own business," Grandma D finished for her with a chuckle. "For some strange reason, I have a hard time doin' that."

Dani entered the room then and helped with the preparations while she reported on the activity outside. The rest of the morning passed pleasantly, as did the meal everyone shared. There was an especially touching moment when Dani announced that Sam was going to be a father in six months. The look of shock, followed immediately by utter delight on the man's face, was truly priceless.

Though Emily enjoyed getting acquainted with the Dawsons, her frustration and irritation with Hank grew as the hours passed. Tina shadowed Emily's movements, as if she was afraid to let her out of sight. He appeared to be oblivious to his daughter's possessive attitude toward her. He also took great pleasure in demonstrating his affection for Emily, without the least concern for the expectations he was raising in the relatives who obviously loved him a great deal.

Emily was grateful for his family's warm acceptance, but she didn't know how she would ever face them without cringing in embarrassment if things didn't work out the way everyone obviously hoped they would. By the time they all left, she felt ready to whack him over the head.

"It was kinda fun havin' everybody over," he said, letting the screen door swing shut.

"You have a wonderful family," Emily replied. "Where's Tina?"

"In the yard playin' with Ivan." His eyes glittering with devilish intent, he crossed the room and put his arms around her waist. "I didn't get my good-night kiss last night, and I heard you say the 'S' word at least four times."

Putting her hands on his chest, she held him off. "Hank, we need to talk."

"We can do that anytime. I'd rather smooch."

His lips covered hers, stirring the familiar magic inside her. She couldn't resist tasting him, holding him this one time. Lord, she hoped it wouldn't be the last. Before he sidetracked her completely, she pulled away and gazed up at him. When he tried to kiss her again, she put two fingers over his mouth.

He raised an eyebrow in query, then released her. "That looks like your serious face, Em."

"I told you. We need to talk."

"All right. What is it?"

Anxiety welling inside her, she waited for him to sit at one end of the sofa. The hundred speeches she'd rehearsed the previous night evaporated from her mind while she took the opposite end and turned sideways in order to face him. His silent, intent study of her face unnerved her even more.

Unable to bear the growing tension, she finally blurted, "What would you say if I told you I was in love with you?"

His startled laugh had a nervous ring to it. "That's a helluva question to throw at a guy outta nowhere. Did Grandma D grill you about when you're gonna make an honest man of me or somethin'?"

"Yes, but that's irrelevant. Please, answer the question, Hank. What would you say if I told you I was in love with you?"

A wary expression replaced the amusement in his eyes. "I don't know. I guess I'd say I was flattered, but..."

"But what? You don't love me?"

"Dammit, Emily, don't do this," he warned. He pushed himself to his feet and stalked over to the fireplace.

"Don't ask how you feel about me? Why not?"

"You know I care about you. There's no need to get all analytical about it. Just let it be a while longer."

"Define a while. Two weeks? Two months? Two years?"

"How should I know? Damn, I should've realized my family would get you all spooked about marriage. Just because they like it so much, they think everybody else has to be the same way."

"You make it sound like a terminal disease, Hank."

"Gimme a break. For some of us, it's worse."

"It doesn't have to be that way. Don't you think we've gotten along pretty well together this summer?"

"Yeah. So why wreck it?"

"You're always grumbling about my going home at night. I wouldn't have to do that if we were married."

"You could stay here if you really wanted to. What do we need marriage for?"

"I can think of several reasons. Tina's the most important one."

"What do you mean by that? She's crazy about you."

"That's part of the problem, Hank. She's gotten too attached to me this summer. I didn't realize it until she called me Mom yesterday."

He crossed the room again and resumed his place on the sofa. "Tell me what happened."

When Emily finished recounting her conversation with his daughter, he rammed the fingers of one hand through his hair in frustration. "I'll talk to her."

"That won't help. Don't you see? She needs to know if I'm going to be a permanent part of her life. Besides, children learn by example. Do you really want to give her the message that it's okay to live with a man she's not married to?"

"You might have a point there."

"I know I do. If our relationship isn't going anywhere, then I think we need to stop seeing each other for her sake."

"I don't want to do that."

"I don't, either. But I don't see that we have any choice."

Hank propped his elbows on his knees, his forehead furrowed with concentration. "Look, I've already had one failed marriage, and I came within spittin' distance of a second one. I can't afford to make another mistake."

"I've had a failed marriage, too," Emily replied, her voice sounding as hollow as she felt inside. "I understand."

"I don't think you do, Emmie." He scooted over and took both of her hands in his. "I think our relationship *is* goin' somewhere. I've loved havin' you here, and I think maybe we could make it together. But I'm just not ready to pull the trigger. I need more time.''

''But what if it doesn't work out? I won't be responsible for making Tina feel abandoned again.''

''Well, instead of pullin' away just when things are gettin' interesting, why don't you move in with us? We could have separate bedrooms.''

''Oh, *right*, Hank.''

''Well, we could. At least as far as Tina's concerned. Then we'd know what it's like to really live together. If I enjoy it half as much as I think I'm goin' to, we'll just run over to Idaho and tie the knot when we're ready. No muss, no fuss.''

''You know I can't do that.''

''Why not? Millions of people do it every day.''

''I'm not millions of people. If we lived in a big city, I might be willing to try it. But here in Pinedale, it would be professional suicide for me.''

''Aw, come *on*, Emily. Don't trot out that old excuse—''

''It's not an excuse! There's a morals clause in my contract. There are rules I have to live by. I don't always like it, but that's reality, Hank.''

''And Lord knows, you couldn't possibly break a rule.''

''I've already broken a zillion rules with you. Do you want me to get fired?''

''It'd sure make life easier, wouldn't it?''

She stared at him in amazement. ''I can't believe you actually said that.''

''Why not? At least you could stop lookin' over your shoulder for gossips all the time.''

''Good Lord, you *do* want me to get fired. That's why—''

''No, I don't, Emily. Not really. But do you realize that every time we talk about doin' something, you always think about how it would affect your job first, and me second?''

"That's not true."

"Sure it is. What if you *did* lose your job? Would that be such a tragedy? Hell, you can stay on here and be my business manager."

His *business manager?* After all this time, the man *still* didn't have any idea of how long and hard she'd worked to reach this level in her profession? She might as well get a job cleaning motel rooms. It was all the same to him.

"I *like* being a principal, Hank."

"What you *like* is your precious respectability. You care about that more than you do about me and Tina. If it's all that important to you, well, fine. Go be respectable, and I hope you enjoy it."

Angry tears blurred her vision. Her chest felt so tight, she could barely breathe. She swiped at her eyes with her fingertips, then leveled a long, steady glare at him.

"That is so unfair. You're not even trying to see my side of this."

"I am, too."

"No, you're not. You're asking me to assume all the risks in this relationship. You think I'm not scared of making a commitment? You think I'm not scared of being hurt again? Well, I'm just as terrified as you are."

"If you feel that way, why rush into this?"

"Because I love you, and I think you love me. But it goes beyond the two of us, Hank. I have to consider Tina, and all the other kids who go to my school. Call me egotistical, if you want, but I'm good at what I do. I have an opportunity to make a positive impact on a lot of kids' lives, and that's important to me."

"I'm not questioning your abilities," he said, heaving a sigh that reeked with impatience. "But I still think you're bein' unreasonable. We don't have to get married to please a bunch of old busybodies."

"What if you're wrong, Hank? How am I supposed to pay my bills if my career is destroyed?"

"Man, you really trust me, don't you? You think I'd just walk away from you."

Emily paused and took two deep breaths, then continued more quietly despite the pain ripping her apart. "It's not as if we were strangers, Hank. We've spent a lot of time together in the last five months. If you honestly don't know how you feel about me after everything we've shared, I have to wonder if you ever will."

"It's easy to say, 'I love you,' Emily, but they're just words. Half the time they don't mean anything."

"You didn't believe me when I said them to you?"

He shrugged. "Shoot, you were half-lit."

"No, I wasn't. But you didn't believe me. And that's what this is all about, isn't it? You want me to prove that I love you by giving up my job."

"That's ridiculous."

His gaze slid away from hers, telling her she was right. Incensed by that realization, she stood, hands clenched at her sides.

"You're right. It's absolutely ridiculous. My getting fired won't prove anything. You can't prove something like love. You have to accept it on faith."

"Pardon me if I'm a little short on faith when it comes to women."

"Don't you think you're lovable, Hank?"

"Save the psychology for somebody who needs it."

"Oh, Hank." She sat down again and held out her palms in a plea for understanding. "You're one of the most lovable people I've ever known. You're charming and handsome—"

"Big hairy deal," he muttered.

Ignoring that idiotic remark, she continued. "You have a marvelous sense of humor and you're exciting to be with. You're a loving father. You have a lot of empathy for other people and dream big dreams, like this ranch."

"Yeah, that's me, all right. Mr. Wonderful."

"You *are* wonderful," she said, shaking her head in exasperation. "When I'm with other people, I'm always supposed to be the authority figure, a dignified adult. But with you, I can be a kid if I want. Or a brazen hussy. Or a goofball. I feel . . . free. That's a precious gift, Hank. And I love you for it and a lot of other things, too."

"Stop it. You're makin' me blush," he grumbled.

Seeing it was true, but that he wasn't accepting anything she'd said, Emily smiled sadly. "No, I like telling you this. Now, where was I? Oh yes. Then there's Hank the lover. He's gentle and sensitive, unselfish and uninhibited. I can be honest about what I want with him and not worry that he'll think I'm too kinky. I never thought of sex as fun before I made love with you."

"That's just fine, Emily. I'm glad you enjoyed it. But all this flattery's not gonna change my mind about marriage."

"It wasn't flattery, Hank," she said quietly. "I meant every word."

"Yeah, well, I'd be more inclined to believe that if you'd had enough faith in me to tell me about Larry Paxon, before it was all over."

"There was nothing you could have done that the sheriff didn't do."

"How do you know that? You never gave me a chance to try. It was fine for you to come in here and help poor, dumb Hank with his problems, but you didn't share yours with me."

"That makes you think I don't love you?"

"Hell, yes, it does. I'm just some guy who can show you a good time and make you happy in bed. You don't want a man in your life, Emily. You want a playmate. When you're tired of playin', you'll be damn glad I didn't marry you."

"Well, I guess that settles it, then." Feeling as if he'd slapped her, Emily stood slowly and looked down at his face. Her heart contracted at the angry, stubborn set to his jaw. "I'm glad we had this discussion. It's cleared up a lot of things for me."

He climbed to his feet, as if looking up at her made him uncomfortable. Propping his hands on his hips, he assumed a challenging stance. "Like what?"

"Since I'm not exactly your usual type, I've wondered from the beginning why you ever got involved with me. Now I know."

"What is it you think you know?"

"You really don't love me," she whispered. She gulped, then said more forcefully, "You needed help with Tina and getting your business started, and I was available. I was...convenient. But you never intended to have anything more than an affair with me."

"Are you tryin' to say I've been *usin'* you?"

"I'm not trying to say it, I *am* saying it. I can't believe I didn't see it before. It's just like it was back in algebra class."

"That's bull."

She walked to the front door and turned back to face him. Determined to stave off the humiliating tears scorching the backs of her eyes, she inhaled a deep, shuddering breath.

"I think I loved you even way back then, but I wasn't any more to you than a learning tool. I should have remembered that."

"Dammit, Emily—"

"No. Please, don't say anything else. I suggest you work on your self-esteem, Hank. You won't be able to love anyone until you learn how to love yourself. Good luck with Tina."

Hank crossed the living room and ran out onto the porch, shouting, "Emily, come back here!"

He was too late. Emily scooted down the front steps and across the yard as though her shorts were on fire. Ivan galloped over to her and jumped into the car. She cranked the steering wheel hard to the right and peeled out, sending up a shower of gravel. Then she drove off without a backward glance.

Fear for her safety closed his throat. Dammit, she wasn't in any shape to be driving. He tried to tell himself the unfamiliar moisture in his eyes came from the cloud of dust she'd left behind, but he didn't really believe it.

He didn't believe all the awful things he'd said to her, either, but the boulder-size ache in his gut told its own story. How in the hell had everything gotten out of hand so damn fast? None of it made sense. The woman must be havin' PMS to come up with such crazy notions.

Sighing, he walked back inside. A muffled sob drew his attention to the kitchen doorway. Hank took one look at his daughter, standing there trembling with fury, and knew she'd heard everything. Cursing under his breath, he approached her with the same caution he would an enraged horse.

"I wanted Ms. Franklin to be my mom an' you wrecked everything," she said, piercing him with an accusing glare. "You hurt her feelings and made her go away."

Hank squatted on his heels, bringing himself close to eye level with the kid. "We just had a fight. She'll come back when she cools off."

"No, she won't. She hates you now, an' I do, too. I don't want you for my dad no more."

"That's tough, 'cause you're stuck with me. You can't go around choosin' your parents like you're in a toy store."

"Well, how come I had ta get *you?*" Her chin quivered, and fat tears leaked out of her eyes. She doubled up her fists and pounded on his chest. "I wish I'da gotten Uncle Sam or Uncle Pete. They don't make ladies cry."

"Stop it, Tina."

He grabbed her hands before she could hit him again, then pulled her into his arms and carried her to the sofa.

She kicked and screeched at him, but he managed to plunk her down on the center cushion. He sat on the coffee table directly in front of her. Lord, how could he make her understand what had happened, when he didn't understand it himself?

"Look," he said, struggling to keep the fear out of his voice, "you have fights with your friends and still make up, don'tcha?"

"Sometimes."

"Grown-ups do that, too. It may take a while, but we'll get this straightened out."

Tina wiped her nose with the back of her hand. "No, you w-won't. You don't love her, an' I don't get it. She told me she loves you, an' she even said she'd be proud to have me for a daughter."

"Of course she would, honey."

"Well, you were gonna marry that dumb ol' Janice, an' she didn't like me at all. So how come you won't marry Ms. Franklin? Is it 'cause I got Janice in trouble an' the sheriff took her away?"

Hank had to gulp at the block of concrete lodged in his throat before he could answer. "No, baby. That wasn't your fault. I'm glad I found out what she was up to before I married her."

"Why can't you see Ms. Franklin's not like her?"

"I never said she was."

"But that's what you're afraid of, an' I think it's stupid. Ms. Franklin's the neatest lady I ever met. I'll never forgive you for not marryin' her."

"It's not your place to decide who I should marry, Tina."

"I don't see why not. You're doin' a pretty lousy job of it."

"Don't take that tone of voice with me," Hank warned her. "I'm still your dad, whether you like me or not."

She scrambled off the sofa and ran for the stairs before he could grab her. When she was halfway up, she turned and stuck her tongue out at him. "Well, I *don't* like you, an' I'm never gonna call you Dad again unless you marry Ms. Franklin. So there."

Hank let her go. The little varmint deserved a spanking for that, but he didn't dare get anywhere near her until he'd calmed down one helluva lot. Her footsteps pounded down the hall overhead and her bedroom door slammed hard enough to rattle every window in the lodge.

He propped his elbows on his knees. Holding his head in his hands, he sucked in deep, harsh breaths. Damned if he wasn't right back where he'd started, and it was all Emily's fault.

C'mon, Dawson, his conscience shouted. *You don't believe that. You weren't gettin' to square one with Tina before Emily stepped in.*

"Yeah, yeah," Hank grumbled.

Why don't you make it easy on yourself for a change? Just get off your behind and go ask Emily to marry you. That's what you really want to do, anyway.

Hank got off his behind, but not to go after Emily. He went into the kitchen instead, and got himself a beer. A man had to have a little pride. He'd apologize eventually, but if he caved in this fast, those two females would push him around for the rest of his life.

Besides, Emily wouldn't be in any mood to talk to him now. Hell, he'd be lucky if she didn't knock his head off and hand it back to him on a platter. He swallowed a sip of beer, remembering when he'd made that God-awful spaghetti sauce. Lord, he'd enjoyed her that night.

Other memories flooded in, each one more special than the last—Emily helping Tina with her homework at the kitchen table; Emily pounding away on the nails up at cabin one; Emily painting the fence; Emily perched on one of those silly saddles at the Million Dollar Cowboy Bar; Emily, naked and vulnerable, looking at him as if he were the best thing invented since books.

The beer can trembled in his hand. Dammit, he didn't want to lose her.

"She'll come back," he whispered. "She has to."

Chapter Sixteen

Emily didn't come back, though. Not that week or the following one, either. The word, *desperation,* was beginning to take on a whole new meaning for Hank. For one thing, Tina had taxed his patience to the point where he was about ready to put her up for adoption, preferably to some nice family who lived in Florida. Maybe Japan.

The kid flat-out refused to do any of her chores, sassed him at every opportunity and called him Hank no matter what he threatened her with. He'd sent her to her room so many times, she was starting to lose her tan. As if all that wasn't bad enough, she cried herself to sleep every night and wouldn't let him in to comfort her. Lord, if he had to listen to those gut-wrenching sobs much longer, he was gonna have to check himself into the state mental hospital at Evanston.

For another thing, he'd finally run out of rationalizations to defend himself with, and he'd done some mighty hard thinkin'. He didn't much like what he'd figured out about himself.

He'd already swallowed his pride and damn near worn out his dialing finger trying to get through to Emily during the past two days. She'd put an answering machine on her phone at home and hadn't returned one message. The instant the school secretary recognized his voice, she frosted his shorts with icy politeness, but she wouldn't put Emily on the line.

He couldn't go into town and camp on Emily's doorstep, because he didn't want Tina blabbing to the rest of the family about what a jerk he'd been. They'd all called to tell him how much they liked Emily, and they were gonna show him about as much affection as they would a rabid skunk when they found out he'd driven her away.

He refused to believe she really intended to end their relationship after one stupid fight. Yeah, he'd been rough on her, and he knew he'd hurt her feelings pretty bad, but he knew she'd understand if she'd just let him explain why he'd been so damn pigheaded. But was she ever gonna let him get close enough to do that?

Dammit, he missed her more than he'd ever dreamed it was possible to miss a woman. She hadn't been just a lover or an employee or a baby-sitter, although he sure as hell missed her in all those areas. Night after night, he'd tortured himself, listing all the things he loved about her.

Her loved her blushes and her smiles and her laughter. He loved it when she teased him. He loved her for being finicky and neat all the time. He loved her marshmallow heart when it came to kids and animals. He even loved her complicated mind, though he didn't always understand it.

She'd been a serene, calming presence for him when he'd needed it most. Her methodical approach to solving problems had made the overwhelming job of whipping this battered old ranch into shape seem possible. He'd never be

able to find the right words to tell her how much her un-
failing support for his dream had meant to him.

Without her, all his old doubts and fears about his ability to stick to a goal, whether it was raising Tina or opening his ranch for business, rose up and socked him in the
face. And those old, restless feelings that had driven him to
the rodeo circuit haunted him night and day.

Well, he'd had enough. He put on a clean pair of jeans
and his best shirt, shined his boots and combed his hair
about forty times, as if he were still in junior high, for
God's sake. Since he didn't even want to think about raising Tina's hopes when his own were so shaky, he made sure
she was still in her room, hurried downstairs and called
Becky.

When he dropped Tina off half an hour later, his sister
greeted him with a warm, sympathetic look in her eyes.
Hank figured she must have already heard about his
breakup with Emily. She grabbed his arm when he turned
to leave, and glanced over her shoulder at Tina, who was
kneeling on the floor beside Jonathan's blanket.

"Be sure and tell Emily good luck for us," she said quietly.

"I think I'm the one who's gonna need it," he answered.

"Well, don't lose your temper. I know it'll be hard when
that old biddy starts in on Emily, but—"

"What old biddy?" Hank asked, suddenly confused.

She shot him an equally confused look. "Aren't you
goin' to Emily's hearing?"

"Emily's hearing? What are you talkin' about?"

"You don't know?"

"I haven't talked to her for a while."

"But I thought you two were so close."

"It's a long story. I'm sure Tina'll be glad to tell you all
about it. Now, shut up and tell me what the hell's goin' on,
will ya?"

Her mouth turned up at both corners. "If I shut up, how can I tell you anything?"

"Dammit, Becky—"

"All right, all right. Vi Matheson's charged Emily with immoral conduct, or some such ridiculous thing. The school board's holding a hearing this morning."

"When?"

She glanced at her watch. "In about ten minutes."

Hank didn't bother to say goodbye. He ran to his pickup, climbed in and took off before he had the door completely closed. Guilt lashed him with every revolution of the tires. God, no wonder Emily wouldn't take his calls. No wonder her secretary hated his guts.

Memories of every time he'd made fun of Emily when she'd fussed about gossip hurting her career flashed through his mind. Damn. He hated himself for every single one. Why the hell hadn't he believed her?

'Cause you didn't wanta believe her, his conscience replied. *You wanted her to get fired so you could have her all to yourself, you miserable SOB.*

His stomach churned with the thought of how humiliated she would feel at having her private life paraded in front of the school board, and eventually the whole damn town. She'd never forgive him for this, and he couldn't blame her.

Well, when a guy hung out in the local bars the way he had during his wilder days, he learned who had skeletons in their closets. If he had to rattle every damned one of 'em, he'd save Emily's job for her.

It was a good twenty-five minutes from Becky's house into town if he obeyed the speed limit. Hank made it in fifteen. He parked in front of the administration building and raced inside to the board room. After taking a deep breath, he yanked open the door.

A conference table occupied the middle of the room. The superintendent and the seven board members took up one side. Their heads swiveled toward him in unison, and Keith Daniels said, "You can't come in here, Dawson."

Ignoring him, Hank focused on the two women sitting on the opposite side of the table. Vi Matheson was at the north end, her mouth hanging open as if he'd cut her off in the middle of a sentence. Her eyes widened when she saw him, then narrowed with what he suspected was pure, venomous calculation.

A guy Hank had never seen before sat beside Emily at the south end. Judging by his three-piece suit, Hank figured he must be a lawyer. Jeez, it was even worse than he'd imagined. Emily shot him a pained look that clearly said, "Go away. You'll only make things worse."

Hank ignored her, too, and went back to checking out the rest of the board members. He recognized Doc Miller, who practiced medicine with Peter Sinclair and served as the board president; the local vet; a minister, though not the one from Emily's church; Eric Jordan, the real estate agent; Johnny Conrad, another rancher; and the gal who owned the fabric store. What was her name? Oh yeah, Mavis, somethin'. Not a bad mix, all things considered.

Doc Miller managed a reasonable imitation of a scowl, but Hank could tell he was tickled to death to see him. "You'll have to leave, Hank. This is a personnel matter, and it's closed to the public."

"Good. I wouldn't want my reputation tarnished by a bunch of vicious gossip, Doc." Hank closed the door and walked over to the chair beside Emily's lawyer. "But I'm not just the public, now, am I? My name's gonna come up in this personnel matter, and I think that gives me the right to be here to defend myself."

The board members looked at each other. Three of them nodded. Two others shrugged. That was all the invitation Hank needed. He pulled out the chair and turned it sideways, then plunked himself down so he had a clear view of

Vi's face. Though he'd love to wring her scrawny neck, he gave her his most charming smile.

"Please, go on, Mrs. Matheson," Doc Miller said.

The old bat sniffed and rolled her eyes, as though being in the same room with Hank Dawson was more than she should be expected to tolerate. "Well, I've completely lost my train of thought. Let's see. Oh yes, as I was saying, I've called Ms. Franklin frequently, offering my advice, since she was new to the school district, but she wasn't at all receptive."

"Was she ever rude to you?" Keith Daniels asked.

Vi pursed her lips and thought that over for a while. "Not really. Although she was awfully abrupt when I tried to warn her about her behavior with Mr. Dawson."

"Now, why would you wanta do that, Miz Matheson?" Hank drawled. "Don't tell me you still haven't forgiven me for gettin' Harold drunk back when we were in high school. I've settled down a whole lot since then, honest."

Discreet coughs that sounded more like chuckles came from the other side of the table. Vi glared at Hank.

"Poor Harold was sick as a dog for two days."

"Yeah, but he had one heck of a good time that night."

"That's enough, Hank," Doc Miller said. "In the hope of saving time, Mrs. Matheson, what exactly is your complaint against Ms. Franklin?"

"You know darn well what it is, Doc. She's been havin' an immoral affair with that man," Vi retorted, shooting a snooty glance at Hank. "It's been such a scandal, everyone's talkin' about it. A woman like that can't have a positive influence on the children."

Hank clapped one hand over his heart and pushed his eyebrows up under his hat brim. "Our affair was *immoral?* I didn't know that! Golly, Miz Matheson, if you'd just told me that instead of blabberin' it all over town, I'da stopped it right away."

"Don't you make fun of me, Hank Dawson. You're a disgrace to your whole family. If your mama was still alive—"

"She'd tell you to mind your own damn business."

Vi gasped. "Why, I've never been so insulted in my life."

"Then it's high time you were," Hank told her. "Emily Franklin's one of the finest women I've ever known, and the best principal this town's ever had. You've got no call to be tryin' to destroy her career. You're just jealous 'cause Harold didn't get her job."

"She's indecent, and I've got proof." Vi waved a white envelope under Hank's nose.

"Oh yeah? Let's see it."

Her hands trembling with outrage, she opened the envelope and slapped a color photograph in the center of the table. Hank grabbed it before anyone else could. By God, the old bat *had* stood outside their motel with a camera. She'd caught them kissing in the doorway, and from the heated expressions on both of their faces, it was a wonder they hadn't fogged up the camera lens.

"You got an extra copy of this, Miz Matheson? I'd love to have one. Of course, it's too bad you cut off Emily's cute li'l fanny like that, 'cause I had my left hand on it."

He grinned at Vi just to needle her some more, then said, "Tell me, how long did you slink around outside waitin' for us? Don'tcha think that was kind of a sick thing to do?"

Vi snatched at the photograph, but Hank held it out of her reach. He heard a groan from Emily's end of the table.

"Give it back," Vi screeched. "It's evidence. When the board sees it, they'll know I'm not lyin'."

"Are you *sure* you want me to do that?"

"Of course I'm sure. Why wouldn't I be?"

"There's somethin' about poor Harold you probably don't know. He talks when he drinks, Vi. He talks a lot."

"I'm not interested in your lies about my son. Give me that picture."

"Fine," Hank said, handing it over, "but I've gotta warn you, if you show it to the folks sittin' over there or anybody else, my next stop's gonna be the county courthouse."

"That won't help you any."

"They keep all kinds of records over there, ya know? Like marriage licenses and birth certificates. With dates on 'em. Might be some *real* interesting facts'll turn up about the Matheson family. Tell me, Vi, was your affair as immoral as ours was?"

"Why, you—" the woman sputtered. "I never—"

Hank laughed and shook his index finger at her. "Oh yes, you did, you little devil. Least that's what Harold told me."

Vi stared at him, her eyes bulging out of their sockets. When Hank didn't even blink, she picked up her pocketbook, shoved the photograph inside and left the room without another word. A moment of stunned silence followed her exit. Finally, Johnny Conrad's shoulders started to shake. A high-pitched cackle came out of Doc Miller's mouth, and the whole room erupted with laughter.

Hank waited for everyone to quiet down. "I assume this hearing will be dismissed for lack of evidence."

"Whatever Vi's personal history might be, I still have doubts about Ms. Franklin staying on as our principal," Keith Daniels said, opening a file folder to reveal a stack of correspondence. "Vi's not the only one who's complained. You can read these letters yourself."

"I know for a fact she hasn't done one thing every darn one of you hasn't done, except maybe the reverend, there," Hank said. "Exactly what behavior has you so worried, Keith? That she might have a little fun once in a while? Or is it just that she's been goin' out with me?"

"Any woman who'd date a man with your reputation doesn't give a hang about her own, Dawson. She hasn't got any business working with kids."

"Why, you hypocritical..." Hank pulled back his fist and would have smashed Daniels's face in, but Emily was suddenly standing beside him, holding on to his arm.

"Hank, stop it."

"Didn't you hear what he said?"

"It doesn't matter. Please, sit down. I have something to say."

Hank grudgingly lowered himself back onto his chair and tucked his hands under the table so Emily couldn't see they were still ready for action. If Daniels said one more nasty word about her, he'd cream him. Emily looked at Doc Miller, as if asking for permission to speak.

"Go ahead, Ms. Franklin," Doc said.

"Thank you." She cleared her throat, then squared her shoulders and faced the board with a dignity that made Hank so proud, he wanted to kiss her.

"I've enjoyed working in this school district, and I'd like to continue to do so," she said. "Some of you may not feel that's a wise decision, and you're certainly entitled to your opinions. However, I want to point out that I haven't heard any complaints about my job performance, only my choice of friends. Frankly, I'm offended by that."

"People are known by the company they keep, Ms. Franklin," the minister said, earning himself an icy stare from Hank.

Emily laid her hand on Hank's shoulder and squeezed it in warning. "In that case, Reverend Jacobs, I don't see what the problem is. Hank Dawson is a gentleman, and he's been a wonderful friend to me."

"You know what the reverend means," Daniels said with a sneer.

That did it. Hank started to come out of his chair.

"Yes, I do, Mr. Daniels," she replied, pushing Hank right back down, as though he were a hyperactive first grader. "But Reverend Jacobs is wrong about Hank, and so are you."

"Baloney. Everybody knows what a hell-raising stud he's always been. I'm surprised your dad hasn't given you what-for, for messin' around with him."

Emily's fingernails bit into Hank's shoulder, hard enough to draw blood if he hadn't had a shirt on.

"My father happens to like and respect Hank very much. And I don't care about Hank's so-called reputation. He's hardly the only one in this room who has ever tipped over an outhouse when he was in high school, or driven too fast, or gotten drunk or kissed as many girls as he possibly could. He simply did all those things with more flair than anyone else."

"The way I heard it, he did a helluva lot more than that."

"The way you *heard* it, Mr. Daniels? So you've never actually seen him do any of the terrible things he's supposedly done? Hank's an awfully handsome man. Women love to talk about handsome men. Do you suppose it's possible some of the stories you've heard just might have been a little bit exaggerated?"

"Not likely," Daniels muttered.

"Well, maybe not. That's one of the great things about gossip. You're free to believe whatever you want about the victim. Here's a juicy tidbit for you. The man I've come to know is decent, honest and a wonderful father. He's working extremely hard to start a new business that will bring in more tourists and benefit the entire community. He pays his bills and his taxes, and he minds his own business. If this board has a problem with my dating as nice a man as Hank Dawson, you won't have to fire me. I'll resign."

"Thank you, Ms. Franklin," Doc Miller said as she walked back to her chair. "Does anybody else have any questions or comments?"

"Yeah, I do," Hank said, though he was so touched by Emily's sincere defense of him, he wasn't sure he could say anything coherent. He stood and planted both palms on the edge of the table, studying each member of the board.

"If any of you are holdin' on to any doubts about Ms. Franklin, you can forget 'em. We love each other, and we'll be gettin' married by the end of the week."

Chair legs screeched on the tile floor as Emily leaped to her feet. Glaring at Hank over the top of her lawyer's head, she said, "We most certainly will not," and marched out of the room.

The board cracked up again. Hank shrugged. "She's a little mad at me for pokin' my nose in here," he said with a sheepish grin. "Looks like I've got some more talkin' to do."

"You'd better get to it, boy," Johnny Conrad said. "And you tell Ms. Franklin, she's got a job whether she marries you or not. Isn't that right, folks?"

A chorus of agreement went up around the table. Hank turned and hurried down the hallway, waving in acknowledgement at the shouts of, "Good luck, Hank," and "Invite us to the wedding," that followed him out of the building.

Emily was already halfway down the block, heading in the direction of her house when he stepped outside. Man, she was really burnin' up the old sidewalk. Deciding to give her a little time to cool off, he followed on foot, his longer stride gradually closing the distance between them.

The kick pleat at the back of her pale pink suit skirt opened with every step she took. He hung back for a while, enjoying each glimpse of her thighs, each angry switch of her hips. What a woman. Damned if he wasn't gettin' hard just watchin' her strut along.

Suspecting she might lock him out of her house, he caught up with her when she turned onto her street. She sent him a frigid glance, then faced forward again.

"We've gotta talk, Emmie," he said.

"We have nothing to talk about," she retorted, enunciating each word clearly and distinctly, as though he weren't too bright. He figured she might have a point there.

"Sure we do," he said. "There's the weddin', and how many babies we're gonna make together, and how we're gonna get you moved out to the ranch before school starts."

She cut across the lawn, her spike heels sinking into the grass. He took her arm to steady her. She nearly fell jerking away from his touch. He shrugged and followed her up the front steps.

Her keys rattled in her hands, but she finally got the door unlocked. Hank reached around and opened it, then nudged her inside and slipped over the threshold right behind her. She turned on him, eyes blazing with indignation.

"Get out of my house and stay away from me."

He poked his hands into his pockets and leaned against the wall of the entryway. "Can't do that, Emmie."

"*Don't* call me that."

"Why not? It's just a little love name. And I *do* love you, Emmie."

She looked away, but not before he saw the flash of pain in her eyes. "Give me a break. I'm not stupid."

"No, you're not. But I sure as hell have been." He reached out and tucked her hair behind her right ear. "I've loved you for a long time, and I should've told you that when you wanted me to."

"Stop it, Hank. It's too late for that." She turned away from him and walked into the living room, her arms crossed over her breasts. "I don't need your pity or your damn noble gestures."

Once again, he followed her. "The only noble gesture I made was puttin' Vi Matheson in her place. She's the one everybody feels sorry for, Em. Not you."

"Right. That's why you had to tack on your lie about us getting married to save my job?"

"It wasn't a lie. I was on my way to apologize to you when I heard about the hearing. I'm ready to pull the trigger anytime you are."

"I think you got bucked off on your head one too many times, Dawson. I wouldn't marry you if—"

"Careful, now. Don't say somethin' you don't mean until you've had a chance to hear me out."

He strolled over to the overstuffed chair. Emily studied him for a moment, then seated herself on the sofa.

"All right. I'm listening."

Drumming his fingertips on the chair arm, Hank searched for the right place to start. "I've done a lot of thinkin' about what you said there at the end about my self-esteem. I know you were right about that. I was takin' a lot of anger that belonged to other folks out on you. That wasn't fair, and I'm sorry I hurt you."

She nodded, but didn't say anything. Hank cleared his throat and went on.

"You know, my mom always called me her problem kid. I've told you some about my dad and how I could never measure up to Sam. I guess I learned early on that the way to get attention was to be obnoxious. You get attention, all right, but it doesn't exactly make folks love you a whole lot."

"Your family loves you, Hank," Emily said quietly. "It was obvious to me the day you brought the horses home."

"Yeah, I know they do. But it's kinda like they're always holdin' their breath, waitin' for the next time they're gonna have to bail me outta trouble."

"It takes time for other people to notice when you're trying to change."

"That's for sure. What I'm tryin' to say, though, is that I haven't always felt real lovable. And, after Christine and Janice, well, it was hard for me to believe a woman like you really could love me."

"Do you believe it now, Hank?"

"Yeah. I did even before the hearing, 'cause I finally figured out you wouldn't have gone to bed with me if you didn't love me. I don't think you'd have taken so much guff from me, either. You sure didn't take any from ol' Keith."

"I didn't see any reason to."

"You took a helluva risk there, Em, tellin' 'em you'd resign."

She shrugged. "It seemed like the appropriate thing to do at the time."

"I hope you didn't do it to prove anything to me. It made me feel about ten feet tall, but I don't need that from you now."

"I was proving something to myself, Hank."

"Oh yeah? What was that?"

"I've been thinking, too, and I realized you were right about some things. I didn't *feel* my job was more important than you and Tina, but I can see that I acted that way. It's been the only important thing in my life for a long time. I don't want to live that way anymore."

"Well, I'm sorry for all the times I didn't take you seriously when you were worried about it." He sighed and shook his head. "Shoot, no wonder you didn't tell me about Paxon. You probably didn't think I'd believe you, but I will from now on, Emmie. It sure could have gone the other way this morning."

"Did they make a decision while you were there?"

"You've still got a job if you want it."

"That's nice."

"I wish you'd told me about the hearing. I would've felt awful if they'd fired you."

"I was still angry, Hank. Knowing how you felt about my job, I didn't think you'd want to help. I was surprised to see you there."

He chuckled at that. "Yeah, I imagine. I was pretty good in there, though. Wasn't I?"

"You certainly were. Lord, the look on Vi's face when you asked if her affair was as immoral as ours was..."

Emily tipped back her head and laughed. "I'd give month's salary for a picture of that."

"I don't reckon Vi'll give you any more trouble."

"I don't think so, either. I couldn't believe what you wer implying."

"Aw, shoot, Emily. It's like reformed smokers. The one who enjoyed it the most are the most self-righteous abou giving it up. I'll betcha twenty bucks ol' Keith's got som dirty little secrets in his background."

"And wouldn't you just love to know what they are?"

"I've got more important things on my mind right now."

"Such as?"

"Such as, can you ever forgive me for bein' such an idiot Em?"

"Maybe. I'll have to think about it."

Hank scowled at her. As far as he was concerned, they'(done enough of this serious talkin', and it was time to mov on to the fun stuff. Like kissin' and makin' up.

"Well, jeez, Franklin, how much longer are you gonna make me grovel?"

"I don't know," she answered with a sassy grin tha warmed him in some mighty private places. "How mucl longer are you willing to grovel, Dawson?"

"As long as it takes to get a yes out of you."

"Did you ask me a specific question?"

Oh. So *that's* what she wanted. Fear clogged his throa for an instant. He could see a touch of it in her eyes, too This was a big step for both of them, but he couldn't ever begin to imagine ever loving anyone else half as much as h loved her. Pushing himself to his feet, he crossed the roon and knelt in front of her. Then he took her hands between his and pressed them to his chest.

"I love you, Emily Franklin. Will you please marry me?"

To his chagrin, tears filled her eyes and she had to gulp before she could speak. "Are you sure, Hank? You're not doing this because you feel guilty about the hearing?"

"The only thing I feel guilty about is makin' you cry. I'll never do it again if I can help it. I've been miserable since you left, babe. C'mon, now, and admit you still love me, and that we'll always share all our troubles from here on out. Life's just not any fun without you."

Throwing her arms around his neck, she hugged him fiercely. "Yes," she whispered. "Yes, I still love you, and yes, I'll marry you."

Hank wrapped his arms around her waist and stood, pulling her up with him. His hands suddenly shaking with relief and the need to touch her everywhere, he stroked her hair, her face, her back. He wanted to run outside and holler the news to all of her nosy neighbors, but he couldn't let go of her, not for a second.

Her lips found his in a deep, possessive kiss, setting off shock waves of pleasure, right down to the soles of his boots. He slid one arm behind her knees and swept her up against his chest.

"Hank, no," she yelped. "You'll hurt your leg."

"What leg?" He carried her into the bedroom and set her down beside the bed.

Tipping her head to one side, she smiled up at him, and his knees nearly buckled when she caressed him through his jeans. Thoughts of a slow, tender bout of lovemaking vanished like raindrops on parched land. Emily seemed to feel the same way. Neither of them could get naked fast enough.

They stretched out on her bed, kissing, touching, stoking a fire already verging on the edge of control. He needed to rediscover her, reconnect with her, forge ties that couldn't be broken, no matter what. Sensations meshed with emotions, creating something new and exhilarating, something beyond anything he'd ever experienced before.

Wanting to see her face more clearly, he rolled onto his back and pulled her above him. She straddled his hips and braced her arms on either side of his head, gazing down at him with those big, serious green eyes that he'd swear could see right down into the darkest corners of his soul.

He'd expected to see the excitement and desire he found in her eyes. He also saw a depth of love and trust and acceptance that filled him with a desperate ache to be inside her, as if, somehow, he could physically touch all those emotions. Grasping her hips, he lifted her slightly, probing for the entrance to her body.

Her head fell back. Her eyes closed, and a gusty little sigh came out of her smiling mouth as she welcomed him. The pleasure was so intense, he almost lost it right then. He gritted his teeth with the effort to hold back, make it last long enough to please her.

She leaned forward, rubbing her breasts against his chest as she kissed him again and again. The citrus scent of her shampoo surrounded him. Her silky hair caressed his arms and shoulders. Her soft, husky voice murmured heady, erotic words he'd never heard from her before. Her hips made slow, tantalizing circular motions.

It was like walking on a tightrope between heaven and hell, testing the limits of his endurance for a prize he had to win and drowning in sweetness, all at the same time.

Filling his hands with her breasts, he drank in her little moans and gasps of pleasure. Now she was meeting him thrust for thrust, urging him into a faster, more violent tempo. Her fingertips sank into his shoulders; his sank into her buttocks, clutching, as if at life itself.

Suddenly she stiffened. A shriek of satisfaction ripped out of her throat. Her body contracted around him, propelling him to an explosive release. She collapsed on top of him, her muscles quivering with the effort she'd expended.

He caressed her back and shoulders, feeling her heart thumping against his sternum. An emotion he barely recognized surged through him. The word he finally chose to describe it, after searching the scattered pieces of his mind, was *contentment*.

Emily stretched her spine, then kissed the side of his neck. She would have rolled off him, but he liked her right where she was, and he told her so. She stacked one hand on top of the other and rested her chin on both, giving him a gratified smile that bordered on smugness.

Lazily weaving his fingers through her hair, Hank chuckled at her. "You look like a conquering warrior."

"I feel like one. I think I like this position a lot."

"I'm glad to hear that. So do I. Oh, but how I love you, Em."

"I'm counting on that." She raised up, propping one elbow on his chest and resting her head in her hand. "And I'm counting on you to make a go of the Happy Trails Ranch. I may not want my job much longer."

"Why's that?"

"Because when we start making those babies you mentioned, I won't want to be so involved at work that I miss all the fun. I might go back to teaching or substituting to keep my hand in, but being a principal demands too much time," she said, her eyes sparkling with happy anticipation.

Lord, that had to be the sexiest smile he'd ever seen on a woman's face. He felt himself hardening inside her, and the delighted look that crept into her eyes told him she'd felt it, too. She leaned down and kissed him, her tongue sweeping the length of his.

"Mmm, eager to get started, are we?" she murmured.

"How many babies do you want?"

"Two. If they're as wonderful as Tina, maybe more."

Hank scowled at the mention of his daughter's name.

"What is it?" she asked. "Are you worried she'll be jealous if we have more children?"

He grinned and shook his head. "Nah, she's gotten real attached to little Jonathan lately. I think she's figured out a new baby can't take her place."

"Then why did you frown like that?"

"I've been havin' a little problem with her. She heard that fight we had, and she's been mad at me ever since."

"Is there anything I can do to help?"

"Yeah. See if you can convince her to call me Dad again, will ya?"

Emily's lips twitched and laughter gurgled out of her throat. Hank put his arms around her waist and rolled over, reversing their positions.

"It's not funny, Emily. She likes you better than me. Every time we have a fight, she's gonna be on your side. How am I supposed to take on two ornery women at once?"

"I'm sure you'll think of something." She petted his chest and shoulders, sending fresh surges of arousal to his groin, starting the fire all over again.

"I think I just did," he said, thrusting more deeply into her body.

Her hips rose to meet his. Her breathing became short and choppy. "Oh, really? What did you come up with?"

"I'm gonna have to even the odds." His own voice started to sound a little breathless. "With any luck at all, we'll have a boy inside of a year."

"That sounds like fun."

"Oh, it will be, sweetheart. I promise."

"Well, then. You should get busy, Mr. Dawson."

"Think so?"

"Oh, you definitely *should*."

"Oh, Em," he said, resting his forehead against hers, "I love it when you talk dirty."

Laughing, she swatted his behind. He closed his eyes and let the sound of laughter surround him, thanking the big dude upstairs for bringing her back into his life. His restless days were over. Heartbreak Hank had finally found himself a mighty fine wife.

*   *   *   *   *

Silhouette Special Edition®

Concluding in July...

The stories of the men and women who ride the range, keep the home fires burning and live to love.

Cowboy Country

by Myrna Temte

FOR PETE'S SAKE (SE #739 - May 1992)
SILENT SAM'S SALVATION (SE #745 - June 1992)
HEARTBREAK HANK (SE #751 - July 1992)

Where the soul is free and the heart unbound... and the good guys still win. Rustled up with love from Silhouette Special Edition...